WITHDRAWN

Season of the Assassin

Also by Thomas Laird

Cutter

Season of the Assassin

THOMAS LAIRD

CARROLL & GRAF PUBLISHERS
New York

Carroll & Graf Publishers
An imprint of Avalon Publishing Group, Inc.
161 William Street
NY 10038-2607
www.carrollandgraf.com

First Carroll & Graf edition 2003

First published in the UK by Constable,
an imprint of Constable & Robinson Ltd 2003

ISBN 0-7867-1124-8

Printed and bound in the EU

PART ONE

Chapter One

[April 1968]

Pictures are never the same as being on scene. You walk into their dorm room – it's like a slaughterhouse. Blood. Matted hair atop the crushed skulls. Their facial expressions look either as if they're asleep or as if they've been caught in the middle of a scream. It varies from girl to girl.

Seven of them. One has survived by hiding beneath her bed. She's in the grip of hysteria at the moment, so there's no interview for a while.

What he's done to them. Plenty of violence after they were dead. It's as if he couldn't get enough of them. It appears that they were repeatedly raped. Which is why I wonder if it was more than one man. Semen is present on at least three of the bodies. One guy could've done all this. But how did he go from girl to girl, seven of them? And not one of them fights back?

Veteran Homicide cops have had to leave the room. I feel the push of today's lunch against my gorge, but I am able to hold it down. First comes the nausea, and then it turns into anger. A bad thing for a Homicide detective to feel. It's got to stay business. When it gets to someplace else, you have to remove your ass from the scene. You get angry, you make mistakes. Killers get themselves sprung on technicalities.

'Jake? You finished here?' my partner, Eddie Lezniak, asks. 'Because they're about ready to clean up the scene if you've got everything we need.'

Eddie the Polack. Not exactly my best friend, but a competent copper. We never hit it off the way a lot of partners do, but we get along well enough that we finish the day's work. He's smart. Not like the usual South Side Polski you find in the taverns. Eddie's a teetotaler. Never imbibes. Not even on the holidays. But working with Eddie is better than being stuck with a spic or a spade. I got nothing against these 'dudes of color', but my life is sometimes in the hands of my partner, and some of these swarthy types don't work out too well in the field.

'Worst thing I've ever seen,' Eddie says. It's like he's talking to no one in particular. Like I'm not standing right next to him, peering at the remains of Selena Moreno. A dead young woman, a nursing student, who never even made it to the adult age of twenty-one.

'That's because it's a multiple homicide,' I tell him. 'It always seems worse when it's more than one. It's like with airplane crashes. Two hundred die, and it seems like some kind of holocaust.'

'Yeah, that's the word, Jake. Holocaust. Like with the Jews. This is a little holocaust on the West Side.'

He walks away as if he's about ready to burst out bawling. He's an emotional Polack, too. These Eastern European guys tend to hang their hearts on their sleeves a little too often.

Seven student nurses. He's used something very sharp on their throats. Each of them has had her jugular slashed several times. Small, precise incisions. Like a razor or some other finely honed piece of steel. We'll have to wait and see what the evidence specialists come up with.

'The work of one man?' Captain Quigley asks me as he arrives on scene.

'I don't know how it could've been. Unless . . .'

'Unless what, Lieutenant Parisi?' the sandy-haired commander asks me.

'Unless he isolated them. Tied them up as he worked his way from bedroom to bedroom.'

'And only one lived to tell the tale. Is that it, Jake?'

'It appears so, sir. She's just this side of shock, so it'll be some time before we can talk to her.'

'Be there waiting, Lieutenant. I do not want the newspapers to get to her before we do. It has happened that way before, and I'll not tolerate it happening again . . . My God, this man was a fucking savage.'

He looks around the room one more time, just as the body bags arrive. They're going to remove the seven corpses now. It's time to get out of their way.

The Greek's is almost empty. It's the closest place I know on the South Side, so I come here when my shift is finally finished. Eighteen hours because of this multiple. Usually it's eight to ten on a normal shift. Some big headline-grabber and it takes forever to get the hell away from the job.

'The usual?' The Greek, Jimmy Karras smiles.

He knows I'm a cop and he thinks we all talk in clichés, so I let him enjoy his illusions.

'What's wrong, Jake? You look a little sour.'

'Bad business, this. Today, I mean. Seven young girls. None of them twenty-one years old. What he did I can't repeat. And I *won't* repeat it, Greek, so this time there'll be no story to tell.'

He looks me over and knows this well is dry for the long afternoon ahead of us. He'll just have to keep the shots and the beers coming and he'll have to hope I'll loosen up with the booze so that the two of us won't have to sit here in silence.

I take the moisture-beaded glass of Old Style and I drain the twelve ounces in one extended tug. I follow the beer with a quick pop at the Jim Beam.

Five doubleheaders is my limit. A police lieutenant is always on call, so I can't turn out my own lights with liquor.

I remember the look on Lezniak's face. It really was a look of horror that crossed his puss as we entered that dormitory room. Just as well it was a weekend. Otherwise there would've been more young girls present, but a number of the residents were gone until Sunday night. He'd caught them on a Saturday evening. All seven of them had been Hispanics. They'd been too far away from their homes to visit for the weekend. They likely saw their families only at Christmas or during the summer break. Mexican and Cuban girls, getting their educations in nursing, up here in El Norte. Now they'd be getting a trip back south long before they'd expected one. I can see why there'd be horror on Eddie's face. What troubles me is that a similiar look never crossed my own face. Maybe it's because I'm not well educated. Just a high-school diploma. Not like my kid, who's going to get a degree on his way to where he's going. I'm just a semi-ignorant wop who picked up his trade by being on the street. Jimmy, my kid, is more what they call 'contemplative' – a fancy word for a thinker.

The Greek is still patiently awaiting the loosening of my tongue. He even stands me a free round – which is an occasion in this saloon.

I hit my fifth round and the force of the alcohol finally registers. This is the warmth I've been looking toward. Eighteen hours on my feet. Eighteen hours on shift. Time to go home and collapse.

Eleanor is there for me at the top of our stairs. Twenty-six stairs to the top landing.

'I can smell you from here.'

'What a lovely sniffer it is as well, Eleanor.'

'You spend everything you make at that goddamned Greek's. Doesn't it bother you that Jimmy's putting himself through college?'

She knows the sore spots. She knows where to probe. I stop halfway up the flight.

'He said he wants to do it on his own. I offered—'

'You offered him nothing. You let him do it. God knows you wouldn't want to share your paycheck with anyone other than that Greek on the South Side.'

'You make a very poor nag, Eleanor. You're far too good-looking.'

I start up the stairs again.

'That avenue is permanently closed, Jake. You closed it yourself. So don't bother with the blather. You don't want me. You don't want your son—'

'My son? Is that what you said?'

Her face goes sullen. We've been here before, too.

'Go to bed, Jake. You're drunk.'

'No. I'm not drunk. Wish I were. I'm just very, very tired and I'm going to bed alone, which is the usual state of affairs in this unhappy house.'

She backs away from me at the top of the flight. I look over at her, but her gaze falls away from mine.

I throw open the door to what used to be our guest room, which is now my room. I fling myself face forward onto the mattress, and I'm asleep before I can remember what it was like to feel Eleanor lying next to me in bed.

A man is reported to have been seen near the dormitory on Saturday night. The dishwasher from the soul-food restaurant across the street had been taking a smoke and had seen a tall, stringy, white male hanging around the dorm's back exit. The dishwasher never saw the man enter the dormitory, but he tells us it would've been easy for him to gain entry if he'd waited long enough, and if one of the other nurses had walked out that door that evening.

Which was what had happened, Eddie discovers. Carmen Espinoza, student nurse, walked out that exit at about 10.25 p.m. on Saturday evening, which would've been around the time the skinny creep had been lurking outside at the back.

So we canvass every bar and bodega on the West Side. Everything within walking distance. Even a good stretch of the legs away from the dorm.

Again it is Eddie who strikes pay dirt. He hits Wesley's Tap, two blocks from the scene, and Wesley himself knows the guy we're talking about. Tall, gangly. The guy's a fucking mess, Wesley says. Wesley himself is a large black male who keeps a sawed-off shotgun behind his bar. He's been fined for keeping the artillery, but I can't blame him for being loaded up. Not in this neighborhood.

The guy in question has been in here numerous times, Wesley continues. He's some kind of merchant-marine guy who's lost his sea papers or whatever and now he's bumming around as a landlubber until he can get his shit together. His name is Carl, Wesley remembers. Carl Anglin.

'He's been in every night the last week. Hadda throw him outta here the last two evenin's,' the big black man tells us.

So now Eddie and I are inside Wesley's Tap, and there are four unmarked cars outside with the backup troops.

My partner is angry. I can see it in his face.

'You ain't going to shoot this guy, polack. This is far too high-profile, and anyways that's not what we're about.'

He smiles stiffly like he's shrugging it off, but I know he'd like to pump all six rounds from his .38 Special into Carl Anglin's crotch.

'Besides. What if he isn't the guy we think he might be?'

'He's the guy, Jake. You and I both know he's the guy. In our guts we know he's the one who did all the young girls.'

I can't summon the resolve to dispute him. I take a tug at the twelve-ounce draft that Wesley has supplied me, on the house. Eddie sips away at a ginger ale.

Eddie takes out his piece and makes sure the chambers all contain slugs. I know that my own weapon is ready. I check it every morning or afternoon or before every shift. I carry a snub-nosed .38 in an ankle holster, and I've got one of those box-cutters in my pants pocket. We've got pump-action shotguns in the squad, but they're only for when we're busting down a door, so to speak.

Anglin usually comes in between 9.00 and 9.30, Wesley tells us. It's just nine, right now.

My handheld two-way goes off. I pick it up.

'Subject is coming your way, Lieutenant.'

It's Harry Sandstrom, sitting in one of the squads outside.

'Got it,' I tell him. Eddie and I turn off our two-ways.

'He ain't gonna like the looks of you two in suits,' Wesley tells us.

Eddie takes off his jacket and then remembers he's got his holster showing.

'Fuck him,' I tell Eddie. 'I want him to know we're here for him.'

The door to the tap opens. Carl Anglin's hair hangs in long bangs over his eyes. He's wearing a peacoat even though it's April and it's unseasonably warm.

As soon as he walks in, he looks our way. He turns his eyes toward me. I can see their green color even in this dim atmosphere. They're a bright green, a cat's-eye green.

I've got the .38 pointed directly at those scraggy-assed bangs.

'You even wiggle and I'll blow your brains all over Wesley's oak bar,' I tell him.

Wesley steps back and knocks two bourbon bottles sideways. The clatter makes Anglin pivot toward his left, toward the exit.

I pull back the hammer on the .38.

'Think,' I tell him.

He stops and turns back toward me.

'Now wait, I didn't do a goddamned thing.'

'Then you won't have a problem, will you?'

'Get down on your knees,' Eddie tells him.

Anglin has been here before. He hits the deck, knees first.

'Hands behind you, lie flat on your face,' Lezniak continues.

Anglin raises his head toward me as my partner cuffs him. I can see the strange green eyes.

'You don't know what you're gettin' into,' he says and smiles. Then he puts his face against the floor.

'We've got you at the back door right before the killings,' I tell Anglin. 'We've got a positive ID on you . You were there and we've got you made standing at that exit.'

He smiles wearily and tugs at a half-burned Camel filter.

He hasn't asked for a lawyer. I think he's enjoying this.

'The worst thing we saved for last,' I explain.

Lezniak is seated across the table from him. I'm standing behind him.

'We have a witness inside. You missed her, Carl. You left her alive. She puts you inside the dormitory. We have the death penalty in Illinois. I don't know how long you've been a resident . . .'

I've got his attention now. The careless hard-on has deflated. He's frightened. I can smell a new odor on him.

'You're thinking I'm making this up, about the witness inside. The one you missed. She's in the hospital, but she's healthy. Getting stronger all the time. And think how that lovely senorita is going to tear you all to hell on the witness stand. She saw what you did. She was under a bed. She heard them pleading with you. But you carved them all up anyhow.

'I don't imagine you were in the war, were you, Carl?' I ask him.

'Hell, how old you think I am?'

'Yeah. You were lucky. Born lucky. Not like that tattoo you're sporting on your left arm.'

It reads 'BORN BAD'.

'I fought at Normandy and at a lot of other places,' I tell him.

'You were at the invasion?'

Anglin's suddenly interested.

'Yeah. Army Rangers. Airborne.'

'So you greased a lot of Krauts,' he sneers.

I look at him quietly. He becomes uncomfortable. Eddie knows the war is a subject that rarely comes up between us. Eddie was a Marine on Iwo Jima. Silver and Bronze Stars. I have some hardware in a box somewhere at home. As I say, the subject does not come up often. We lived through it once. It was enough.

'I've seen a lot of dead bodies. None displayed the craftsmanship I saw with your work.'

'That's very cute. But I ain't buyin', Lieutenant. Like I already said, I ain't done nothin'.'

'We'll note that, what you just said, Carl. We'll remember all your cooperation – right before that young lady comes into the courtroom and nails your dick to the plaster ceiling,' I remind him.

'Fuck it . . . I want a lawyer.'

'You don't want to talk to us no more?' Eddie smiles.

'I want a lawyer. Fuck y'all.'

Eddie jumps up and cuffs him on his forehead before Anglin is able to dodge the blow. Eddie Lezniak was also middleweight champ of the South Pacific during the war. Wrong guy to piss off. Quick as a cobra with those hands.

'Oh, excuse me. I didn't mean to make you bleed,' Eddie says, straight-faced.

There is a trickle of blood coming down from Anglin's left eyebrow. I hope he doesn't need stitches. That'll require more paperwork on our part. And this is the 1960s. Peace 'n Love. We're not supposed to manhandle subjects anymore.

They've taken a lot of the fun out of this line of work.

Anglin lawyers-up. He goes to court and gets a bond that's too expensive for his empty wallet. We all sweat out the weeks before his trial, but we've got Arthur Marchand, a very good prosecutor, going for our side.

Theresa Rojas is the survivor. But the news about her is not so good. She's gone from shock to catatonia. There is no communicating with her. When Eddie and I go visit her at County Hospital, she stares right through us. And County Psychiatric is one of the top psycho hospitals in the country. They've got their best people with her, but she has gone into a zombie state. When she comes off the sedatives, she flies up to the ceiling. They've pumped enough morphine into her to give her the consciousness of a turnip, and court begins in a week.

Then Marchand's witness from the restaurant across the street gets himself shot dead in a drive-by episode just outside work. The dishwasher owed for illegal pharmaceuticals, and the people he owed didn't care about his star status as one of our witnesses.

Carl Anglin walks. We've got nobody to put him on scene. One drugged-up zombie and one for-real stiff. Marchand can't prosecute. It's out of his hands. The stringy-haired monster gets a free pass out of jail, and now Eddie and I are the ones holding our dicks.

We're right there when they open the jail door for him.

'You two war heroes take it easy,' he says and grins, his bag of personal items underneath his arm.

I grab hold of Lezniak before he can deliver a blow. There are too many witnesses here. Too many photographers and news people.

'Your nightmare just started,' I tell Anglin.

'Oh, yeah?' He grins.

I keep my voice low. 'You don't know me. But trust me on this. I'm never going to stop. I don't care how many years it takes. I'll be there waiting for you. That girl isn't going to stay all balled-up in a hospital bed forever. I'll find someone else, something else, Carl. Believe me.'

I hadn't realized that my hand had encircled his left wrist. When Anglin finally winces, I know it actually is my own grip that's causing that greasy brow to crease in pain.

'I know the law. I know what harassment is, Lieutenant. You can't do this. I mean, you can't—'

I grab hold of that wrist even harder, until I'm sure it's just this side of snapping.

'Ahhh . . .' he cries out.

Now Eddie is holding *me* back.

'You're a fish, Anglin. You're not even a lizard. I'm going to be there when the smoke rises right out of your fucking gills.'

Anglin shoves away from us, here at the accepting desk. But he won't look back at me as he heads toward the exit doors.

Chapter Two

[December 1998]

I looked down at the dead body at my feet. She'd been twenty years old, her driver's license revealed as I held it up to the dim-wattage bulb above us.

'Jimmy, she's had her throat cut,' Doc told me. 'Twice. In the area of the jugular. This guy took his time and did some nice, precise cutting. Something like our previous buddy.'

He was referring to Marco Karrios, the so-called 'Farmer'. He'd cut women for their internal organs – until my wife met up with him at our house. She shot him in the chest, and I was lucky enough to arrive on the scene and pop him with a head shot that ruined our brand-new mauve sofa. My wife Natalie worked Burglary / Auto Theft as a detective. She was on the fast track to becoming a Homicide cop, like Doc Gibron and me already were.

'Lieutenant Parisi, the photographers are here,' one of the uniforms told me.

We got out of their way for the moment.

'There's something familiar about those cuts,' Doc said.

'The Farmer's dead. I was there.'

Doc looked over at me. 'I don't mean him. I mean there's something familiar about this guy's whole situation here. She was a student nurse,' he said, indicating the corpse.

'My God, Harold, that guy must be either dead or pushing sixty by now. He left town. I ought to know. My old man was on that case, what, thirty years ago. Anglin. Carl Anglin.'

'I'm simply saying it looks like the case file for him. I was just getting off the street when your dad took him down.'

'And they had to let him go.'

'It wasn't your old man's fault, Jimmy.'

My old man, the boozing Homicide cop. I'd been embarrassed to bring friends to the house because he'd be there in one of his 'states'. But I also joined the police because of him. Jake Parisi. When he was straight he was good. I tried to break away from him, but everything that happened to me pulled me closer to the old man's world. The streets. The stiffs. Christ knows he could be brutal and unpitying, but he always had a look he threw my way that brought me to him like there was some secret he wanted to whisper to me.

'I know. Circumstances. A Homicide cop's nightmare. Main witness goes looey-looey. Goes into a coma-like state, and then the other witness who puts Anglin near the dorm gets himself popped in a drive-by before the trial. They have to let Anglin walk . . . But there's another problem here.'

'What's that?'

'There's only the one victim, Doc. Anglin slaughtered several girls at one go. He was one of the first "spree" killers.'

Doc was laid back when it got to my father. He knew the pain involved with the old man and me. He understood what the shrinks call lack of 'closure'. There certainly was that – lack of finality, I mean. The way he left us . . .

My mother, Eleanor, survived. The old man went some years back. But as I said, there was no closure.

We were at St. Emily's School for Nursing. It was on the northwestern fringe of the city. Anglin did his thing on the West Side, all those years ago. This couldn't have been him. He disappeared. He was smart enough to know that he had to if he was going to dodge the big slug. My father was on him. On him enough that Anglin knew that even this huge city wouldn't hide him. Jake wouldn't give up on him. Hell, he *didn't* give up on him.

But Anglin would be an old man now. Too old and too cautious to carve up a young woman like the girl we saw on the floor.

Someone must have been thinking on the same wavelength as my partner because the Feds showed up. The FBI. They asked permission to cross our yellow tape, and naturally we were generous enough to grant them access.

'The vultures have landed.'

Doc had no use for the Fibbies. He thought they were generally incompetent. He much preferred to work with US Marshals if he had to work with Federal law enforcement agents at all, and I tended to agree with him.

Jim Mason was the special agent who appeared on scene with an assistant I didn't recognize.

'What's the big interest here in one dead girl?' I asked Mason.

'Oh, just what you might call a passing interest,' Mason said.

He was about six feet five, an ex-Duke University basketball player. Had a cup of coffee with the Seattle NBA club. Fucked up his knees, I heard.

He was also one of the few black Feds we knew in this town.

'In other words, you ain't telling us,' Doc said as he smiled over at him.

Mason pointed a finger, like a gun barrel, at my partner and grinned himself.

So we ignored Mason and his girlfriend – his partner was a white female – and we finished up our end before the body-bag people toted the student nurse's remains away.

Her name was Martha Eisner. She was from LaSalle, Illinois. We had the task of telling her mother and father that their daughter had been raped and murdered and that we didn't have any idea, at the moment, who had killed their girl.

This was the worst aspect of Homicide. Doc and I had a long ride to north central Illinois, and there was no use stalling.

They lived in a ranch-style place. Simple, not very expensive. Working class. LaSalle seemed to be a blue-collar area. At least, where the Eisners lived it was. It was 10.00 a.m. by the time we arrived at their door. Doc rang the bell, but I'd do the talking.

We identified ourselves as soon as a woman in her mid-forties opened the door. When she saw the shields, her mouth dropped open.

She let us in. Her husband was at work. She would have been at work, she told us, but she'd taken a sick day. A migraine, she explained.

'I'm afraid we have to inform you that your daughter's been killed.'

I didn't know any way to soften the blow except by being direct and getting it over with.

Her knees buckled and I caught her before she hit the well-worn carpet.

Doc helped me get her to the couch. Then my partner went into the kitchen to get her a glass of water. What good water did, I'd never understood, but Mrs. Jane Eisner took a sip before her emotions bubbled out of her. She sobbed for a good long time. Then the sound subsided and I asked her if she was able to answer any questions.

No, there was no steady boyfriend. No, there'd been no messy breakup with any male friend she knew of. She couldn't imagine anyone wanting to harm her child – I couldn't understand why anyone would want to take her girl's life either. Not yet, at least.

But we would. We almost always found out why.

The interview lasted another twenty minutes. We waited until the husband, Eric, arrived home. His reaction was more hostile.

'I knew that goddamn city would kill her. You don't see that kind of thing going on around here . . . How can you stand to handle the . . . the filth you have to deal with? Doesn't it tire you . . . Doesn't it—?'

Then he began to sob. Jane rose off the couch and went over to console him, but he forced her away. And none too gently, I saw. I wondered if this was a happy marriage. Her migraines. His attitude. But that was a dead end. If I asked I'd find out that he was home all night, got up for work around six . . . No, he hadn't killed his girl. We were the ones who'd have to find out who had. It had been a long, hard drive up here, and now we'd have to head back to Chicago to find out who'd really killed Martha Eisner.

'How can you stand to deal with all the animals up there?' the grieving father wanted to know.

We told him we were sorry for his loss, and then we got back into the Taurus and headed toward the Interstate and home.

Home. Indeed. The city, where I'd lived my whole life.

I was staring out my office window, looking at Lake Michigan. This view was the only perk of my job. Other than catching the pricks that committed murder. This kid had been a junior. One more year to go to get her bachelor's degree in nursing. She'd wanted to help people and a morgue was where she'd wound up.

I began to wonder if her father hadn't been right. Maybe life in some small town would be safer. I had two grown children and one infant – via Natalie, my second wife. Maybe it would be more secure for all of them if we moved.

But I loved this place in spite of its ability to depress the hell out of me. The killings did pile up, on occasion.

My father, Jake, had been in Homicide in the 1950s and 1960s. He'd been good at it, too. Put lots of bad people off the streets. But he'd liked to drink. Excessively. To the point that he and my mother did not share a bedroom the last few years of their marriage.

My father had left me with the ultimate mystery. I'd been trying to solve the puzzle of his death since the day he'd left us, but the answer did not come. I'd been through therapy. I'd endured counseling. Nothing straightened it out.

And I'd taken the case to the source itself.

My mother.

The murder of the second young nurse was called in the

next day. The people on her floor thought she'd gone home for the weekend, so no one thought to knock on her door until late Monday afternoon when she was supposed to have returned from morning classes.

This one's name was Renee Jackson, a black female from the West Side.

She had been cut in the same way as the Eisner girl. Deep penetration at the jugular. Twice.

'I think that son of a bitch Anglin is back,' Doc told me as the flashes from the cameras of the scene-of-crime photographers popped around us.

'He was supposed to be in Utah after he wrote that book about being the accused killer of the original seven girls. He was a cause célèbre or whatever for all those sixties liberals. You remember?'

'Remember? Hell, I'm still one of them . . .,' Doc reminded me. 'Yeah. He went out west with the book money. Then there was the movie. The cops were picking on an indigent sailor. Anglin the victim. All that shit. He made some good dough. Enough to hide out in the mountains, with occasional side trips to Las Vegas and Nevada to visit the chicken farms. He had a penchant for whores, I think I read.'

'So the Feds are thinking the same way you are.'

'Why else would they show up on scene like that, unannounced?'

'Because they're Fibbie geeks with minimal caseloads, Doc. Too much money. All dressed up and nowhere to go.'

'You sound highly prejudicial,' my partner said, smiling wryly.

'You think the captain'll pop for two round trips to the Rockies?'

We flew economy to Salt Lake City. We had to rent a four-wheel, all-terrain vehicle to make the trip up into the mountains from there. The Captain would not be happy about the extra expense, but we'd been warned by the local police that other transportation would get us stuck and maybe even frozen to death.

The Utah locals had Anglin living just three miles east of Wheeler. Wheeler itself was not even on the map, so they had to give us directions.

And the worst part was that Anglin hadn't been heard from or spotted in ten months. The mailman was the first to notice when all the mail began to pile up uncollected.

The higher we went on this highway, the colder it became. When we reached the snow line, we were close to the small town. There was a Seven Eleven at the far edge of Wheeler. We stopped there to pee and to get directions to Anglin's shack or whatever it was he lived in.

The geezer behind the counter knew Anglin. He said he was one of the few in town who would be able to remember this recluse who had once been accused of murder. The kids in town were glued to their video screens, he explained. They didn't read newspapers or even watch the TV news.

Doc tapped his kidney and so did I. I was glad I was wearing my flight jacket. The cold was brutal up there, even allowing for the fact that it was winter. They must have missed summer altogether.

'Nah, it warms up into the forties in August,' the geezer behind the counter said, grinning.

I was so preoccupied with getting to Anglin that I hadn't noticed the beauties of the Utah scenery. It was awesome. Big sky, big mountains. Clear air to breathe. No stench of chemicals here. God's country.

But it was being shared by a man my father had pursued all through the final years of his life.

When we got to the turnoff where the old man at the Seven Eleven had told us to turn right, we saw the house set back about a quarter-mile from the highway. It was no shack, but it wasn't paradise either. It was a modest one-level ranch-style place with a large front picture window.

We approached the house more slowly now in our dark green Jimmy.

When we arrived in front of the structure, we saw that there were no cars or vehicles in front of Anglin's place. Doc was driving. He stopped the Jimmy right in front of the doorway.

I knocked on the door. Repeatedly. No one answered. I remembered the mailman. I went out to the mailbox by the road and I found it crammed with junk mail. Then I walked back to the door and Doc.

'Got your little bag of tricks?' I asked him.

I was referring to his burglar's tools.

'Yeah. I'm always prepared.'

He took a pouch out of his winter-coat pocket. He reached in for a slim piece of metal that reminded me of a scalpel. He inserted the blade into the front door's lock and then he turned it back and forth. He popped the dead bolt in less than forty-five seconds. Professional speed.

'I used to be faster,' he apologized, smiling rather embarrassedly.

We took out our weapons. We entered the living room slowly and quietly.

Doc tried to turn on the overhead light in the room, but nothing happened when the switch clicked. I took out the flashlight from my flight jacket, and turned its beam toward the floor.

We worked our way toward the kitchen. In the kitchen we found a large refrigerator. It seemed Anglin had done fairly well from his novel about the oppression he'd experienced from the Chicago Police Department.

When Doc opened the refrigerator's door, he hopped back in fright.

'What?' I asked.

'Shit. The son of a bitch has left an opened can of tomato juice. It's turning fucking black. Christ, has the man no sense of hygiene?'

'You scared the shit out of me. I thought you'd found somebody's goddamn body parts.'

'Nah. That was that other homicidal fuck from Milwaukee.'

I heard a soft sound coming from farther back in the house.

Doc touched my sleeve. He put a finger to his lips, and then he removed his nine-millimeter from his shoulder holster.

I had the Bulldog still tucked into in my ankle holster, but I had my own nine in my right hand now.

We made our way quickly and quietly into the interior of Anglin's house. It was cold in there. His heating must have been turned off after he'd been gone a few months.

Doc directed me toward the single bedroom on the left, at the back of the house.

He checked his weapon and I checked mine. Then we kicked open the door and found Special Agent Mason and his attractive female assistant aiming their own guns directly at our noggins.

Chapter Three

[June 1968]

The girl is still traumatized by whatever horrors she endured at the hands of Carl Anglin. Now the Federal Bureau of Investigation has joined the fight to put the nails into Anglin. We are required to assist them, but we do not like to share the playing field with the FBI investigators. It's a matter of pride and territory. They're pissing on our trees. The fucking government has to intrude into the job. They can't just fuck up their own patch. Eddie thinks I'm paranoid about the Feds because they're staring over our shoulders. I'm not sure what 'paranoid' means, but I know when someone's breathing down my neck. This is the 1960s. Racial harmony, understanding, integration, Martin Luther King . . . I'm all for equal rights. I've seen the work some of our black men in blue have done on the streets – when I start talking race, everyone assumes I hate blacks or anybody darker than a wop. Truth is, I hate any guy who blames his load on his background. Sink or swim, motherfucker, on your own.

Things come up with the aid of all that government money, though. We find out unusual information about our subject. Anglin's not the ignorant hillbilly we thought he was. He graduated high school in the upper third of his class and he has two years of college behind him. He studied languages at a junior college, and his grades were high. Then he entered the US Navy and saw duty just after the Korean

War. It appears he was a member of an elite force in the Navy, but his active-duty records are 'classified'. Which disturbs the shit out of me. I was in the Rangers, but everything we did was on record. Practically everything, anyway. When they start showing you 'classified', it means that this guy was part of something that would probably embarrass the US Government. Which means he was probably in the murder-for-hire business, but it's not called that because he was wearing a uniform when it took place. I'm talking about a well-trained assassin. I understand that I'm doing a lot of guesswork here, but there's got to be a reason Anglin's under the veil.

Eddie thinks the guy works for the Spooks – the CIA. Eddie reads a lot of fiction.

But it gets my nose turned upwind. Isn't it remarkable that one witness turns up dead and another has two-way conversations with her thumbs in a mental ward? It's too remarkable.

So we set out to examine the demise of Johnnie Robinson, the dishwasher. When we talk to the people at the rib joint where he worked, across the street from the infamous death dorm, they give us a sullen look when we ask questions. It seems they've been grilled by the top people in Homicide and now they don't want to go through the procedure again. It's as if they were frightened by the previous investigators.

I find out that Captain Quigley, my boss, did the preliminary investigation of Robinson's killing. It is very unusual for a police captain to be doing such routine fieldwork. So after Eddie and I get done talking to the brothers at the rib joint, I go back downtown for a talk with Quigley.

'I hope you don't mind answering a few questions I have about the Anglin case,' I say to the balding, six-foot-two captain.

'The case is over. We need to catch the real killer,' he informs me, a very sour look on his face.

'I don't think it is . . . over, sir. I think we got the right guy. But what troubles me is losing two witnesses in such a short time-span . . . It makes me smell a fix.'

'Are you accusing me of something, Lieutenant Parisi?'

'Of course not, sir.'

I can sense Eddie squirming behind me.

I'm sitting in the chair in front of the captain's desk, and Eddie is standing a pace or two back.

'Then what is this bullshit you're throwing at me?'

'Why would a police captain investigate a murder that would normally be processed by somebody like me or my partner here? Was it considered high-profile? The popping of a dishwasher on the west side?'

'All murders are high-priority, Lieutenant. You should know that.'

I don't grant him the courtesy of agreeing because we both know it's a lie. All deaths are not equal. Just like all lives aren't – in the real world of the streets.

'I find it strange that you'd have the time or opportunity to investigate the death of one witness in a case that's already been tanked, for all practical purposes.'

'I don't much care what you find odd about what I do, Parisi. And if you don't want some hot jets to scorch your ass, you better find a new angle on this case, Lieutenant.'

The captain is a fucking harp. A Mick. He thinks all of us goombahs are connected to the Outfit. Like most Irish, he can't distinguish one Italian from another. We're all freaking Sicilians, to him.

End of discussion. I stand and we leave.

Eddie sips at his coffee in my office. I prefer Coca-Cola. There are no windows in my cubicle. The room seems perpetually dark, even with the lights on.

'Carl Anglin was into something. I think Robinson was a pro job, not a drive-by. I think somebody got to any witnesses on scene when Johnnie caught his death of cold,' I tell my partner.

'I don't like all this sidelight shit. I liked it better when it was a simple multiple homicide.'

'I'm sorry to screw up your day.'

'Why would anyone want Anglin off the hook?' Eddie demands.

'Because he's done something somebody thinks is worse. Something a lot more embarrassing to somebody.'

Eddie sips at his black coffee again, and then he puts the paper cup into my wastebasket.

'I hate fucking complicated shit like this. We catch a killer, they get lit up. That's how it's supposed to work, Jake. This is bat shit, this.'

He walks out the door, announcing that he's going to take a dump and read the sports page. It'll clear his mind, he says.

'Hello, Greek.'

This time it's gone beyond the usual limit of five.

'Maybe I better get you a cab, Jake,' the Greek says from out of some corner where I can barely see him. 'You're wrecked, buddy. Let me call you a ride,' he repeats.

Again words of refusal come out of me from some unknown place.

I stagger out of the Greek's and make my way to the unmarked car that I use. I stop suddenly and start vomiting beside the driver's door.

Puking is unusual for me. But it clears my head a bit, and I think I'll be able to navigate home now. I get inside the car and open all the windows in the four-door Ford. But I can still smell myself when I get inside, so I reach into the glove compartment for the mints I stash in there, just in case. My badge'll get me by if I bob and weave, but you never know if some hard-on'll try to make a name for himself by busting a cop for Driving While Intoxicated. So the breath mints are insurance.

I make it home without incident. But the vomiting frightens me.

Eleanor is not up waiting for me at this hour – it's 4.35 a.m. So I go directly to my bedroom.

My son Jimmy is going to the university downtown to get his bachelor's degree, but he says he wants to join the police force when he graduates. I try to dissuade him every way I can. I tell him about the corruption on the job, about all the assholes who make it on sheer politics rather than ability. But he won't listen. He has wanted to be a cop since he was twelve, I think. All the way through high school until now. And there's nothing I can think to say that'll point him in a different direction. He's a smart boy, Jimmy. Good grades.

He reads a lot. I don't have the time or the will. He's quieter than I am, too. My wife told me that when Jimmy turned six. He's the thinker in the clan, his mother insists. He'll be a better husband and father, I guess. He seems to have a lot more patience than the old man.

I can't say 'nigger' or 'spic' or 'wop' or anything with a flavor of the street in front of the kid. Eleanor has threatened to shoot me.

I think of him as I drift off on top of my mattress. I can smell the puke again, but I wander off in spite of the odor.

'I've been drafted,' my son tells me at the dinner table the next evening. Eating dinner with both of them is an event which takes place only rarely.

'What're you talking about? You haven't graduated yet.'

'They've taken the 2-S away. I'm 1-A. Took the physical last week.'

'So?'

'So I lied to you. I dropped out at the end of the semester. I let myself be drafted.'

'You're shitting me.'

'No, Pa. I'm not lying.'

'But your grades . . . They were real good.'

'Yeah. A three-point GPA.'

'What the hell's the matter with you?'

My wife pours him another coffee.

'Didn't you try to stop him?' I ask her.

She ignores me.

'What is this? Some kind of goddamn conspiracy?'

'You never gave him a nickel for his education. You got nothing to say to him,' Eleanor finally tells me.

'Don't start that again—'

'It was my call, Pa. Mom had nothing to do with this . . . Look, the Second World War was yours. This one is mine. I feel like I'm avoiding something I ought to be part of.'

'Everybody hates this war, Junior. You read the papers?'

'Did anybody fall in love with *your* fight?'

He's clever, this kid. He'll make a fine interrogator. He knows how to counterpunch.

'I was hoping you'd miss this one, Sonny.'

He hates being called 'Sonny'.

'It's my turn. I was putting off what had to happen. That's all.'

Eleanor's crying.

'Momma. Stop it.'

'Shut up,' she warns him.

'Can't you sign back up for school? Can't you change your mind?'

'He hates living here! Are you a fool? Can't you see?' she cries.

I look down at my half-eaten steak.

'I'll cut back, if that's what this is all—'

'He's afraid to bring Erin home. He's afraid they'll run into you. Drunk. You, Jake. Do you understand?'

'I . . . I can stop. I can change. You don't need to go to a goddamned war to get me to—'

'I'm not going for that reason. I already told you. It's my turn. You don't get to pick your battles. They pick you, Pa. How many times you told me just that?'

'I can stop, Jimmy. For Christ's sake, all you had to do was tell me that I was . . . embarrassing—'

'You don't embarrass me, Pa.'

'You're a horseshit liar, Jimmy'

He doesn't try to keep it up. I get up from the table and walk directly out the door. The moist air smacks my face with its spring lushness, but all I can remember is my son being embarrassed by me. What angers me is that I've known it all along. I could see him directing that girlfriend of his – Erin – out our front door as soon as he saw I was home in the evening. I barely got a look at her. And she's the one he's in love with, Eleanor tells me. Whenever she's speaking to me.

I've driven my son out of the house. My son. My flesh and blood—

I know better. She can't fool me. She never could lie to me. Jimmy's not mine, except in name. He's my brother Nick's child. I had mumps when I was a teenager. The doctor thinks the mumps was why Eleanor and I were unable to have a baby, the first few years after we were married. Suddenly she's pregnant with Jimmy, but I remember we'd been sleeping together very infrequently after the doctor told me I might be sterile. The marriage was going bad. We were drifting apart.

She knew Nick before she began dating me. My younger brother Nick. Then he takes off for the oil fields to make his pot of gold. He fails completely, but when he gets back the two of us are together. Engaged.

He still carries the heat for Eleanor to this day. Somehow she convinced him to help her have a baby. Neither of them have ever confessed and I've never put the question directly to them, but I know.

Jimmy's Nick's boy. Not mine. I can see his father in his eyes.

But we pretend, the three of us. We play that I got divine fertility on just one night and I made him from one creative burst of sperm.

Jimmy. Nick's boy. Pretending to be my dutiful son. I love him, but he's not mine. We look like a family but we're not.

She wants reasons for the drink? Do I need another? I know it's a crutch. I ought to confront her and my brother, get it out in the open. But more than twenty years have passed, and I'm afraid if I ask I'll get the answer I dread the most. This is one interrogation I can't handle.

Nick made Eleanor pregnant to console her. So she'd get at least something out of this marriage. It's more like an arrangement for the both of us. She cleans and cooks and says she wants to get herself a job when Jimmy's finally out on his own.

I drove my own boy out of the house. Even if I'm not his natural father, I've been a father to him for two decades. Nick hasn't. He's stayed respectfully out of the way. He rarely comes over here.

Jimmy's going off to the war in Vietnam. It's a lousy war and no one likes it.

My war was a lousy war and I hated it. It frightened me, it twisted me, it wrung me out. There was nothing good about it until it was history.

I've lost my kid. Now I'll spend twenty-four months in hell, waiting for him to get out of southeast Asia.

This is my judgment, my penance, my punishment. I don't need a padre to explain it to me. God's kicking my ass for all my faults. And even though Jimmy doesn't really belong to me, the illusion was better than nothing. Better than no son at all. Better than sterility and an unhappy marriage. He was there for a while, and now he's about to leave.

The rain begins to fall gently as I'm halfway down our block of bungalows. House after house is identical to its neighbor.

I feel the warm droplets soak my shoulders. I've forgotten to put on my jacket.

The waitress at the rib joint doesn't want to talk in front of the boss. So Eddie and I take her for a short drive when her break comes up at 7.30 p.m.

Her name is Estella Johnson. Black, thirty-five years old, divorced, she lets us know.

She sits in the back of the car with Eddie. She's big-bosomed and very sexy. Eddie is already red in the puss.

Estella smiles perfect pearlies at my Polack partner.

'This po-lice captain makes a big deal of the fact that we all agree what we saw the night Robinson got tapped.'

'What did you all agree on?' I ask from behind the driver's wheel.

Eddie's about ready to swallow his tongue from lust. Estella's got to be a big draw for the rib joint.

'That it was fo' black mens in the car that drive by and pop Johnnie Robinson.'

'And you disagreed with that story?' I ask.

'I has my doubts.'

'About what part?' Eddie finally queries.

I look in the rear view and see him smiling and squirming. He's single and he's wondering what a black woman would be like after all those lily-white Polish girls from the southwest part of town.

'It might be that the dudes in the car were a little lighter in the complexion than your captain would want us to believe.'

'You think they were white shooters?' Eddie asks.

'There were only two in that car. Not four. I could see them right out the front window. They must've knew what time Johnny go outside for his nicotine addiction. They were there the second Johnny walk out, and then I see the passenger's window roll down and then I hear the pops. Motherfuckers usin' a .22. Everybody in this neighborhood know that a small piece like that is used by them pro-fessional killahs. Them slugs go all crazy when they gets inside you.'

'You think they were white,' I repeat.

'Didn't look like brothas to me. But I could be wrong.'

'And there were two, not three or four?' I ask.

'Both of them was sittin' up front. I couldn't see them all that clear, but I know they wasn't from this goddamn neighborhood. Y'all need to check closer to home.'

Estella takes hold of Eddie's hand and pulls it to her left breast. I have to tear my gaze away immediately from the two of them. Estella giggles. I pity my partner.

Chapter Four

[January 1999]

The Feds eventually lowered their weapons, as did Doc and I. But they gave us no information – what we found we discovered on our own. What my partner and I did locate was Anglin's yearbook. I stuffed it into my briefcase, and we carried it off the premises of Anglin's Utah dwelling before the Fibbies could scream foul.

Back in Chicago, I took a good look at our subject. He'd been an athlete and a scholar and had seemed to get along well with his peers. A member of the swimming and cross-country teams. Honor roll, several times. The guy fit a more modern kind of serial profile – like a Ted Bundy.

We needed to interview Anglin's mother. Perhaps he'd contacted her in the ten months since he'd disappeared.

The man could be dead. This could be some other player that we hadn't picked up on. It could be a copycat. Someone who'd read all the literature on Anglin.

I didn't think so. I thought he was geared up for a come-back. He was having all that fun being a celebrity killer who got off the hook. Doing the talk shows, appearing in the tabloids. Playing the victim to the hilt. And all the while *his* seven victims, the seven nurses, had no one to speak for them. Once that had been the role of my father, Jake. But after his accident, if that was what it was, the Department had put Anglin on the back burner. Life went on, everyone kept insisting. You couldn't keep kicking a dead pooch. The son of a bitch got off. We didn't nab him. My father went to his death and never had the satisfaction of Carl Anglin's incarceration.

The problem with Anglin's mother was that she'd be very old if she had indeed survived. Had to be in her eighties, Doc figured, reasoning that Anglin was in his sixties. If Carl was still breathing.

Yeah, he was alive. I could feel his pulse off in the corner of my office. I could remember my dad telling me about the greenness of his eyes. Like some jungle cat's, Jake had said.

My old man did not tell horror tales. He wasn't trying to spook me. I'd heard about those eyes from my father's partner, Eddie Lezniak, as well. Eddie had retired and now lived in Indiana on a ten-acre piece of land with his own pond full of fish.

Jake Parisi never talked much to me at all. It was like he was keeping me at arm's length because he was afraid I'd get too close. When I found out I was really Nick's son, I understood why Jake had never let me close any distance between us. But I always felt he loved me in spite of my biology.

The first thing we found out was where Anglin's mother worked. She was a single parent, my old man's files informed us. She lived in Cleveland and worked at Richardson, Robinson and Trask, it read. A law firm. She was a legal secretary. When we contacted the Cleveland firm, we found she'd moved to Chicago fifteen years ago. We got her address at her new firm from the old group. When we called Smith, Talbot and Turner, we heard that Patricia Anglin had left that legal group six years ago. They had an address for her, and we decided to visit her in person.

Patricia Anglin was in her early eighties, as Doc had guessed. But she seemed very bright. When we asked a question she responded promptly, even briskly. There was obvious antagonism in her eyes as she answered our questions, here at her retirement complex. She had an apartment in this village of senior citizens.

'You hounded Carl thirty years ago, and now you want to start up with him all over again.'

'We want to talk to him. Yes,' Doc told her. He smiled at her, but her response wasn't exactly amiable.

'You were after him and you couldn't prove anything because my Carl is not a murderer. Did you know he was in the Navy?'

I nodded.

'Did you know that he was involved in secret operations for our government?'

'Yes,' I told her.

'My son was a hero . . . And then he decided he wanted to get out of the service. But they didn't want to release him. They said what he did was too "classified". Whatever that meant. So he stayed on for two more years, and then he really quit. It was like they'd kidnapped him. I don't know where he served or what he did, but he came back different. He wasn't the same boy they'd signed up. He was quieter. More sullen . . . But he wasn't the monster who killed those nurses. If he killed anyone, it was while he was wearing a uniform . . . Now, I'm very tired and I haven't anything else to say to you, and if you ever come back I'll need to have an attorney present.'

She stood as straight-backed as an Army drill instructor.

'You don't have any idea where your son can be located, then?' I asked, trying to smile encouragingly.

She huffed, we said thank you – and we got the hell out.

'Tough. She made you, you know,' Doc said to me as we drove the Taurus back to the Lake Shore.

'Made me?'

'She recognized your name as soon as she heard it. I saw it on her face. Instant recognition, Jimmy. She made you as Jake's boy. That old broad's got a bear trap for a memory. She knows where sonny boy's at, too.'

'You think so?'

'Enough to have her eyeballed until further notice.'

'Surveillance?'

'Indeed, Lieutenant Parisi.'

'So be it,' I agreed. 'We'll set up the shifts when we get back to the office.'

The stages of the drive from the retirement home back into town were marked by changes in the smells. When we reached the outskirts of Chicago, we sniffed the stink of the chemical plants on the western edge. As we changed direction and headed eastward, there was the smell of the icy lake water. The Loop had a scent of its own. There was nothing exactly like it.

We pulled into the parking lot next to the central downtown headquarters. I halted the navy blue Taurus in its marked spot, we hopped out, and then we headed up in the elevator to the floor that housed Homicide.

He'd cut their throats twice. That had been to kill. The other damage was done postmortem. That was the style of the newest slayings as well. It looked like Anglin, and I had a feeling my father would have said it felt like him, too. Maybe he was getting too old to do multiples simultaneously, the way he'd murdered the nurses. Or maybe he was working himself up to another grand finale-type multiple homicide. I was trying to figure it his way. He was tantalizing us. He knew, if he read the papers, that I was on this investigation. My name had been in print more often than I'd have liked it to appear. It didn't help us for him to know who was coming after him, but it was a free press.

Perhaps, after all, it was to my advantage, his being aware of me. Maybe he'd remember my dad and Eddie Lezniak. Maybe he'd recall how he got lucky with them, losing two witnesses against him. Or maybe he knew why it was a fix. A sure thing.

We headed back to the point of origin. To the location of the original killings. We stopped at the rib joint across the street from the girls' dormitory, there on the West Side. It was thirty years later, but we found out that Billie Lee still owned and operated the restaurant. Billie Lee was close to retirement age. She appeared to be about sixty-five. Black woman, medium height, natural 'do'. They used to call that style 'unconked'.

We took a walk outside the small rib house with Billie. She looked a little sullen and suspicious when Doc explained what two Homicide cops were there for.

'That been over for, what – thirty years?' she complained.

'It ain't over 'til it's over,' Doc said and smiled at her. The two of them. Senior citizens, I was thinking. Doc was sixty-three. They were both Korean War-era.

'What you expec' me to recall about somethin' been gone for three ten-spots?' she asked, smiling. She was trying to appear relaxed. Even nonchalant.

'I think you gave the police some bad evidence the night your man got popped out here on the street. You said you saw a car full of African-Americans drive by and kill our witness. I think you saw something else,' I told her.

My bluntness seemed to have frightened her.

'I told the po-lice just exactly what I saw.'

'I think you're lying,' I said, grinning wolfishly.

Doc stepped in to become her pal in time of need.

'Easy, Jimmy. I don't see why Billie here would fabricate anything.'

'Fabricate? What the fuck do "fabricate" mean?' Billie blurted out.

'It means lie. It means to bullshit a police officer. You know where that leads, Billie?' I was bullying her now.

'Take it easy, Lieutenant,' Doc said. He gave me a sly wink.

He walked down the street with Billie. They were alone for a couple of minutes, about a half-block from where I stood. Then they headed back my way.

'Jimmy, I think the lady was strong-armed into giving false evidence. I think we can help her,' Doc said, his face straight.

'This all go down thirty fucking years ago. Why you want to mess wid me now?'

'There've been more since Carl Anglin did his thing, Billie. Two more that we know about. And one of the new ones was a sister. I mean she was black, an African-American.

And no one's paid for those seven young girls. You haven't forgotten them, have you, Billie?' I asked.

'I ain't forgotten them, no. That was a terrible thing. Terrible. I never forget it. We was all scared to take a smoke outside here after it happened . . . Look. A white po-lice come up to me after the first po-lice—'

'That was my father, Lieutenant Jake Parisi.'

'Yeah. I remember his name . . . The next po-lice don't give me no name. Don't show no badge, neither. But he tell me all about the Health Department and how they can find rats in most any bidness, and I figure I ought to cooperate wid this po-lice. Him and his fuckin' rats. This place all I got, and this man say I'm gonna go on fuckin' food stamps if I don't cooperate.'

'You cooperate with us and I'll guarantee nobody's going to shut you down for rats or any other damn thing. You have my word,' I told Billie.

'Maybe . . . maybe it wadn't no black men killed your witness. Maybe it was just two white men wearin' ski masks to cover their faces.'

'You sure, Billie?' Doc asked. 'Don't just tell us something you think's gonna make us happy.'

'Nah. That's the way it was. I was lookin' out that glass front door, about ready to tell the lazy son of a bitch to get his ass back to work, and along come this unmarked car—'

'You mean like a squad car?'

'Like a detective's car, yeah . . . They pull up to him, he turn around like he's gonna bolt away when he see them ski masks, and they put two shots in him from a .22. I could tell it was a .22. Heard enough gunfire in this neighborhood to know the difference.'

I could see the fear in her dark face, even out there with only the streetlights illuminating this West Side side street.

'You gonna get me killed, Lieutenant.'

'Nobody's going to know we ever talked to you, Billie,' Doc assured her.

'That's right. We're going to keep an eye on you. Don't worry.'

'Don't worry. That's what my two ex-husbands say. First one choke on my own spare ribs. The other one fall flat on his face in Vegas with the only blackjack winner he hit after losin' three thousand dollars . . . Don't worry.'

We walked her back inside, and then we came back out to the car.

On the drive back Doc started to put pieces into the puzzle.

'Were they ours or were they Feds?'

'I don't think they were ours. I know how prejudiced we both are against the government issue, so let's try to be reasonable. Something's connected to Anglin's military service. He was involved in classified operations, so we assume that the spooks were trying to protect one of their own. Maybe Carl threatened to blab everything on *Sixty Minutes*. Who knows? They saved his ass on the seven nurses because he was involved in something very touchy. Something sensitive enough that they figure it's national security.'

'Maybe we're widening the scenario,' Doc mused.

'Could be. Maybe Billie is full of shit. Maybe she gave us what she thinks we wanted to hear . . . But I don't think so. I think Anglin was involved in something someone thinks is extremely significant.'

'What would that be, Jimmy? Did he whack some dictator? Make some despot disappear?'

'He's into something they don't want us to know about . . . We need to see the workup on the witness's shooting.'

I made the call to Evidence, and they said they'd expedite.

The return call came in a half-hour.

They had a file for me to see, so Doc and I took the elevator downstairs. We entered their cubicle, and Randy Smithson had the file ready.

Doc and I took the lift back up to Homicide. We went back into my office. Doc didn't like his space – said it was too small. So that was why he hung out with me so often, even when we weren't working the streets.

The information about the caliber of the weapon had been razored out. It'd been excised.

'What's the story on the cutouts?' I asked Smithson on the phone.

He professed ignorance, as I'd supposed he would. I hung up. It was no use. The trail was three decades old, and I was trying to follow along as if my father were still around, ending his shift with all those shots and beers at the Greek's saloon.

'Where now?' Doc said and smiled sadly.

The Redhead had no advice for me. She was my wife – Detective Natalie Parisi.

'Seems like it's a no-winner, Jimmy. Everybody loses. The nurses, your dad. You, too. This thing with Anglin, sometimes it happens that way.'

She sounded like a thirty-year vet. So I humored her.

'Yeah, sometimes.'

'You're not quitting though, are you?' she asked, smiling quizzically.

She was bent over the crib wherein our newest addition lay. My daughter's name was Mary. A fitting Mick moniker for a redhead, born of a redhead whose maiden name was Manion. Half guinea, half harp. Should turn out to be a drunken kidnapper, Doc wisecracked.

She had auburn-colored hair, actually, what little there was of it. My wife's hair's hue was the same. It was the most beautiful color for a topknot that I could imagine.

'He doesn't walk. He doesn't get a free pass. He's going to pay for the seven young women he killed and the two new additions to his lists. My old man was still after him when he died. Jake Parisi didn't let go and, by Christ, neither will I.'

The baby began to cry, so I picked her up.

'Hey. All that wasn't directed at you, toots.'

'Toots? What the hell is that?' Natalie demanded.

'It means sweet, in the old country. My mother used to call me that before I wouldn't let her anymore.'

My girl Mary had green eyes, but they were nothing like the way Jake told me Anglin's eyes were. My girl's eyes put you at ease, they were so soft and muted. Carl Anglin's shade of green was intense, the old man had said. It came out of the dark corners of a room and found you wherever you hid. Like a jungle cat's eyes. Stalking. Preying. Looking for any kind of a weakness, any kind of hole in your defenses.

He massacred those seven young women. He hog-tied them and then he went to work on each of the gagged girls. They were killed in a line, like at a slaughterhouse. Each of them had to wait their turn. He ungagged them as he worked his way down the row, but he made sure they wouldn't scream too loud or too long. He cut their throats down to the bone, you see. He severed the larynx, making it impossible for them to sustain any loud sounds. Anglin cut the jugular twice to make sure the bleeding would be at maximum flow. They'd die quickly, but he would take copious amounts of time with the dying and dead victims. The torture was taking place between life and death, I'd say. When they stopped, he didn't, necessarily.

Jake, my father, told me about Anglin because he didn't want me to follow in his professional footsteps.

'This is the kind of work I do, Jimmy,' he told me, just before I went to Vietnam. 'This is the kind of shitty business I'm in.'

'Then why do you do it?' I asked.

'Because I'm good at it. I've got a nose for shit. Human excrement walking on two legs, I mean. I know when people lie. I have a nose for lies, too. I smell all the odors in both nostrils, Jimmy. That's my gift. It's like a sense. An extra one past the usual sense of smell. I've got an educated schnoz, sonny. The crap had better stay downwind when I'm around.' He smiled.

Then he took a tug at his sweating quart of Old Style.

I went to Vietnam where I killed several men. I'm not proud of those killings. I came home and married my first wife, Erin. I became a policeman after graduating from the Academy. Twelve years later, I had a Homicide cop's shield, and I was trying to finish a thirty-year-old murder case that had made my father old before his time and perhaps had even helped fling him backwards down a flight of twenty-six stairs.

Chapter Five

[July 1968]

I see Jimmy off at the airport. Eleanor accompanies us, as does Jimmy's girl, Erin. Erin's the one he's going to marry when he gets out of the Academy. He's going to the police training facility as soon as his hitch in the Army is over. He'll be able to finish his degree at nights, he says. The kid seems to have himself aimed at something. My son wants to be a Homicide cop, like me.

We don't hear from him for two weeks. Then we get a letter every week. He's settling into Basic Training in some hot place in Georgia. The people tend to be very dumb or very smart, he tells us in his letters. It's much the same impression I had of the men in the Army in 1944 and 1945 when I served.

Estella the waitress tells us a very different tale about the night of the murders than does Billie, the co-owner of the rib joint. Billie goes along with the original version of the four black guys in the car. When we go back to talk to Estella again, her ass has been fired. It seems very disappointing for Eddie Lezniak who was sort of hoping to be able to flirt with the big-breasted waitress once more.

Billie must have heard from some people who helped her confirm her story. And we can't locate Estella. She's been swallowed up by the West Side, something which happens frequently.

The city is getting hot. Racially and temperature-wise. These are bad times here in Chicago and bad times most everywhere else. Assassinations. Overheated inner cities. Hell, we've had bricks tossed at our unmarked vehicles here on the West Side. Blacks have been burning each other out on this side of the city, and it's scary to be a policeman where your skin makes you a target.

Shots have been fired at uniforms, and there's been talk of bringing in the National Guard if things explode. They feel like they're at the boiling point to me. Eddie's frightened, too. He keeps the pump-action shotguns in our back seat wherever we go, and our least favorite place to tour is the West Side.

Anglin lives in an apartment in the city's north-central district. He hasn't disappeared since we had to let him go. He keeps what you'd call a high profile after the case is dismissed. He shows up on local talk shows on the radio. There are a few TV spots about what happened to the man accused of butchering seven student nurses. He seems sympathetic to some people.

Eddie and I cruise Anglin's new neighborhood whenever we get the chance. There seems to be little reason to continue after him other than the obvious one: The motherfucker killed those girls. We both know it, so we continue to let Anglin see us from time to time.

We try wrenching information out of the Navy about Anglin, but they are very closemouthed about intelligence-related matters since they're embroiled in southeast Asia at the moment. Everyone in any Federal department is very tight-lipped about everything, at the moment. Things are not going well for us in the Orient, and things are going even worse here at home. As I said. Gunfire on the West Side. It's in the open now. Like Dodge City after a cattle drive. There doesn't seem to be any stopping it.

The Convention ignites that final conflagration. Every available cop in town is sent into the line at that park near where the Democratic gathering is taking place. This park used to be a place I'd take Jimmy on my days off when my son was a little guy. Now there are three million apes loose here, and there are thousands of cops with batons and guns and plastic shields. This can't be Chicago. These guys can't be from here. This is a place you come to on Saturdays and Sundays in the summer with a cold quart of brew hidden in a paper sack. This park is where you swing your kid on the swings and where you balance him on the teeter-totters. Not this ugly little jungle where the freaks are squaring off with the 'pigs'.

I'm not a real fan of being called a porker. I don't see the humor in it, even though some of my brethren in blue do. Some of them have little pig dolls fixed to the dashboards of their squads. It's their way of coping with the longhairs who throw feces at our windshields, here at the park.

We're close to the Lake, so we can smell the water. The heat and humidity are oppressive. But there's no place to hide.

The violence starts in the late afternoon and builds to its crescendo by 9.00 p.m. or so. I don't have time to look at my watch. I'm dressed in my blues, like everyone else out here. When our line of cops withstands the first charge of punks and paid 'revolutionaries', it's dusk. It's a wave of freaks against a double line of coppers. We get aggressive and drive them back. Only a few of them offer any real competition. Some of our guys get out of control and they beat the snot out of several of the protesters. I have to grab one uniform who's about to club a female into submission. The little shit calls me a pig motherfucker for my trouble, so I kick her in the ass hard, and she retreats to her own lines.

They throw some bottles and bricks, but where we are is fairly stable for the rest of the long night. The brutality some of our number use seems sufficient to slow these kids down. But they're not all kids. Some of them are much older, much more mature. They're the ones with a cause stuck up their asses. Or they're on the payroll of someone who wants to change the world. The usual assholes.

All I know is Eddie and I are prevented from doing our work because the Convention and the yips and dips and freaks are all standing in our way.

The weeks that follow seem to be a simmering down. The rads are still in the streets, the war is still slogging in the wrong direction in Vietnam, and Carl Anglin is still living the good life on the North Side.

He has babes wandering in and out of his apartment. Amazing. These women must know his reputation, but they are attracted to him nonetheless. Some very nice-looking women, too. Maybe it's the rush of danger. Maybe it's the times. Maybe he's got a foot-long schwantz. Who knows?

Eddie and I book two dozen no-brainers in July. Mostly domestic squabbles that went bloody. Husbands stabbing wives. Wives poisoning the old man, siblings blowing each other away. Nothing remotely out of the ordinary.

Carl Anglin is *the* case. There is no other. Not before. Not now. Even my partner thinks I'm beginning to 'obsess' about him. Every time we're free from an overload of murders we find ourselves surveilling Anglin's apartment.

Carl throws a party at the end of the month. He's just signed a book contract. Six figures, major publisher. And I hear there is a possibility of a movie tie-in. The son of a bitch even has a literary agent.

'No, Jake. Don't do it.'

'It's an open bash, Eddie. Why wouldn't we be invited?'

I convince him to get out of the car with me. We walk up to Anglin's apartment building and I ring his doorbell at the front door. He buzzes us in immediately and we're on our way up to his third-floor flat.

The smell of dope is thick in the air. I see men and women of all colors crowding his small place. They are primarily younger people. Mid to late twenties, mostly.

'Jesus, Jake. Let's get the hell out of here,' Eddie moans.

We have to squeeze to get through the entry.

'Somebody call the pigs?' a well-endowed topless blonde giggles.

'Yeah. Someone called about a public indecency rap,' I tell her.

'You mean someone called because I'm giving my breasts a little night air?' she asks teasingly.

Eddie's got his stare fixed on her melons.

'Nah. No one called. Just kidding.'

'Would you like to find out if they're as tasty as they look?'

'Nah. I'm just here to support Carl.'

'A cop here to support Carl?' she asks. Her tits bob as she takes a deep breath of this marijuana-laden air. There's plenty of beer and hard stuff on scene as well.

The blonde comes closer. Close enough to brush her nipples against my sleeve. I look over her shoulder and I see some male performing oral sex on a brunette female. The brown-haired sweetie is on top of the dining-room table with her legs straight up in the air, and this guy is going at her like a starved hog at a trough. Which reminds me that Eddie and I are both 'pigs' here.

'You like what you see?' the blonde inquires.

'Very interesting,' I reply, smiling. 'But I'm married.'

'So'm I,' she grins.

She is very blown out. The stench of weed is heavy on her hair and face. She almost makes me gag with the acrid stench.

'You've got great breasts,' I tell her.

We move into the apartment past her. Past the guy performing cunnilingus, and then into the kitchenette. There must be fifty people crammed into Anglin's one-bedroom apartment.

A man in a suit stands by the refrigerator.

'You want a beer?' the suit asks.

He goes into the icebox and gets out two for us. Eddie takes his and I grab hold of mine. We're on duty, but we don't need to stick out anymore than we already do.

'James Henry,' the suit says. 'I'm Carl's literary agent. I'm from New York,' he explains.

'Hear Carl made big money with his book,' Eddie says and grins.

'Six figures. But there'll be a paperback and, we hope, a movie.'

'Why would you dirty your hands with blood money?' I ask.

'Pardon?'

'I said, why would you dirty your hands with blood money made from the murders of seven young women?'

'Who . . . who are you?'

'I'm Jake Parisi.'

'And what's your line?' he continues.

'You mean what do I do? Oh. I'm a police officer.'

Suddenly the small group around Eddie and me is very quiet.

'I'm in Homicide. Like my partner Eddie here.'

'Jesus,' James Henry moans.

'No. Jesus ain't anywhere in the vicinity tonight,' I tell him.

The brunette is bucking up against the face of her boyfriend. Apparently she's arrived at wherever he's taking her.

'I'll bet this book's going to be a best-seller. No?' I ask him.

'Look—'

'Look nothing, asshole. Where's Carl?'

James Henry looks both of us over. The brunette's moaning inside her afterglow.

'He's in the bedroom.'

Eddie and I squeeze by the literary agent and the half-dozen fans of the beer in the fridge.

'Excuse me,' I say.

We wade through the tokers and the smokers and the midnight jokers and we find Carl right where the agent said he'd be. The door to the bedroom's open and Carl Anglin's on the bed without his pants or Jockeys and he's being fellated while his female partner is getting it from another male in what is generally referred to as doggie-style.

We break up their little three-way, however. The female and male grumble and then walk off back to the party.

I can see Anglin's green eyes even in the haze of the smoke and summer humidity.

'Well, hello,' he says. He rises to put on his underwear and pants.

'How you doin', Carl?' Eddie asks.

'I was doing just fine until you two broke it up. That girl is a swallower, by God. Ain't many of them wandering these mean streets.'

'Well, she can come back and gargle with it in a minute,' I tell him. 'We just came by to pay our respects.'

'Did you come to partake, or are you here to pinch us all?' he asks, grinning slyly. He leans back against the headboard of his bed. He's sitting up now, attentive.

'We're Homicide. We don't bust up community blow jobs,' Eddie reminds him.

'Oh, yeah. You two were the policemen who cracked the big case of the seven nurses . . . You know, I hear those girls partied heavily. I mean, I heard they threw some downright orgies at that dormitory.'

'How would you know anything like that, Carl?' I ask him.

'Oh, word of mouth . . . Get it?'

'So you're soaring high here. Women you don't have to rape. All the dope you can smoke . . . This the kind of life you lived when you were in the service, Carl?'

Anglin's grin disappears. It appears I've found his sensitive spot.

'What are you referring to, specifically?' he wants to know.

'Oh, nothing. It's just that I was impressed reading about your exploits with the CIA.' I smile.

'You don't know nothing about no CIA because I never been a part of them. You're trying to get a little rise out of me by showing up here and now I'm getting bored with both of you so why don't you just get the fuck out?'

'We could screw up your little party in a big way, Carl,' I remind him. 'There's a whole lot of illegality goin' on around here.'

'You're not that chickenshit, Parisi.'

'Buck buck, motherfucker.'

Then I smile at him and Eddie and I move out of his bedroom. His bright green eyes watch us all the way out.

The blonde is now masturbating the literary agent. She's taken out his cock from his trousers, and she's working him with both hands. By the time we pass the two of them, she's on her knees and he's moaning with his back up against the refrigerator.

The brunette is now lying atop her partner in what is known as the sixty-nine configuration.

'Must be hell,' Eddie concludes. 'Going to all those parties and having to perform. He must be one tired snatch-sucker at the end of the shift.'

We muscle our way out of the stifling-hot apartment and down to the car.

'We may never get him, Jake. He doesn't need to kill anybody now that he's got all this attention. He gets the cooze, the booze, the dope. It's all legit, so why take chances?'

'Because he likes it, Eddie. He's going to get bored with all this celebrity shit and he's going to want to lay out the challenge. He's being protected by somebody for something and he thinks he's invincible. Like some Indian in his ghost shirt. He thinks he can stick our faces in it and have all the good little things his newfound fame has brought him . . . No, Eddie. He won't stay happy with what he's got. You always want what you can't have. I'm trying to convince him that he can't have it the old way. I want to push him out the door and make him grab at it.'

'That could be real dangerous for the local population, Jake.'

'I understand. This guy's a loose cannon – with a quarter-inch fuse, no less. He'll go back to it because he likes it. I'm just trying to make things seem easier for him.' I aim us in the direction of the Loop. 'But if he kills again, Eddie, and we can't bring him in front of the man . . . then I'll just naturally have to shoot him right in the head.'

Chapter Six

[February 1999]

Doc had an in at the military archives. He wouldn't give me the guy's name. All he'd say about this source was that he was reliable and that he'd served alongside Doc in South Korea during the mid-1950s. We'd used this mystery man as a source before, so I couldn't complain about his anonymity.

Doc had found out Anglin's affiliation in the Navy. He had also found out the addresses of two Chicago-area vets who'd served with Carl.

John Grinder lived in the northwest part of the city. He was the owner of a liquor store in Ravenswood, a North Side neighborhood. Doc and I got into our unmarked vehicle, the Taurus, and we headed out to Grinder's store.

Grinder was a big man. Much heftier than Carl Anglin. He had a middle-aged paunch sticking out in front of him.

'Gentlemen,' he greeted us, smiling as we approached him at his counter. The place was called, very simply, 'John's'.

We showed him our ID. He blinked, but he smiled again.

'I didn't kill the old lady. She's at home and in the fuckin' pink,' he cracked.

'We'd like to ask you about Carl Anglin,' Doc said.

His face darkened.

'Anglin? That son of a bitch?'

'Yeah,' I told him. 'But we'd like to talk to you off the premises. Can you arrange that?'

'Sure. I guess. I haven't talked about him in— Shit, since I left the service twenty-five years ago . . . Let me get my son to watch the counter.'

He called out 'Danny,' and his son promptly came up front. Good-looking kid in his mid-twenties.

'I'll be out for a few minutes. Watch the goods.'

Danny smiled and said, 'Sure.'

John Grinder asked us if we could talk somewhere other than police headquarters, downtown. He didn't like to leave the business for too long. Since he was being cooperative, we settled on going over to the Garv Comeback Inn in Berwyn. It was Doc's hangout. He called the Comeback 'a noir saloon'. Claimed he did all his best thinking there. It was really because he liked John Garvin's bratwurst.

It was truly a saloon, standing near the railroad tracks in this western suburb of Chicago. It was a middle-class Slovak neighborhood that never seemed to change.

Garv himself was a survivor of the Battle of the Bulge. His limp, as he plodded toward the three of us, gave an indication of the price John Garvin had paid to run this sawdust-floored bar until he hit retirement age.

'What can I do you for?'

His opener was another thing that had never changed *chez* Garvin.

'I'll have a Diet Coke,' I told the old World War II vet. Doc had a Sprite, and John Grinder ordered a black coffee.

The barman ambled toward the cooler.

'We'll try to keep this brief,' Doc started. 'Anything you can tell us about Carl Anglin?'

'Anything?' Grinder said. 'Where would I start . . . The guy was a natural-born killer. He did those seven nurses, didn't he?'

We didn't answer him.

'I understand. Ongoing investigation.'

'Yes. He killed them,' I said.

Grinder looked surprised at my candor.

'He was part of a special force that I was a member of. Sort of like the Seals, but not exactly. We did the things the papers never print. The embarrassing little jobs. You know, the cut throats in the hotel rooms. The dead camel jockeys who show up disemboweled in their sandy little tents out in the middle of fucking nowhere. We did the covert stuff the CIA wouldn't or couldn't do. They always invoked the "National Security" flag to cover everything we did, whenever Congress got a whiff of it . . . But we were disbanded officially during the Eisenhower administration, right before Nixon lost to JFK. But that didn't stop the Navy from using us – unofficially. Look, I won't get specific with you because I signed an oath and, believe it or not, I love my country. I thought I was doing my duty, back then. Sometimes I wonder about it all now, but I gave my word. You understand?'

I nodded.

'We were in the service, too. Doc was in South Korea with you, and I was in Vietnam for two tours.'

'Outstanding,' Grinder said and smiled.

'Just stick to Anglin,' Doc offered. 'You don't have to name names or places or dates. And everything you tell us is between us. You'll never have to repeat it.'

'No witness chair?'

Doc shook his head.

'I remember Anglin. He was the one with the big-time grudge when the end came for us. We were called Tactical Five. I got no clue why. That's all we were ever called. We did a lot of assassination stuff in Asia. In places like Hong Kong. Singapore. Places peripheral to the actual thing in Korea. They flew us in by helicopter, dropped us close to shore, and then we swam the rest of the distance. We made our assigned kill, swam back to the meeting place and a chopper or some other form of transport'd pick us up.'

'You said Anglin was angry about the end of Tactical Five?' I asked.

'Yeah. The rest of us just saw it as duty. Or at least the guys I was close to felt that way. And when it was over, we didn't question it. Orders were orders. Anglin couldn't accept it. And he never came home with the rest of the outfit.'

'He stayed on in Asia?' Doc asked.

Garvin arrived with our drinks, set them down, and then shuffled away.

'He remained. Went AWOL, far as I remember. The MP's went searching for him, but when Carl wanted to, he was one of the best I ever knew for going deep under.'

'That sounds great,' I moaned at my partner.

'You'll have a lot of trouble trying to find that fuck if he wants to go invisible. I saw him do it more than once. He's better than a magician. Blends in like one of those little lizards.'

'He never arrived Stateside?' Doc queried.

'Not that I know of . . . But what I heard from a member of the old crew was that somebody picked up his contract in Hong Kong. That was where Carl wound up. The prick was off making himself a new career was what I heard. Gun for hire . . . Now that was just rumor, you understand. I can't personally verify it.'

'He didn't go home, but he started to contract out to private outfits,' I repeated.

'Yeah. That's what I heard . . . He killed those girls. I know he did. I wasn't surprised when they arrested him all those years back. He had a reputation for going physical on any on-scene females that happened to be in our area of operation.'

'You ever see him kill or rape anyone?' Doc asked.

'I would've shot the fuck myself if I had. No. I never saw that. But everyone knew about it. He liked to cut them when he was through with them, the word was . . . Look, I gotta get back. I got a business to run . . . But one last thing. You want to find Anglin, you might want to find Renny Charles. That was Anglin's number one bro' in Tactical Five. They were what you would call inseparable. Renny took off when Anglin did. They were partners. And I heard Renny was living somewhere in the city. I heard that a little while ago. So . . . '

We finished our drinks, went out to the car and began the drive back to Ravenswood.

Doc contacted his anonymous friend about Renny Charles. It was true that Charles had served in a classified outfit with Carl Anglin, but we got no further information about him. So we went to Computer Services and set their gears in motion.

We tried credit cards. We tried Division of Motor Vehicles. We came up with a zero for our efforts.

Then Doc reached out to the IRS. He found Renny Charles through an audit that had taken place just a few months ago. The address was on the near North Side.

We sat in the car outside the apartment where Charles supposedly resided. Before we got out, we both checked our weapons. Doc didn't want backup and neither did I. We wanted to keep Charles and his location quiet because of his background. If this guy was the killer he'd been made out to be, then he was probably being watched by his own folks. The Government was exceedingly paranoid about its covert personnel. We didn't want this to become a media event. So we were going in alone in spite of the potential danger.

I had the Bulldog .38 strapped to my ankle. It had remarkable stopping power. It'd drive a melon-sized hole out of the back of you as it blasted through. The Nine was in my shoulder holster. I used an automatic so that I had firepower comparable to what was on the street. I had a straight razor in my jacket pocket and a sap in my pants. Doc had a snub-nosed .38 on his ankle and a .45 Colt in his shoulder holster. He also carried a switchblade in his shirt pocket and a sap in his pants.

'Ready?' I asked.

He nodded and we got out of the car.

It was a chill and rotten night. Snow flurries, penetrating damp. A dead cold. Made the bones quiver.

Renny lived on the third floor of a three-flat, there on the North Side. The flurries made it all but impossible to see three feet ahead of us. The wind was blowing a gale, straight into our faces. We got to the front door and made it inside. It was a relief to be able to catch our breath in the entryway.

We were not going in the usual way, of course. Doc buzzed the tenant on the first floor.

No response. So he tried tenant number two.

Same silence.

Out came his toolbox. He had the lock popped in less than one minute forty-five, and the reason it took so long, he said, was because it was so damn dark in there.

We were up the two flights quickly. We'd noticed a light on in the apartment while we'd sat in the car checking our weapons. I was hoping it was not just Charles's night-lite.

Doc knocked on Charles's door. We didn't hear anything.

'Renny Charles . . . Police! Open up!'

I heard something moving inside. Doc raised his size twelve foot and smashed the front door open. We lunged into the room, both of us hunched over, and there was a burst of orange flame and an accompanying *crack*! as we stumbled to the floor.

I scrambled toward the shot and let loose with the Nine as I went. Six shots, scattered all over the living room. Another flame roared out at us and Doc emptied five rounds into the darkened room.

Then we heard a crash. The window in the front room had been shattered, and there was a blast of icy air rushing at us from the hole the body made as Renny Charles had apparently plunged three storeys to the lawn below.

We rose and raced toward the landing. Then it was down the three flights of stairs and out that entrance door, Doc huffing directly behind me, and we saw a man lying on the snow-glazed grass in front of us.

'Stop!' I yelled as soon as I had enough breath. The snow was flinging itself into my eyes. I had to put up a hand in front of my face.

Doc saw the .22 pistol on the ground, three feet away from Charles.

He picked it up as Charles writhed in agony.

'My fuckin' leg. I broke my fuckin' right leg. Call an ambulance,' he pleaded.

I went to the car and called 911.

'So why'd you cut loose on us?' Doc asked.

'It must have been that illegal entry,' Charles said and smiled grimly, his cast-covered leg held up by taut wires.

We were at St Luke's.

Renny Charles was a six-foot three-inch cracker whose parents obviously never beat him enough. He was easy to hate. I could see how Anglin would find this guy a soul mate.

'We identified ourselves as police officers. You didn't respond,' Doc told him.

'You didn't have a search warrant,' Charles responded.

'Who says?' I grinned at him.

The bluff seemed to work.

'Why would you want a search warrant to get to me?' he asked, a little less sure of himself.

'Because we want to find your old buddy Carl Anglin, asshole,' I explained.

'Anglin? Christ, I haven't seen him in—'

'That's not what we heard . . . You're up for attempted murder, right now. But we can make all of your immediate problems disappear.'

'If I hand you Carl.'

'Very perceptive, dickless,' Doc said dryly.

'You two can go hump yourselves.'

Doc unhooked the bracelet over his right wrist and attached Renny Charles to the frame of the hospital bed.

We turned and walked to the door.

'Wait a minute,' Charles said.

'You have a change of heart?' I queried.

'I saw Carl Anglin two weeks ago. He was living near the El tracks. Just south of Evanston . . . Christ, I'm not tight with the prick. I'm not into the shit he's into. Killing those girls. That's why I'm here. That's why you made me bust my leg. I'm in my fuckin' sixties! I'm a veteran! You know that?'

'You better be a little more specific with an address, Renny. And maybe you're a stranger to this town. Policemen here aren't fond of getting shot at, cheesedick.'

'How'd I know who you really were? Anybody can say he's a copper . . . Look, Anglin lived at an apartment on something like Kensington Place. That's all I remember . . . You're not really gonna bust me for attempted homicide, are you?'

'You were in the service with Anglin. You saw the little things he liked to do. Especially to women who were in the wrong place at the wrong time.'

'Yeah. He had strange tastes. I don't deny it—'

'Maybe you've become a suspect in his last two jobs, Renny,' I continued. 'Maybe at his advanced age he needs a little help to get to those young things. He's not as spry as he was when he roped up those seven nurses and tore them all up. That was thirty years ago when you were both in your primes. Lean, mean killing machines. That's what you both were, but now time's dulled you. All that bad hooch and even worse dope . . . They've blunted you both. Taken pieces out of you . . . No. Maybe we'll look into where you've been the last few months. We'll see when you really saw Carl Anglin last, and if you've been lying, then we'll let you spend those sunset years in a hole like Menard.'

We walked out the hospital room before Charles could whine at us again.

'You really think he worked with Carl?' Doc asked as we passed one especially attractive blonde nurse.

'He did once. It doesn't really matter. He has more to tell us. He's gonna be a fount of information, I'd say, Doctor.'

Doc turned his head and tried to catch another glimpse of the Nordic beauty who just a moment before had crossed our paths.

Chapter Seven

[August 1968]

The summer gets hotter and so do the times. The streets are no place to be. They're sweltering with distrust and outright hatred. There's even open bad blood between white and black policemen. That kind of thing was kept under pretty tight wraps until recently.

Jimmy writes us from a place called Bong Son in Vietnam. He's in the bush, he says. On active service. He's already made corporal, Stateside, and he says he might have a shot at sergeant before long. If he stays healthy, he explains. I write him a letter and tell him not to talk about shit like that when he knows Eleanor is going to read the letter. Jimmy shoots me back a note and apologizes, saying it won't happen again – that business about his health being included in his correspondence. From then on his weekly letters sound much more upbeat. So I know he's lying for his mother's sake.

He keeps talking about how many black soldiers are stuck in the bush with him. Jimmy the Liberal. He says there are too few white guys in the shit. He says they, the Anglos, find their way to the rear echelon. I never knew my kid would turn out to be a Democrat.

I wrote a few letters myself from Europe during the Second World War, so I understand why Jimmy'd be interested in his 'health'. It's just that you can't share any of that with mothers or wives or girlfriends. It only makes them more frightened than they already are.

I close the Greek's regularly these nights. There's nothing to go home for except to sleep. I usually eat out with Eddie, except for dinner when we're on days.

We received the predictable warning from our Captain that we were not to harass Carl Anglin any longer. Anglin's lawyer has been on the blower to downtown, so we're supposed to lay off his star client.

I visited the cemetery where two of the girls were buried, in the southwest part of town. It seems two of them were distant cousins, so they wound up in the same churchyard. Big crosses over their remains. The families went all out on the funerals. The victims were both Hispanic, both Catholics – like me and my family. Guineas from Sicily tend to go Roman.

There isn't much to do at their resting place. I read the inscriptions. The date of birth and death on each tombstone. The little quotes of Bible poetry they elect to leave as remembrance on the stones. That's not a whole lot to stand for a couple of lifetimes, even ones as short as theirs were.

And then I would start remembering Anglin's jungle-green eyes and I'd want to go find him and kill him. But that, of course, would have put me in the same league as this ex-Navy thug whose military record is closed and whose history is unavailable to the CPD because of what the military calls 'National Security'. I know and Eddie knows that there's something in his files that'd help us understand why Carl Anglin has eluded us.

He's done something very bad, I'm thinking. Something bad enough for the government to hang tough in the face of our court orders and injunctions – all of which have failed to open the book on Anglin.

There are people I know who could find out what it was they have to hide, but I don't deal with that branch of my family. Some of my clan turned left when they got to this country. In other words, some of my cousins are members of the Outfit, the Chicago version of the Mafia, Cosa Nostra, or whatever you want to call them. I call them thieves and murderers. We've never gotten along, and I ask no favors of them. I've never attended family reunions, weddings, or any gatherings where any of them might show up.

I've had my opportunities to go on their books. There are lots of cops who take money. It's a standing joke in Chicago about payoffs to police from taverns and nightclubs. I could've had Jimmy's college tuition paid ten times over if I'd nodded my head to them. It's not because I'm a pristine virgin. It's because I know them too well. I know what they're like. Once you say 'Yes' to them, it's yes for the rest of your life. I'm afraid of a debt that large. I'm afraid of owing my soul to them. Perhaps it's the Catholic in me, but I know what they're like, and it's not what you see in the movies. They have no honor. They kill their own people for money. They murdered a whole lot of the male population of Sicily, and now they're trawling more fertile waters here in this country.

So I won't use those connections to find out what Carl Anglin was doing in Asia during the Korean War, and the government shows no inclination to help us get him back into court. Two witnesses. One dead, one might as well be.

I visit the Rojas girl at least every two weeks. I saw her most recently last Thursday. Eddie does not come into the room with me. He had a sister who had a nervous disorder, so he's not too fond of the surroundings at Elgin State Mental Hospital.

When I went into the room, I found her sitting down. She was staring out the window. The sun was shining that day, so her room was bright, maybe even cheerful – to someone who didn't have to live there.

'Hello,' I say to her softly.

She doesn't turn toward me or the nurse. The nurse signals for me to make it brief. The girl will be taking her meds pretty soon, she explains, before she turns and leaves me alone with the sole survivor of the massacre.

'I'm Detective Parisi. Jake Parisi. I've talked to you before . . . I know you can hear me and I promise I won't stay long and bother you . . . If you are hearing me inside somewhere, I want you to know that I won't think you've done anything wrong if you can't respond to my questions. I know he frightened you. I know it's worse than I or anybody else can know . . . But I have to tell you that you're all we've got to get to Carl Anglin. He's the man who killed the other girls. He's the man who would've killed you too. If you hear me, think. I know you're hiding deep inside yourself. I'd be hiding too. I know these doctors know a lot more about just exactly where you are, but I'm asking you to come on back out and help me. Help me – and help the families of those girls who were your friends. Don't let Carl Anglin get away with this. I have to tell you the truth. If you don't come on back to the surface, he's going to get away with killing your friends.'

There's not even a tremor in her face. She hasn't heard me or she's simply not even in the same room with me, which is what the nurse continually tries to explain to me. Theresa Rojas has left us. Her body is all that remains.

'Don't let him do this, Theresa. Don't let him wipe them out. Let me speak for them, and for you. You can do it if you come back. Please try. Please . . . I'll come back in another couple of weeks. You rest. Get strong . . . God help you, Theresa.'

I turn and walk out of her private room toward my waiting partner.

'Can we leave now?' Eddie asks.

The place makes him frantic, so I hurry him out the doors.

We can't tap Anglin's phones. We can't search his North Side apartment. We're not welcome at his orgies. Even Narco has been warned not to get a hard-on about raiding one of his little dope-athons. Anglin is strictly hands-off. Which makes me work twice as hard keeping him in our sights. I do some stakeouts on my own time. He comes and goes like a normal blue-collar resident of this blue-collar neighborhood. But the locals know him and seem to give him a lot of distance. The locals don't go to his parties. It's the wealthy, affected North

Shore crowd that hangs out at his gatherings. He's a magnet for every bored Gold Coaster who's looking for a little toot to snoot. Some city celebrities show up at his place from time to time, and so do some of the literary figures in this town. It seems he's got them buffaloed into believing he's the new Ernest Hemingway of Chicago. His book has had excellent reviews. It's sold well, which is why he can afford his new lifestyle. It's unfortunate that no one seems to realize that his 'memoirs' or whatever are strictly fiction. There's no mention of his days in the service, and according to him the killings happened while he was home working on a collection of his poetry – which is forthcoming from his publisher in New York.

It would be justice if I shot him. But perhaps I'm just not the kind of hero who would take matters into his own hands. Set things right, like some cowboy legend. I believe too much in the system. My job is to catch them, not kill them.

I come through the door at 12.35 a.m. on this Thursday morning. Eleanor is waiting for me at the top of the stairs.

'You can't keep this up,' she tells me.

'Keep what up?'

I begin my tired ascent of the twenty-six stairs.

'You haven't written Jimmy in two months. I haven't seen you in over a week. This is not a marriage. It's not even an arrangement anymore.'

'Divorce me, then.'

'I can't. I'm a Catholic, just like you.'

'To hell with the Church! Divorce me, marry Nick, give Jimmy his real father back!'

I stop halfway up. I have to grab hold of the banister.

'You don't want that and neither do I, Jake. Nick gave me a child. You couldn't. I wanted to ask your forgiveness a thousand times, but I can't do it. You could've got the marriage annulled for it. Why didn't you?'

'Why didn't I? Let me think.'

'Stop it! Nick gave us *both* a child. It was for *us*, not just for me. The doctor said we could never conceive and I did the only thing I knew that would give us a family. My God, Jake, what's more important than our son?'

'He's not mine! He belongs to you and my brother!'

I straighten up and let go of the banister, but my feet aren't steady because of the six beers and their chasers.

'Why can't you forgive me, Jake? Why won't you believe me when I tell you I did it for us. I love *you*, not Nick. Your brother knows it, too. He was doing it for—'

'Don't you say it! He wants you. He wants you now, this day. And you stand there wondering why I live the way I do. Is it too difficult? I'm sterile, just like the two of us together are . . . But I made my bed, even if it's not in your room anymore. I keep my word, Eleanor. I don't betray people. I don't knife them in the back when they least expect it. I don't go to another man to change what God set up. We should've stayed childless.'

'What would Jimmy think if he heard you? You love your son. Don't lie to me, you drunk! You've always loved him. But your pride won't back down. You act like you're impotent. You're not impotent. You simply had a disease in young adulthood that—'

'Don't say it again. Don't . . . Jesus, Eleanor, I'm too tired . . . Maybe we ought to separate. I can find an apartment—'

'This is our house. I'd rather go on this way than have to explain to people why you're living somewhere else. I told you I was sorry . . . I love you. I always will.'

She turns and walks away from me. I want to stop her, but I am too weary to lift my arms. I sit down on the midway stair of the flight. I put my head in my hands.

'Oh Jesus. Jesus.'

Then I summon the will to rise, and I walk up the remaining stairs.

Anglin takes a bust for drunk-and-disorderly. Apparently his neighbors are tiring of his all-nighters. They call the gendarmes and the police are compelled to respond.

I go down to the lockup to have a look at him. Eddie warns me not to, but I feel compelled to see him.

'Well, I'm happy to have a visitor,' he says and smiles. Then he looks up and gives me the full treatment with his eyes. They are shockingly bright and intelligent and . . . evil.

'I'm no visitor. Just happened to be in your vicinity.'

'Well, I'm glad you came anyway. I have this unavoidable desire to get you to believe I'm not the guy you think I am.'

'Who do I think you are?'

He smiles and flashes a stare at me.

'I'm the guy in the ninth concentric ring. I am Legion, I am the Antichrist! There! Satisfied?'

'When they fit the hood over your face, I'll be satisfied. When they turn on the circuits and the smoke rises from all of your facial orifices, then I'll be at peace.'

'I'm getting out on bond. My lawyer's in there now. I'll be out by lunch.'

'I'm sure you will be . . . I just saw someone who knows all about your innocence.'

'Yeah? Who's that?'

'The nurse you left behind.'

'You keep insisting that there was someone who actually saw me do those seven young ladies. I keep telling you she saw someone else. Why is it impossible for you to come to terms with the notion that you got the wrong man?'

'When she comes out of it, we'll have you back here. But your bondsman won't be able to afford you when I come for you then . . . By the way—'

'Yeah?'

'Why'd you kill them? I mean you could've raped them and done your disappearing act. The way they trained you in Special Forces.'

'I don't know anything about Special—'

'You could've had them and you could've let them live. You know how to leave the scene of a crime, like I said. So why not just have all that sex and leave?'

'I told you I don't know what you're talking about . . . But as far as rapists go – and I only know what I've read – they sometimes can't get the full effect with just a normal climax. Some of them enjoy the thrill of control. The control over the very life of the victim . . . But then, you're a Homicide lieutenant. You don't need me to explain basic criminal psychology to you. You know about control. How many rape/murders have you presided over, Lieutenant?'

'I just wanted to hear your slant, your version.'

'Very clever, Detective. Very clever indeed. Astute, even. But I didn't do those girls. There are all kinds of killers out there, and the man who did the nurses is still out there.'

Anglin's wearing a T-shirt with the American flag all over the front. It's obvious he doesn't plan on staying here very often.

'The food's lousy in jail,' I tell him. 'You'll have to make adjustments to your sexual habits when we lock you up the next time, the final time. By then you'll be hoping they give you death. Everybody's gonna want a piece of your scrawny ass when they hear there's a celebrity in the jailhouse . . . Wherever you turn, you'll see me out the corner of an eye. I'll be there, right there. When they spring you, I'll be behind you or just off to the side—'

'My lawyer has already told you that—'

'I don't give a shit what your lawyer said or who he said it to. So sue me, shitbird. I'll never give you up. Maybe you better do one of your jungle ops on me when you get out.'

'You got the wrong guy, Lieutenant. You just made a mistake and you're having trouble living with it. So I like pussy. I don't need to force them to fuck me . . . You got the wrong perpetrator. You'll see, if you ever go after the real guy.'

'Remember what I told you.'

I turn and walk away from his cage. I hear what sounds like soft, almost gentle laughter following me on my way out of the lockup.

Jimmy's been hit. Not badly enough to be sent home. Says it was just some hot shrapnel that cut through the bottom of his Chinook helicopter when they were sent into the bush for an engagement with the NVA and the Viet Cong. Jimmy says he didn't even feel the piece of metal that hit him and didn't realize he'd been wounded until he saw the red stain on the knee of his pants.

Eleanor cries when she reads Jimmy's note. But I tell her that he'll get some time off in the hospital. Maybe even some R-and-R in Japan. She looks up at me and I tell her that being in the hospital will keep him out of combat, at least for a little while.

I touch her hand, but when she looks up at me I withdraw my fingertips.

Chapter Eight

[February 1999]

Renny Charles came up with an address for Anglin. It was the most positive information we'd had in weeks, so we didn't hesitate to get some cops over to the location. We had to scan the neighborhood and interview several dozen people before we found a woman who'd seen Carl Anglin coming out of an apartment not two blocks from where we stood and this young college girl who said she'd noticed his distinctive weird eyes 'looking me up and down'.

It was 4412 East End Avenue, right by the Elevated tracks.

I had six squads waiting for Doc and me at the address.

'Isn't this a little showy, just for an interview?' Doc asked me on the ride over.

'We're just going to talk, yeah. We don't have any evidence from the two murders to put Anglin on scene, but he doesn't know that. Let's just go in like we mean business.'

Doc smiled and turned off his all-day all-night jazz station from Evanston.

We were at the point, the lead, as we walked up the steps at 4412 East End Avenue. I had my Nine in my hand and Doc had his standard police-issue piece in his right mitt. There were six uniformed patrolmen on the stairs coming up with us to the third floor. Anglin was bold enough to have his name on the mailbox by the entrance.

'Police. Open up,' Doc yelled as he beat on the door. We didn't have a warrant to break in so were hoping we'd caught him at home.

Doc hit the door with his knuckles again, and this time we heard movement from within. The remaining two patrolmen we'd brought along were standing outside in the alley, watching the rear exit. There was no way Anglin could evade us.

The door opened slowly to reveal a young female, naked to the waist. Her eyes appeared bleary, blown-out.

'There ain't no party here,' she said, a glazed smile on her lips.

'We're police. We'd like to come in, honeydew,' Doc grinned.

She fell for his Slovak charm.

The door opened all the way. All she was wearing was thong bikini underwear.

'Oh my,' Doc said, admiringly.

She was a stunning brunette.

'Where's the head of the house?' Doc asked her. We shut the door behind the three of us and I thought I heard one of the uniforms groan.

'Would you be more comfortable if you put something on?' I asked her.

'Don't you like to look?' she slurred, grinning dopily.

I raised my hands in surrender. Either she was a little more than liberated or she was displaying herself in order to distract us. If she was trying to distract us she was doing a first-rate job. My wife would have slapped my face if she'd heard I'd let this kid stand naked in front of us this way.

'Carl ain't here, as you can see. I don't know where he is. Sometimes he don't come home at all.'

She switched her stare to Doc.

'You using?' Doc smiled.

'Yeah. How 'bout you?'

'What's your name, darlin'?' Doc asked.

'Cherilyn . . . You wouldn't turn prick and send your narco buddies this way, would you?'

'Not unless we feel you're being unresponsive.'

She whipped off her bikini bottom before I could tell her what we really meant by 'responsive'.

'Jesus Christ,' Doc laughed. 'We mean that we want you to help us find Carl. We aren't asking for, ah, professional courtesy.'

'Oh,' she said. Her face had gone blank. It was as if she really had mistaken what we were after here.

'Because we do have friends in narcotics, and those needle tracks in your arm give us probable cause to have this apartment flopped. And those guys don't give a shit if you bend over and shoot the moon at them while they tear this place apart. So do you want to cut the crap and tell us where Carl Anglin is?' I explained.

We found him in conference with his Chicago agent. This was the guy who set up his personal appearances.

'Excuse me,' Ralph Martin, the agent, cautioned us. 'We're in the middle of some private business—'

'Sit down, chubby,' Doc told him. You could see Martin was very much offended by the 'chubby' remark. He was one of these North Shore yups who worked out daily at some health club in the city. Racquetball was probably his sport. But he did sport a paunch.

'We need to talk to you, Carl. We've been looking for you for a long, long time,' I told Anglin.

He shot the green, mean stare at me.

'I'll need a lawyer,' he said.

'Call him. There's the phone. Tell him to meet us downtown. Homicide floor. You remember, don't you, Carl?' Doc asked.

'I remember.'

Anglin picked up the phone and then he pushed the buttons. It was a Chicago number, I saw.

'Come on, Carl. Let's go for a ride.'

'I'll get back to you in an hour, Ralph. Don't worry,' Anglin told the agent.

'Might be a little longer than that,' I told Ralph.

'You heard the names Martha Eisner or Renee Jackson?' I asked Anglin.

He sat in the interrogation room with his lawyer, Paul Jackson. Jackson nodded that he could answer.

'No. Neither. Never heard of them.'

Anglin was sucking hard at a Camel filter until I informed him that there was no smoking in this building. He put out the butt and looked down at the glossy finish of the dark oak table.

'This conversation is about to be aborted,' Jackson said. 'You have shown me nothing that would cause Mr Anglin to go any further with this line of questioning. This appears to be open harassment on account of Mr Anglin's previous incarceration for the murder of those seven student nurses – a crime he was found not guilty of.'

'I remember,' I told him.

'It was your father who arrested him, was it not?' the lawyer asked, smiling greasily.

Jackson wanted me to hit him. He had a hard-on thinking about the litigation he could bring against me.

'It was my father, yes. But he has nothing to do with these two current murders. I'm not lame enough to bring up a thirty-year-old dead case.'

'Splendid. Then you understand we have nothing further to say to you.'

'I brought you down here for a reason, Carl,' I told Anglin.

'Tell it to my lawyer.'

'We don't have anything except your mode of operation to connect you with these two young women, Anglin. But we'll have more soon. You can be sure we will. And one other thing.'

'What's that, Lieutenant?' Anglin stared at me.

'It isn't over with the seven nurses. Don't ever think it's over. We know the government likes you for some damn reason. But that won't stop me from getting you. I'm not a political policeman, Carl. I don't give a shit about my pension. I'll keep working until I collapse with a stroke over a case file. Which should tell you that I'll never stop. The case is never closed. I won't talk about it anymore now, but I'll be in your face again. If you'd just stayed out of business, all this might not have come to a boil. But you really pissed me off when you came back into your old hunting grounds and thought you were untouchable. Whatever you have with the Feds won't cut jack shit with me. I just wanted you to know . . . Be seeing you soon, Carl.'

'Your old man couldn't catch me. You think you're as good as he was? I heard Jake Parisi was the big dog. Except for the liquor. That's what kept him stuck at lieutenant. Wasn't it? Then he had that tragic accident—'

I was up out of the chair and I had my hands round Anglin's throat. I was squeezing, and his emerald orbs were beginning to bulge when I felt Doc's surprisingly strong grip on the back of my neck – and then I was being hauled back into my own chair.

The lawyer made all the obvious threats about my attack on his client, and then Anglin and his mouthpiece left the interrogation room.

'A mite unprofessional, Jimmy,' Doc said.

The heat in my face was slowly receding.

'Yeah. You're absolutely dead-on.'

'Take it easy, guinea. We just got invited to this dance. It's a brand-new deal. The trail is fresh and the scent is clear. He wants to get your attention away from the details. He wants to make it personal between the two of you, the way it was for your dad and him. That was Jake's only error. He let it get to him, he let it become a vendetta. That's how you guineas operate, ain't it?'

My pulse was still pounding. In my mind I could feel my fingers getting closer to Anglin's windpipe. The man was four or five inches taller than I was, but I had him at the point of no return. And I was glaring into his eyes, and for some odd reason I felt like my rage was feeding off his stare, making me stronger, angrier with each squeeze. I frightened myself in the process.

'Carl Anglin is not the Boogey Dude. He's not Satan. He's a filthy piece of human flesh who'd like you to think he's supernatural. It's part of his bullshit appeal to all these young doper snatches who hang out at his parties. He's like the next step away from the occult. They take him as an evil father replacement because most of them don't have anyone at home . . . He wants to get into your head. *Our* heads. It's part of what they taught him in the military. He wants to scare you. That's why he did the seven girls one at a time. Just so the next one down the line had to wait and think about what he'd be doing to her. He's doing the same thing with that talk about your father. He's stirring you up, James. Don't let him.'

I looked at the one-way mirror. Luckily our captain hadn't been present at the interview. But he'd be hearing from Anglin's lawyer as soon as that pimp found a telephone.

Now that the daytime temperature was in the forties, I took my baby daughter for walks in her stroller. My other two children were approaching adulthood, so I'd never thought I'd be doing that again. I was off shift and my wife Natalie was on. When we both worked simultaneously, my mother, Eleanor, got the job of sitter. She loved taking care of Mary. And I'd noticed that dealing with my kid had made my mother seem younger. She only needed to sit for us two or three days a week, with our schedules, but she still seemed more youthful, maybe even happier.

I walked Mary around the block three or four times. Just enough to get the pink in her cheeks.

Then we went back inside because this was still winter, and the temperature in this city had been known to drop ten degrees and more in less than an hour.

When we got back inside our North Side bungalow, I turned on the TV for her cartoons. She was just beginning to get interested in them. Some of them were too violent for me. So I turned over on the cable to the movie classics station. Those old black and whites put my daughter to sleep in just seconds. I thought maybe it was their lush music scores. The violins and everything. I wasn't sure. But I knew it worked.

Then the familiar pangs crept back into my heart. I saw Mary as a twenty-year-old nursing student, learning all those facts that would help her alleviate human suffering. And along came the big bad wolf and he huffed and he puffed and he put his hands around my own daughter's throat. I saw it in my mind. This vision of the future where Carl Anglin never grew any older. He never got caught, either. He was the devil who always had hell for his refuge, and for some reason we tolerated his existence. We never seemed to do anything to put him permanently out of business. The human predicament – a constant relationship with evil.

Perhaps Doc was wrong. Maybe Anglin *was* the Boogey Dude, the Boogey Man, the horror beneath the bed or inside the closet or wherever he lurked.

Who was I to think I could eradicate Legion? He was too many, even though the Bible said he was really just one. Fallen angel. Would-be God.

I took Mary up out of her crib and embraced her until I made her too warm – and until I pissed her off sufficiently for her to want her old man to feed her some more of that tonsil-pleasing apple juice.

We went over the crime scenes at the locations of the Eisner and Jackson killings. The FBI had been over them several times. All the photographs had been taken, everything had been processed. He'd left nothing behind. He knew how we thought. He was trained to defeat a police examination. The military had taught him to leave nothing of himself behind. What the military called an exchange. Pubic hairs, spittle, semen, body hairs, fibre. Nothing was left on the bodies of the girls.

I was assuming that he was using condoms in the rapes. There was damage to the cervix in each case. He had rammed himself or some object inside them, but there was no trace of sexual climax. He was too smart. As I said, he was too well prepared. He was that organized kind of killer that purposely put together his own slaying scenario before he actually went out into the world and performed his deeds.

I got hold of Mason, the Fibbie, and I asked if we could see his files. We got unexpected cooperation from the Federals. They showed us what they had, which was the same as we had. Nothing.

There was nothing to do but go nose-to-nose with Mason himself.

We were at his office, not far from our own.

'Why are you guys protecting him?' I asked him straight out.

Mason grinned and let the room go quiet.

'You seem to think we're conspiring against the CPD over this man. Why is that?'

Mason's assistant, the FBI babe of the month, was sitting in with us. She had her legs crossed demurely. She was trying to become Agent Starling.

'He's got a closed file. That's why. Because we know he was a trained pop artist for the Spooks or Someone Just Like the Spooks – you know, one of your more covert brethren who goes around the world taking out the trash. Without a trial or any of that legal bullshit.'

'You're a very cynical man, Lieutenant. What makes you think I could get into those papers, even if I wanted to?'

Doc watched the assistant cross and uncross her lovely white legs.

'Because thirty years ago this man destroyed seven young girls. They were a little younger than your buddy over there.'

I could see the girl's quick blush. Then she restored the calm to her expression.

'You know what this man is. I thought we both worked for justice. Or was that just the romantic in me?'

Doc and I got up to leave Mason's office. Doc struggled to stop concentrating on those two beautiful white Fed legs, but he finally mustered the self-discipline necessary for him to join me on my way out.

Chapter Nine

[September 1968]

The long summer is coming to a close, but it isn't coming easily. Naturally, Eddie and I take the heat for not nailing Carl Anglin. The city looks to us for a reason why we couldn't put him away. I can't go public with excuses. Two witnesses, one of them dead and one of them Theresa Rojas, still in some sort of mental coma. I don't want Miss Rojas to have to face the photographers and the news media. Her name has never been released, for her own protection. All the other seven witnesses are silent, of course.

He'll kill again, I keep thinking. We'll catch him on the next round. But that further depresses Eddie and me because it means that someone else will have to get split open like a gutted fish in order for us to get a crack at Carl Anglin.

We try the government over and over to get something about his background, but we come up cold. Just the way it was when we tried to shake the story about the four black gangbangers who supposedly did our witness at the rib joint.

I finally resort to members of my clan that I'm not proud of. 'Resort' is the right word. They're my last stop.

'I would consider it a favor, Marty. A favor that might get returned when one of your brothers gets caught selling from all those chop shops you own,' I tell my cousin, Marty

Genco. He's connected to a crew in the northwest part of town. They're into auto parts, but they're also hooked up to the Genco clan, the main family of Chicago's Outfit. And they have connections with the government on occasion. They were supposedly involved in one of the more notorious plot to kill Castro. The Bay of Pigs screwed things up for them for a while, but they're still close to some good sources.

Marty looks like my side of the family. He's my cousin on the old man's mother's side of the *familia*. He has the same nose and the same facial structure that the Parisis do. People thought we were brothers when we were growing up on the North Side. But I went to the Second World War and he stuck around the city and made a fortune chopping up every loose auto on the northwest side.

'Who is it you want to pop?' Marty asks and smiles.

'You know who the main guy is these days. Don't fuck with me, Martin.'

He hates to be called by his full name.

We're sitting in his office. The office in front of his 'legitimate' muffler repair shop.

Eddie is with me, too, to make it official.

'You think I'm gonna go to the family for you to get dirt on this Carl Anglin.'

'I want you to find out what he did for the government during the 1950s. That's all.'

'That's *all*?' my cousin laughs.

'I can help you with three of your guys who're headed to trial. I can get the price reduced on two of your cousins. I can't get them off, but I can help with their sentences if you do this for me.'

'Jake, I know about this guy.'

'You do?'

'Yeah.'

'How, Marty?'

'He has the biggest connections. You don't wanna know, cousin. This is over both of our heads.'

'Why don't you let me decide how deep the water is?'

'Because it's my ass here too.'

'They're not going to know about this conversation from me or Eddie here.'

Marty looks us over carefully.

'You wouldn't be wired, would you, Jake?'

I stand up and raise my arms.

'Go ahead. Knock yourself out.'

'One thing you never done is lie to me. I'll give you that . . . This guy Anglin was a hit specialist. Good with a rifle. He took out guys in Asia during Korea. He was a government hit man. They sent him all over the Far East to whack guys who pissed us off. Then came all that flap about covert operations – you remember. We were the good guys, we didn't do shit like that. They made the CIA and FBI play fair. All that horseshit. It's no wonder we're losin' in that place where your kid's at . . .'

'So everything Anglin did was in Asia. He never did work closer to home?'

Marty's eyes widen. I look over to Eddie, who has noticed the change on my cousin's face.

'It gets to be what they call conjecture after that, Jake.'

'So give me the story.'

'The story is that he was at the Bay of Pigs. He got himself captured and he got himself escaped. And that's all I know about Carl Anglin in this hemisphere. Gimme a break, Jake. A guy like Anglin can get everyone in his wake killed. Just figure you caught a break by him gettin' off the hook for those girls.'

I show him the file. I let him see the photos. He's impressed. Marty's not all that much into the muscle side of the family.

'He likes the knife, this guy.'

I nod.

'All I heard is what a great shooter he is. Maybe he separates business and pleasure. Knife and gun. You know.'

'I think you know more than you're telling us.'

'I swear I told you everything . . . Are you gonna keep your end of the deal?'

'I am.'

Eddie and I get up and walk out of Marty's office.

We walk toward the street and our vehicle. The heat is on the wane. You can smell the fall creeping into the atmosphere.

I get in and I do the driving. Eddie rides shotgun. He doesn't like traffic anyhow, so I'm usually the wheelman.

'What was he leaving out, Jake?' he asks. He rolls his window down. It isn't that cool yet.

'Something dangerous. Something he's not immune to.'

'Since when has his crew developed a fear of the United States government?'

'There's the everyday people, and then there are the guys you never see or hear from.'

'The covert assholes. The contract killers. They call themselves shit like the Division or the Bureau or whatever.'

'Spooks within the spooks. They're the guys anybody ought to be afraid of. They hide behind the flag. In the dark corners. They're the ones we hire instead of negotiating. You were in the war, Eddie. You know who I'm talking about.'

'You mean the distant cousins of the OSS and the CIA. Their nameless brethren.'

'So Carl is a shooter for some unnamed outfit. He does his business halfway around the world and is successful, but when he comes back home, he gets nailed in that mess in Cuba . . . So what does that tell us?'

'He has a grudge.'

'Big grudge. The vendetta. He does the girls for pleasure, he does the shooting for profit, maybe even because he thinks he's some kind of patriot . . . But killing the nurses has to reel in a lot of big-time favors for Carl. Now he owes them. He owes them his life and his freedom. But he becomes a celebrity instead of a mutt killer, which is what he really is. And the only word we have on his past is what my cousin the auto thief tells us. So how does any of that help us?'

'Maybe we could talk to some of our friends in the media,' Eddie suggests.

So I've humbled myself to the Outfit. I came begging. It's something my wife and son cannot understand. This Sicilian 'thing' that Eleanor says died back in the old country with our grandparents. Maybe Jimmy will leave history behind him, but I'm too close to the old ways, the ways my father taught me. He came here from the island. Jimmy was never taught a lot about Nick's and my ancestors, and maybe it's a good thing. Sicily's the past. The old things are gone. This is the new country. This is a world for my son, even if he really belongs to another man.

We talk to Jack Lescano on the *Tribune*. He's interested in the paramilitary angle on Anglin. We talk also to Milt Kamin at the *Sun-Times*. He is likewise interested. Two weeks go by, but nothing is printed in either paper. So I call the two of them and find out that their editors have canceled the story for lack of supporting documentation. They've heard the tale about 'National Security', then. It has silenced the two reporters, and Eddie and I are on our own, just like at the start.

Until an FBI special agent named Callan contacts us. He wants to meet. Privately. He wants to talk to us about our favorite whacker, Carl Anglin.

We meet Special Agent Callan in a restaurant in Cicero. He orders the lasagna and tells us both to try it. Says it's the best in the city.

'You know why I'm here,' he tells us as the waiter fills our water glasses.

'What do you have on Anglin?' I ask him as Eddie takes a sip of ice water.

'Anglin was a hit man for an agency in the federal government that shall go nameless because even I don't know their working moniker. He killed for hire in Asia during and after Korea. He did hits in South America after that. Then he became involved in Cuba, and he was—'

'Captured at the Bay of Pigs and became very pissed off at everyone's incompetence.'

'So why do you need to listen to me?' Callan asks, smiling.

'What else you got?' I grin back at him.

'He was pissed off, all right. He dumped whatever agency he was affiliated with and he started to go solo. He'd shoot anyone for the right price. The Pope, anybody. Everyone became a target.'

'But The Bay stuck in his throat,' I say.

'Yeah. A permanent bad taste,' Callan confirms.

He's a big man. Six-three or better. No body fat that I can make out. The poster-boy G-man.

'So what does he do that's so terrible that even the Outfit don't want to talk about it?' Eddie throws in.

The lasagna arrives. It's as good as the FBI agent says it is.

'That's all supposition. Nobody knows for sure,' Callan continues. 'But I have a theory. Only I'm not at liberty to share it with you at present because I'm filling in the details.'

'Why did you come to us?' I ask him.

'Because you two took undeserved heat for Anglin's getting away with the nurse murders. I was on scene that afternoon. You don't remember me, do you?'

'There were lots of police there,' Eddie reminds him.

'Yeah. There were. All those cops. And no justice. Anglin did it. Everyone knows he did it. He's probably telling all his celebrity friends about the gruesome details. He's quite the showman now . . . But I'm telling you what you already know anyway.'

'When are you going to have an idea on what it was that Anglin—'

'Lieutenant, I'm just here to find out if I have your confidence.'

'You do. Yes.'

Eddie nods in affirmation.

'I know we at the Bureau don't always get along with local law-enforcement folk . . . but this might be too big for petty grievances to get in the way . . . I don't mean to leave you hanging here, but I want to be sure that I've got my ducks in rows. I want clean details to go to the grand jury with. I don't want a last-minute bailing-out, like there was, unfortunately, with Anglin. When I hook him, I want the tip of the hook to wind up in his guts, all the way to the bottom . . . Anglin's a very bad man. What he's done can't go unpunished. Will you trust me for a little while longer?'

I go to work on the lasagna, but my gaze doesn't leave Callan's. Eddie's watching the two of us watch each other.

The call gets me out of bed at 3.42 a.m. on a Thursday. I get downtown, and Eddie meets me at Headquarters.

'What?' I ask. He looks half asleep – either that or he's about to break into tears.

'I don't know. The captain requested our presence at the address on the sheet there.'

We take the elevator down and then walk out to the car. Traffic is very light, naturally, so we're able to get to the location in just a few minutes. It's on the North Side, only a few miles from the Headquarters.

We get out of the car and walk to the entrance of the apartment building here at 4949 N. Biltmore Avenue. Not far from the Lake. You can smell the morning breeze wafting in off the water. The sun won't rise for a couple of hours, so there's a cool breeze that suggests early fall.

He's sitting on his couch in his one-bedroom apartment. We're early on scene. Just the captain and a few technicians are present so far.

Special Agent Andrew Callan sits slumped on that couch with his eyes closed. In front of him is a bottle of what turns out to have been tranquilizers. There'd been thirty pills, the prescription label reads, and now the bottle is empty. There is a suicide note on the coffee table where the bottle lies. The note reads: 'Not any more. Too much. Too often. Forgive.'

But there's no signature and the words are written in black capitals, in ink. Eddie picks up the note with a pair of tweezers.

I go into his bathroom. There is a shelf full of prescriptions for dealing with depression, the captain tells me over my shoulder.

The captain is rawboned and pale. He tends to blush at

the scene of crimes like this, as if he's embarrassed to be here with us.

'He didn't seem depressed or suicidal when we had dinner,' I tell him. Then I have to explain that Eddie and I had dinner with the special agent.

'What'd you talk about?' the captain wants to know.

For the first time, fear hits me squarely in the middle. I feel almost nauseous. Anglin slithers away from seven murders. We hear about his exploits in Asia only through the underworld of this city. And now an FBI man kills himself because he's depressed.

Our first stop, later this morning, will be at Callan's physician.

Dr Morley tells us that yes, Andrew Callan was suffering from chronic depression, but that he had his condition under control with the use of lithium. As long as he took his prescribed dosage, he didn't plunge to the depths of despair. He had been on lithium for three years and had shown no ill effects. He had also not shown any tendencies toward suicide that the doctor could recall. Morley puts us onto Callan's psychiatrist, Jack Pederson.

Pederson sings the same refrain. Callan was fine while he was on his medication. He'd had only one bad 'episode' in the two years he'd visited the shrink. That had taken place only one month earlier, but it seemed that the special agent had got over the rough patch and carried on with his life.

Andrew Callan was unmarried. It's my job to notify the sister since she's the FBI man's only surviving relation.

'Somebody whacked Callan,' Eddie intones as we drive away from the therapist's.

It's almost noon now, mid-shift, so we head to Garvin's saloon to take our lunch.

We arrive at the railroad tracks, and I park the car out in the weeds that Garvin never cuts. It's like dwarf elephant grass.

We order a couple of sandwiches and two soft drinks. I notice I've been imbibing less alcohol recently. I guess I've tried to convince myself that I need to be sober to catch this son of a bitch Anglin. Maybe I haven't had the time for the booze. Or maybe I'm just becoming immune to its numbing effect, the main reason I drink the stuff. I don't know.

Garvin shambles away to prepare our orders.

'How's Jimmy?' Eddie wants to know.

He'd just got out of the hospital, the last letter had said. 'He's going back into the bush, he says. He told us that things were quieting down, but I think that's for Eleanor's consumption,' I tell Eddie.

'I'm praying for him, Jake.'

We're sitting in a bar in Berwyn in the middle of the day. We're currently the only two patrons. Carl Anglin eludes us like some haunted-house ghost, and a federal agent has committed suicide because he was onto Carl's exploits close to home.

It feels like the end of something. I feel numb even without the booze.

My boy is halfway around the world, being shot at, like I was in 1944 and 1945. The whole planet's gone mad, and here we sit, quietly having lunch.

I change my order from a soft drink to a draft beer.

'Shit,' Eddie says. 'I'm with you. Hit me with a cold one too, Mr Garvin.'

Chapter Ten

[March 1999]

Mason came up with something for Doc and me. The female assistant with the legs presented the material to us in a sealed folder in our office there in Homicide. She didn't say anything, just dropped the envelope on my desk and immediately walked out.

'Jesus, she's good,' Doc moaned.

I opened the file and began to see the maze of cutouts in Anglin's military history. But there was nothing there that we didn't already know.

Except about his capture in the Bay of Pigs. After that he disappeared, it said, and became what the CIA people called a 'rogue'. He was like a marauding elephant that stomped an occasional village or two and then disappeared into the bush.

It fit him perfectly, that description.

What struck me, what intrigued me, was that episode in Cuba. Anglin had to have been scared at being trapped on Castro's island. He had to have been enraged by the lack of backup his own country provided him there. It was almost like a small-scale Vietnam. There they were, on the beach, with their lily-white asses hanging out in the tropical sun. But the troops didn't come to save them.

So how would I react if I were Anglin, this quasi-007 with a license to terminate? I thought about who left my private parts out in the breeze and I thought about ending a few lives, here and there. But who did I rub out? Allen Dulles or some other CIA honcho? Too tough to get at. Some military chief? Who? No one put their name to the Bay of Pigs. It was too big an embarrassment. The Kennedys took some hits for the plan, but those were the guys in Camelot, those were the lords of the realm. Who was a more likely target?

It got me back to where I'd been at the beginning. We were still trying to nab Anglin for a little conversation about the two recent murders.

I remembered reading my father's files on Theresa Rojas. That business had been thirty years ago, and the last I'd heard was that she was still in Elgin. Healthy as a horse physically but just as far from Planet Earth as she had been three decades back.

Doc and I took a ride up to the hospital. The drive from the city took an hour and a half, allowing for traffic. We breezed through because all the road work would begin in April, a month away.

When we showed our badges to the receptionist, she called the on-shift doctor and asked if Theresa Rojas was allowed visitors. She looked up from the phone and told us there had to be a doctor in the room with Theresa and any visitor.

We asked if it could be arranged, and we saw from her look as she asked the shrink that it was a hassle for somebody. But I repeated we were there for a homicide investigation, and the receptionist said the doctor would be down in a minute.

Five minutes passed, and finally a female therapist presented herself at the desk.

'I'm Carrie Johansen. I've worked with Theresa for the last two years.'

Carrie was barely five feet one and weighed maybe 100 pounds. Kinky blonde hair. And she exuded an up-front sexuality, it seemed to me. She carried herself in a manner that was aggressive and in-your-face for someone with an M.D. in psychiatry. I liked her immediately.

She walked us onto the ward.

'What's Miss Rojas's condition?' Doc asked Carrie.

'Compared to what?' she countered, grinning.

'Compared to the way she was when she entered the ward,' Doc said and smiled back.

'She's somewhat improved, but she's still uncommunicative, if that's what you want to know.'

'She's the best-kept secret in the case of those nurses' murders,' I reminded Dr Johansen.

'We're all very aware of that, Lieutenant,' she shot back.

'You've done a nice job of keeping it that way for thirty years,' I stated.

'No small feat. Not when it comes to keeping the press off your back.'

'No. You're right,' I agreed. 'The reason they haven't been around is because she was excluded from all the paperwork,' I continued. 'She was whisked right out of that dorm before the media got on scene. And newsguys were a little more understanding about privacy in years past.'

Carrie nodded as we arrived at Theresa's door.

'The federal people are primarily responsible for keeping her unknown up to now. Not us. There are too many open doors at our place downtown. The Feds are skilled at keeping things from the public.'

She opened the door.

Theresa Rojas, aged fifty-two, sat by her window. Her gaze stayed fixed. She remained peering out the window into the sunshine of a fifty-degree pre-spring day.

'Theresa,' Carrie said softly. 'We have some visitors.'

Theresa Rojas turned toward us. She was strikingly pretty, even in middle age. Her face did not show the wear of five decades. It was as if she'd been frozen in 1968. The only things that betrayed her real age were the silver streaks at her temples amid the otherwise raven-black hair with its blue sheen and the slight markings of crow's-feet beneath her eyes. With a little makeup she'd look thirty, no older.

She looked at us. There was no expression on her face.

'They tried everything. EST—'

'Electroshock therapy?' Doc gasped.

'Everything . . . Nothing rouses her. She seems as if she's only barely connected to the rest of us. We don't know if she's still in that dorm room, hiding under the bed, listening to that man slaughter all her classmates and friends, or whether she's transported herself somewhere else. We just do not know. If you're thinking she might come out of this someday, you might be right. Just as right as supposing she'll go on like this until she dies.'

I noticed the medicine bottles on top of Theresa's desk.

'What's she taking?' I asked.

'Primarily tranquilizers. Nothing too mind-altering.'

I went over to the table, took out my notebook and wrote down the names of the medicines.

'Don't you trust my word, Lieutenant?' Carrie asked, smiling. It was almost lewd, that grin.

'I trust you. I just like to write down the relevant facts. I'm getting progressively more forgetful . . . Just like she would be –' I pointed to Theresa Rojas – 'if she were here in the real world with the rest of us.'

'I think her memory's intact – somewhere.'

'Who picks up the bill here for her?'

'The State of Illinois, partially. She has some money in her family. And there is one other donor.'

'Namely?' Doc asked.

'No name. Anonymous.'

'I don't like that guy,' Doc said to her.

She laughed at his pseudo-tough-guy crack.

'A lot of things about Theresa Rojas are mysterious. She makes her own bed. Refuses to let staff take care of her laundry. She finds her way down to the laundry room where the non-committeds do their own private clothing. She takes me or whoever's taking care of her down there and she does her own wash. Theresa refuses to take meals with anyone else. Meals are taken here, on the bed. She can be very stubborn about whatever it is she has in her head that she needs or demands . . . But she will not speak. She will not communicate. Not in writing, sign language or verbally. She hasn't made a sound that anyone around here has heard in thirty years. I'm told the last utterance she made was a primal shriek aimed at a Homicide detective, thirty years ago.'

'That would have been my father,' I explained.

Carrie's eyebrows rose theatrically.

'Really?'

'Yeah. His name was Jake Parisi.'

'Is he still alive?'

I shook my head.

Did Theresa Rojas remember my gruff-assed old man? Did she recall how he must have been uncomfortable around this brown, beautiful *chica*? Jake had his doubts about everyone but himself. It wasn't just a matter of different skin hues.

'Oh,' Carrie said and lowered her eyes.

'This was the last major piece of business he had before he died. Carl Anglin. It was the only big-time homicide he'd been involved with that he wasn't able to close. It bothered him until his last day. He was the cop who let Carl Anglin go.'

'Jimmy, people didn't blame him for that,' Doc said.

'I read about the case,' Carrie said. 'Extensively. It didn't seem to me that the police bungled anything. It was just that their material witnesses disappeared. First the one was shot, and then we have Ms Rojas here. None of that is connected to your father, Lieutenant.'

'Thanks for the free therapy. I feel better now.'

She snorted, and I had to laugh aloud with her.

'Can I be with her alone for just a moment?'

Carrie looked at me quizzically. But then she relented.

'It's not SOP. But just for a minute. Don't get me in trouble.'

'I won't.'

Carrie and Doc went away.

Then it was Theresa Rojas and me in the room, alone together.

I sat by the window, on the ledge next to her. We sat quietly.

'Theresa, my name is Jimmy Parisi. I know my father talked to you a long time ago when you first came here. My dad's dead. He died not too long after he came to visit you. I know when he came he was hoping for some kind of miracle. Hoping that you'd talk to him so that he could help you get justice for all those girls that Carl Anglin killed. We all know about your trauma, so I'm not going to try and tell you anything stupid, like I know what you went through. Nobody knows that except you. And now you're all alone in that place where no one else is accepted. Nobody's been where you've been. I've been in a war. I've seen as many dead people as you have – probably a lot more, actually. But I'm not saying that gets me an invitation to come inside the place where you're at.'

Theresa was watching a woman outside who was sitting at a park bench. The woman was sobbing. She'd probably just visited a relative, a loved one, who was in Elgin for a long time. That was the way she seemed to me. I was always supposing. It was what Homicide cops did.

'I saw torn-up bodies all over that little country. And I've seen countless more since I've done this job. I don't know what all these therapists tell you, and what I'm saying now is just me taking my best shot in the dark, because I sure as hell am no psychiatrist . . . I'm trying to break down your door. We both know that. You're resisting. You've resisted for thirty years. I know you've heard that one before . . . Theresa, we're no closer to grabbing Carl Anglin than we were when he literally frightened hell out of you when he mutilated your friends in that dormitory. But if you're really in there somewhere and if you can really hear me, I think it's time you came back out. If you think I'm challenging you, you're right. You're about all we've got. Just like my father told you. But he never had time to come back and visit you some more. I'm going to keep coming until you talk to me, Theresa. There's room for you over here, on this side. You're a pretty woman, you're in the prime of your life. I want you to come out. Otherwise Anglin's murder count just went up by one woman.'

She tapped her fingers on the windowsill. The sound was very brief, but I heard the muted thumping clearly.

'Theresa?'

She was still once more. I went to the door to bring Doc and the psychiatrist back in.

'Did you try to talk to her?' Carrie asked.

I simply looked at her.

'Everybody does,' she said.

'She drummed her fingers on the window sill,' I told her.

'Habit,' Carrie replied.

'We'll be back, in any case,' I told her.

There was no smile for me this time.

On the way back to the city, Doc looked over at me from the passenger's side of the Taurus.

'Miracles don't solve homicides,' he uttered.

'No. You're right.'

He sat there and stared out through the windshield.

'Why'd you write down the names of her medications?'

'Because I wanted to see how doped up they've got her.'

'You think someone might be spiking Theresa's meds?'

'It's a possibility.'

'What if she's simply lost, Jimmy? It happens, you know.'

'Sure. It happens. Thirty years, Doc. She looks like some preserved specimen . . . I think we ought to put her under surveillance.'

'What if she already is?'

'What do you mean?'

'I mean if she's being doped by somebody, it's pretty obvious they're also going to keep a close eye on her. They haven't killed her, which they would've done if they didn't think she'd veggied out permanently. They must be convinced, Jimmy. They must be sure. They could've made her disappear a long time ago. That's the kind of thing Anglin's war buddies did so well.'

'They've had plenty of opportunity, sure. And you're right. Why take a chance by whacking her when she's one of the walking dead already?'

'Sure. These guys don't take unnecessary risks.'

'But what if Theresa Rojas came out of it somewhere along the line? What if she recognized the medication they were giving her as prescribed mind control? What if she, a nursing student, realized that someone was trying to keep her locked up in her own psychosis?'

'Jimmy. Wasn't it enough what she went through with Anglin, that night?'

'But she's a survivor, Doc! She held her breath, never made a whimper. She outfoxed him – a professional assassin. She stayed with him all night long, all those hours, and she didn't give it up. I think she's home with the lights on, Doc. I think she was trapped in hysteria for a while after that night in 1968, but I think she gradually came out of it. Then they had to back up their bet by making it all a sure thing, and I think Theresa Rojas got hip to all the pharmaceuticals they were trying to pump into her and she's been allowing herself to be kept captive in the hospital.'

'That's very wild, Lieutenant.'

'No wilder than what Anglin did to get himself protected by some outlaws in the government who're willing to kill anybody just to keep it inside the sack where it hides.'

'Jesus, Jimmy, we're talking about people who've got no scruples at all. They'll kill anybody. Good guys, bad guys – they don't make any distinction.'

'You saw them lurking about in the aftermath of the Korean War, and I saw them in Vietnam.'

Doc nodded.

I went on. 'These creeps. They're like sappers, if only in one way. Slithering through the bush on their bellies. They don't know boundaries, no. Once you let them loose . . . It's like a bacteria. It's got no conscience. It kills and spreads and kills. Nothing stops it except a burning-out. A purge.'

'Or . . . Theresa really is in some kind of mute state and your theory is paranoid bullshit.'

'Yeah, Doc, and I'm pulling for your paranoid bullshit explanation.'

He laughed and turned on the radio. He switched to a

classic-rock FM station rather than his usual jazz preference. Doc turned to me and said that rock and roll helped him turn back time occasionally. Like taking a dip in the Fountain of Youth via the airwaves.

Chapter Eleven

[October 1968]

The Bureau investigates the death of Agent Callan, as do we. I take a close look at the toxicology of his medication, but nothing I discover invalidates the conclusion that he was what the FBI calls a special agent under 'duress'. They tell Eddie and me that this guy Callan's been inside the pressure cooker for too long.

The interesting thing I find out about this Fed is that he was in the Marines before joining the Bureau. He served on board a ship, the *Icon*, during the Bay of Pigs disaster. It makes me wonder if his path crossed Anglin's back then. But I've already received the royal runaround from the government. Getting information from them is like prying open a rusted-out vault. You've got to blow the door off the hinges to get inside.

Callan wanted to do the right thing. He was prepared to help us, and suddenly he was taken out of play. There are too many coincidences, too many odd circumstances. I'm not a conspiracy freak. I don't see the work of the devil in a corrupt City Hall deal. I see human crooks. That's all. Maybe I'm too simple for this job, but I've been hauling out the trash on these streets for a long time, and my arrest record is as good as that of any of my colleagues.

Frustration happens when doors slam in your face. I understand that much psychology. But with this case there are too many doors, too many slams. Callan comes along, and suddenly I'm thinking I see some daylight.

Then, on a Friday afternoon, his sister from Dubuque, Iowa calls me. She wants a meeting, a face-to-face. I arrange it for this afternoon. At Garvin's Comeback Inn in Berwyn. It's a dump, but it probably isn't bugged, either.

Her name is Doris. She's Agent Callan's twin. I can see the resemblance.

She takes a look around the seedy saloon and her nose goes skyward. I have to laugh. Eddie looks at me like I'm laughing at a funeral.

'I know. It's terrible, this place, isn't it?'

She looks at me and smiles. She's a pretty woman, but I don't see a wedding band.

'Andy didn't kill himself.'

'Why do you say that?' Eddie asks her.

'He's my twin. I knew him like no one else knew him. Someone murdered my brother. And I think you know why.'

'Did Agent Callan talk business with you?' I ask.

'He did. I was the only person he ever talked to. Our parents are dead. Neither Andy nor I ever got married. My work – I've got a PhD in English Literature – took me to Iowa, and so we've communicated over the telephone.'

I look over to my partner. We're both thinking a bugged telephone had something to do with Callan's demise. Andy had told Doris things she shouldn't have heard. Now she's as much a target as her brother was, if the conspiracy theory is really true.

'Are you afraid for your safety?' I ask.

'Yes. I think our calls were being listened to. Andy knew something was wrong before he died. He stopped discussing his work, the last three weeks or so. But we met about ten days ago, and he told me it was dangerous to share anything else about this Anglin case with me. He apologized for being stupid enough to have said things over the phone. He told me to quit my job, get out and not leave a forwarding address . . . Was he right? Is all this as dangerous as he said?'

'I think you might want to do what your brother said,' I tell her.

'Oh, my God.'

'You're single, right? You can work anywhere. I'd do what Andrew told you to do. I wouldn't be able to offer you protection here. And I don't have much confidence in any federal aid at the moment. There might be one other way.'

'What's that?' she asks.

'Go public. Get some journalist to write it down. The problem is that they'd have to substantiate all your allegations, and to date we've got nothing to prove your brother didn't kill himself. They've done this thing very cleverly. If they drugged him, they did it with something that leaves no trace. We run into questionable deaths all the time. They don't all get resolved . . . No, if I were you, I'd head out until – maybe – all this comes out in the wash. I wish I could offer you more.'

'Andrew didn't kill himself. Don't let it lie, Lieutenant Parisi.'

'I won't.'

Eddie looks down at his shoes. The three soft drinks we ordered from the owner of Garvin's sit on top of the slab, untouched. Ms. Callan gets up and leaves us there. She's driven all the way in from Dubuque, but I can't guess where she's headed now.

'Would they pop her, too?' Eddie inquires.

'They might. They also might figure she's frightened enough to keep her mouth shut. Too many murders make for too much tidying-up. Even the government can't afford an unlimited mess. Maybe they'll leave her alone. She's just a sister with a grudge and a sad tale to tell. Who's going to listen to her?'

'She still ought to get the hell out of town,' Eddie concludes.

I watch Carl Anglin, as I said, on my free time. I'm careful not to let him catch me at it because we've been warned by the folks downtown not to harass him. Since he is no longer a prime suspect in the nurses' murders, we are to look elsewhere.

Naturally there are no other likely suspects. Anglin did it. Everyone in Homicide knows it. He walks free with all that blood on his hands.

Life and death go on. There are other killers to apprehend. We are kept busy. But now that the outdoor summer months are closing out, the number of homicides decreases. The hot politics of Chicago's summer of '68 is simmering down some, but the anti-war sentiment is growing by the day. The liberals want us to love the North Vietnamese. The guys who've been shooting at my goddamn kid. Jane Fonda, the movie bitch, is talking nice with the communists while our guys are getting chewed up in that weed patch.

Jimmy writes that they're aware that the nation is not behind them, that the troops' morale is low. Mostly everyone wants to saddle up and come home. Winning is not a priority. Survival is. The South Vietnamese – the ARVN – are Number Ten. They have no respect or love for the Americans and they fight poorly. They fight for money when they pull the trigger at all, Jimmy writes, and it feels like our guys are out there on a limb all by themselves. Not optimum prospects for victory in Southeast Asia.

His tour is coming to a close in a few more months, but he thinks he might like to commit for a second go-round. He says the benefits are pretty good. He'll get more money when he gets out and he won't have to do chickenshit Stateside duty for the rest of his hitch when he returns. He'll be out immediately when the Freedom Bird lands in the U.S.

I'm back to spending more time in the Greek's tavern. There's nothing for me at home. Eleanor is only there physically. We do not touch, we do not intersect at any point. The house feels empty without Jimmy.

I embarrassed my son with my drinking. I drove him out when he wanted to spend time with his friends. Jimmy would not bring his buddies or his girlfriend, Erin, inside our walls. And I can't blame him. Drunken old homicide investigator. Failure, in fact. Murderer walks the streets because I couldn't collar him. I know my own excuses. Christ, a dead witness and a fruitcake zombie who lives anonymously in Elgin State. I have the killer's scent fully in my nose, but I cannot bring him down.

I know Anglin was up to his eyebrows in evil with the military. A hired killer who hides today behind his flag, behind his uniform. I understand he's done something big enough for the Spook community to watch his ass end. He's a protected man. His connections go to some major vein in the heart of D.C. or Quantico or Spookville – or wherever.

There's an innocent teacher of English who had better be on the run because her brother confided in her over the telephone. There's a dead FBI agent who I know in my gut never pulled his own plug.

It's no wonder I'm here at the Greek's on the South Side swilling up bourbon and beers by the pair. If you drop a shot glass full of bourbon into a glass of draft beer they call the result a depth charge. Well, I've blown up a whole flotilla of submarines, then, with all the charges I've dropped.

'Jake, you better head on out into the sunset,' the Greek himself tells me.

I've exceeded my limit, he explains. He's the only friend I've got. He's called me a cab. Is sending me home before I get my pension in trouble with a drunk-driving rap. The cabby comes into the bar and hails me.

I wave to the Greek and stagger out into the icy wind. The breeze takes my breath away momentarily, but I'm able to get myself inside the Checker cab.

Eleanor is away for two days, visiting her mother in Indiana. They live in some hick heaven called Oxford.

'Anybody home?' I bellow out. I know there'll be no reply.

I walk up those twenty-six stairs and head toward the guest room, my bedroom.

'Nobody home? You sure?'

I smile with the sound of silence. This is the way it ought to be for Chicago's most outcast copper. There are policemen at headquarters who make a point of ignoring me. The only guys who talk to me are the captain and my partner, Eddie. Fuck the rest of them, I figure. Times like these reveal who your real friends are. I was never all that close with my fellow Centurions.

I lie down on my bed. It is hard and uncompromising, this mattress, the way I want it. Helps relieve the bad back I got, sleeping for two years on the ground in Europe during the Second World War. Nothing eases the pain except this boardlike bed of mine. Eleanor refuses to sleep with me here anyway.

I close my eyes and I see the photographs of the seven nurses. I see the terror in Andrew Callan's sister's eyes. I see the dread in Theresa Rojas's blank stare. And I see the actual corpses I encountered on the floors of those dorm rooms. There is nothing quite like the real thing. The authentic dead body.

They haunt me every night. I cannot drown them out with the booze. Sleep doesn't stop them from invading the surreal territory of the land of dreams. They're with me all day and every night. I'll need a shrink if the booze doesn't do me in first.

Eleanor. When was the last time her warm presence made contact with my own flesh? I can't recall. I love her in spite of her disloyalty. She made me a cuckold and tried to tell me it was for my own good, it was so that we could have the family that I couldn't give her. Nick was simply providing the seed of our happiness, she tried to convince me. Why couldn't I see things for what they really were? She loves me, she says. It was never otherwise. Why couldn't I bend my lofty virtue just once, she pleaded, and let us be happy with our lives and with our son? She digs into her Catholic upbringing and reminds me that Joseph had to live with an immaculate offspring. Well, she wasn't Mary, Eleanor reminded me. If she were to have a child it would have to be via more conventional means. Meaning Nick. Nick's seed, Nick's sperm.

Sleep is God's opium. Sleep puts it behind us, it lets us unload all our burdens. But the price of sleep is dreams – more specifically, nightmares.

I have to close my eyes in spite of that knowledge.

And when I do, I hear a creaking of the floor downstairs. My first reaction is to bolt upright, here in bed. I grab down for the snub-nosed .38 in my ankle holster and yank it out. Then, silently, I get out of bed.

I do not call out. I don't want them – whoever they are – to know I'm aware of them.

So I get to the bedroom door and I walk quietly down the twenty-six stairs. I walk at their far right edge in order to avoid the creaking I heard before.

When I arrive at the first floor, there are no lights on. I've turned them off before going upstairs.

Dumb fuck, I'm thinking. *Trying to boost a copper's house. How stupid can a thief be?*

But maybe it's not a thief.

I work my way slowly through the dark toward the kitchen. My advantage is that it's home turf for me. Whoever this is, he's on foreign ground.

The kitchen is clear. I stand still and listen.

Nothing.

I carry on and make my way toward the living room, just the other side of the dining room that I'm now passing through. I hear another slight squeaking of the floorboards. So I stop in place and try to get a fix on the location. The sound is coming from the kitchen. I hear another faint noise coming from there.

The son of a bitch is following me.

I carefully step back toward where I began, in the kitchen. There's no way he can avoid me if he's still in there. I'm pointing the .38 in front of me like a flashlight. One movement and someone is going to be splattered across my walls.

The weariness is still with me. The alcohol makes the room move eerily in the darkness. I try to fight off the effect of the booze. There is only a swinging door separating me from the kitchen and the intruder inside.

Crouching, I rush through the door, the .38 in my hand moving back and forth to cover the room. There is silence and nothing else. This time I hear the movement coming from back out in the living room. I shove back through the kitchen door and hurry toward the source of this latest sound.

It's the same in here. I hear the noise coming from back in the kitchen.

Fuck him. I'm going to turn on the light. I flip the switch and the brilliance of the bulbs blinds me slightly. But there's no one in here with me. So I walk through the dining room and I flip on that switch. The overhead flares on and I'm still on my own.

I throw open the door to the kitchen, and I fumble until I've switched the light there on. Still there is no one to be seen. I hear the noise in the dining room. I peer through the crack in the swinging door and I see the backside of someone dressed in black. They're headed toward the living room. They're running a game on me, staying one square ahead, but now the game is going to get deadly.

I charge into the dining room at a dead run, hurl myself through the still-lit living-room and finally catch sight of the black-clad figure making his way out of my living-room window. I pump five shots at the fleeing figure, and I know I've only hit with one. I think I've caught him in the buttocks as he bent over in order to get out the window.

If I'd been sober, I would've killed him. My eyesight is 20-20, and I'm a better than fair marksman.

The five shots are noisy. When I look out at my front lawn I see lights coming on in the front windows of several of my neighbors' houses.

I call in for a squad car to get out here. They respond in under five minutes because the car's not far from my house.

The patrolmen want to have a look around, so I show them where everything is. They defer to the fact that I'm a Homicide cop, but I know they can smell the liquor on my breath and maybe even the scent of the fear I'm spreading all over my own house. They're polite – Adams and Lefferts are their names – but I can tell they're thinking I might have hallucinated, me being bombed the way I am.

'I've been drinking,' I tell Lefferts. 'I'm not, however, all fucked up, Patrolman.'

'Yessir.' Lefferts smiles. He goes to find his partner who is searching the upstairs storey now.

I make them some coffee. Mostly I make it for myself. My hands are shaking as I put the grounds into the pot.

'There's no blood anywhere that I can see, Lieutenant,' Adams tells me when he and Lefferts come back into the kitchen.

'I know I hit him once,' I tell the tall, good-looking kid.

'Could be he didn't leak until he got to his ride,' Adams says. 'But there was a set of footprints on the wet grass.'

'We need to get a cast made,' I tell them. He goes out to the squad car to ask for some on-scene help.

'Five shots?' Lefferts asks. 'You'd think he would've bled a little, even if you did only hit him once.'

The electric coffee pot begins to perk, and the noise makes me jerk upright.

Chapter Twelve

[April 1999]

The night in 1968 went something like this. It was after 8.00 p.m. The seven student nurses were in the dorm for the night because they didn't speak English very well. They hadn't been in El Norte long enough to pick up on the directions and whereabouts of things. The girls were pretty much homebodies because this city was big. So big that nothing but Mexico City or Havana in the Hispanic countries compared to this foreign place.

There were Mexican men in Chicago, but not of the same class that the girls were used to. These seven nurses came from educated families, some better off than others. But all of them came from the middle classes. On the West Side of Chicago, there was stark poverty. There was a large black population, and there was also a growing Hispanic community. But the Hispanics lived on the edge of poverty in these barrios. So the girls might not have felt comfortable mixing with the established Spanish-speaking residents. It wasn't necessarily because of snobbishness. These folk were adjusted, more or less, to El Norte. The student nurses were still only visitors to this part of North America.

Chicago could be intimidating. The students knew something of the city from the cases they studied at County Hospital. Gunshot wounds, stabbings, stranglings, poisonings. They'd seen it all come through Emergency. So they might have been a bit scared to venture out into the world immediately around them.

So it was early evening and they had settled in to study or watch television or just hang around and generally be lonely. After a couple of hours the boredom or the weariness had worn them out and several of them were preparing for bed. Since they were all Catholics, they prayed before going to sleep, and perhaps a few of them said the rosary as well. (Later, cops found the beads by three of their beds.)

Carmen Espinoza was the last one out of the dorm, around 10.00 p.m. Everyone else was socked in for the night.

It must have been that last nurse out who made it possible for Anglin to get into the dormitory. The safety door probably swooshed closed just a hair too slowly after her departure, and Carl Anglin was in the alley, just waiting for someone to give him his chance. It came – and he was in.

Anglin began with the first nurse, Angela Trujillo. He bound her with her own sheets and silenced her with a balled-up pillowcase that nearly choked her to death. He moved on to the next room and subdued the two roommates, Maria Colota and Juana Martinez, by punching both of them unconscious with his fists. The ruckus must have lasted only seconds because the other girls down the hall never heard him coming.

He continued in a similar way until he had all seven girls tied up.

He returned to the first room and spent some time with victim number one. When he had raped her several times, he cut her throat twice. Very skillful cutting. Like someone who had done that kind of knifing before. She bled to death very quickly. Her mouth was stuffed with pillowcase, so there was no audible screaming.

Anglin moved on to the pair of student nurses in room two. He sodomized one of the young women, and then he raped the roommate in a more usual fashion before he also anally assaulted the second girl. He cut their throats, one after the other, and then he disemboweled both women, leaving them split open like butchered cattle at the stock-yards.

All this was done without disturbing the student nurses on the floors above or below. There were three floors in this dormitory.

Anglin finally finished the carnage around 1.00 a.m., it was estimated by the Medical Examiner. Give or take an hour either way.

My father arrived on scene early that morning. He told me before I went to Vietnam that he had never seen such savagery, such an absence of pity for the victims, in his entire career. He told me the details of the case before I left for Asia because he wanted to dissuade me from joining the police. I saw some things in my area of operations that might have rivaled in brutality what Anglin did to the girls, but then, I was in a war. Anglin had taken the unbelievable violence of combat and transferred its ugliness into the dormitory where the seven young females perished. My father's story frightened me because of the matter-of-fact way he told it. It was as if this was nothing new, this incredible carnage. But he had seen savagery before, in the streets and in his own war.

So he did not convince me to do anything other than become a policeman. I came back from Vietnam after two tours with a box full of decorations that I stopped wearing as soon as I could find my civvies. I signed up for the remaining hours that I owed for my bachelor's degree, finished up that work and graduated and promptly signed on at the Police Academy. My first assignment was a beat on the West Side – patrolman, of course. Several years later, I had my shield and worked in Burglary/Auto Theft. Finally I landed where I am today: Homicide. That was my own personal evolution. I grew up in the police with the Anglin murders already a matter of history. I saw my father turn gray with the weight of the nurses' deaths. Then he died and I was left alone with this burden. The CPD put Anglin's file in their 'inactive' section and hoped he'd go away.

If I compared Carl Anglin to Evil, I'd be accused of sounding philosophical or even theological. I knew he was a man with two legs, two arms, and all the other usual equipment. Carl was human. It would be facile or naive to explain him away as something supernatural. No, he was one of us, more's the pity. It would make us more comfortable with ourselves to categorize him out of the human species. It'd make things easier for us, more bearable. The presence of evil in men had long been a subject of study and dispute for men far more intelligent than yours truly, so I wouldn't tarry, as they said. But there *was* a dose of something in Carl Anglin that made all those tales of a horned beast with a tail and a pitchfork just a little more credible to us believers who had no trouble embracing notions of angels and the God of Abraham. Still, the bad guy was undoubtedly less acceptable, the product of medieval ignorance, even if Jehovah was okay in some intellectual circles. To me it made no sense to exclude the Devil because there was a helluva lot more evidence for the Beast in action on earth than there was for the presence of this Essence of Good. I was a Catholic, as I said, and we still had that little embarrassment known as the Rite of Exorcism in our book, so I guess modern man hadn't dismissed Old Scratch entirely.

It was difficult to deal with Carl Anglin if I didn't try to see him as human rather than demon. He had the same weaknesses any other perpetrator had, I told myself. He'd escaped punishment because of a glitch in history, not because he was the son of Satan. To think any other way would be ignorance and superstition.

But when I went over in my mind the crime scene my father had encountered thirty years ago, I was left there in my office, alone at 3.30 in the morning, feeling a chill creep up my backbone.

I rose out of my chair and looked out the window at the lake. The sun would not rise for a few hours, but I was feeling an urgent need for the rays from the east to touch my window here sooner than that. All the lights were on in headquarters, but it wasn't bright enough. Only natural sunlight would drive this dank feeling out of my bones.

Doc Gibron was married to a baby-doctor, a pediatrician. She was Indian and outrageously beautiful. Far too good for the likes of my partner. They had adopted an African-American girl who happened to be blind in one eye. The girl was the heart of their happiness. Doc was in his sixties, as I said, and Mari, his wife, was in her early fifties.

They were a unique couple. Doc had his PhD in Literature from Northwestern University in Evanston, not far from where I sat. He kept threatening to quit and chase the coeds, but he said Mari'd slap the shit out of him and he couldn't bear having her angry with him. Besides, he was a father now.

As was I. But I hadn't seen any of my three offspring in thirty-six hours. It was time to go home and leave Carl Anglin for the next shift to worry about.

'You ready to call it a day?' Doc grinned.

'I was born ready.'

I tried to sound as enthusiastic as I could after a day and a half of overtime. The extra hours had turned out to be fruitless. There seemed to be no progress on either of the two homicides. The old adage held true. With a murder, the longer it went, the worse it went.

Doc and I took the elevator down and walked over to the corner cafe where we bought coffee or soft drinks whenever a break was called for. I bought the *Tribune* from a newspaper vending machine before we went inside the cafe.

At 4.00 a.m. the joint was half full. It reminded me of that painting, *Night Owls*.

We ordered a coffee for my partner and a Diet Coke for me. I took the caffeine-free soda pop. Because of my blood pressure.

'We can't shoot him,' Doc said.

'What?' I laughed, looking up from the *Tribune*'s sports page.

'We can't just whack him. But you know some people who could.'

'Quit screwing around.'

I eyeballed him, and he too finally broke out laughing.

'It might just be an option, Jimmy. Tell one of your Sicilian cousins to put one behind his fucking ear.'

'I don't deal with that side of the family. Not anymore.'

One of my underworld cousins had been murdered by the Farmer, Marco Karrios, in that case we'd just finished up last year. The poor son of a bitch had been butchered like some of Carl's victims. Killing Marco Karrios hadn't made me feel any better about the loss of my cheap-thief relative.

'Yeah. I almost forgot about that,' Doc lamented. 'I'm sorry I brought it up, Jimmy.'

'Forget about it. He was a big boy. He understood the danger. If you lie down with dogs, right?'

Doc knew it was a sore spot, so he let it go.

'You know how much trouble and money would be saved if someone popped a cap on the son of a bitch . . .'

'We don't do murders, we solve them,' I recited. It was like a Homicide cop's Pledge of Allegiance.

Doc grinned.

'You did homicides, justifiable though they were, with that other uniform on . . . Anyway, it'd be a sweet way to bring closure to our current caseload.'

The night sky seemed to be turning just a little bit lighter. I was looking out the plate-glass window. Perhaps the lights inside here were playing tricks on me.

'I'm going home, guinea. It's my little girl's birthday. I've got to be at Walmart when they open. Got a $500 budget. Mari says not to spoil her . . . You coming over tonight for the cake and crap?'

I nodded.

'Absolutely,' I affirmed.

Doc patted my hand like he was my loving grandma, and then he left the coffee shop.

I thought I'd stick around until the first rays of the rising sun appeared. I didn't want to walk to my car in the lot by myself in the dark, squeamish as that sounded. I was armed to the teeth, as always, but I didn't want to make that short trip alone, or at least without the sun to light my way.

I was getting old and perhaps more careful with it. Homicides had never bothered me before like this one was doing. I could leave my work at the office, for the most part. Now I was dragging Carl Anglin wherever I went. Natalie had noticed it, around the house. She said I was more moody than usual. I denied her allegations, but I was lying when I did.

'Screw him,' I said to my Coke cup.

The waitress, Arlene, was passing by and overheard me.

'Not you, beautiful,' I told her.

'I'm so disappointed,' she said, pouting.

I left her an extra buck tip, which took away her frown.

The parking lot was deserted. Doc, of course, was long gone, headed for an open Walmart. The overhead lights were on, but the lot was not very well illuminated.

I decided to take my Nine out of my shoulder holster. Usually I touched this piece twice a day. Once when I donned the shoulder rig and went off to work and the second time when I arrived home after a shift and took it off. But now I felt the need so I palmed the piece. My family automobile was a Chevy Cavalier. It sat way in the back, in one of the rows closest to the headquarters entrance doors.

You'd have thought coppers would park out in this lot to give the place additional security, wouldn't you? It was probably our arrogance to think that no one would be foolish enough to assault a police officer on his way to his vehicle, but I was thinking that Carl Anglin probably didn't give a shit who his target was. And I meant to warn Doc to watch himself when he was alone or off duty. I could picture Anglin going for either of us. He was protected, remember? He was untouchable, invincible.

I heard something coming up behind me. I pivoted toward the sound, and I found a squad car with two patrolmen inside pulling into a space behind me. I was glad I was holding my piece against my thigh. It could've been embarrassing if I'd assumed the shooting stance, aiming my gun at two uniforms getting off shift.

'Jesus,' I murmured.

I put the piece back in its holster by my armpit.

I rolled away from her. I couldn't get my breath.

'Jimmy?' Natalie asked gently.

'Oh, my. You take my breath away,' I said, smiling.

She knew I was stealing lyrics from one of her favorite songs. It was in that movie with Tom Cruise. *Top Gun.*

'You do the same for me,' she said softly, and then she ran her fingernails gently through the hairs on my chest.

'You are one hairy guinea,' she teased.

'Indeed . . . You want me to Nair off this shit?'

'Not on your life, wop . . . Your pulse is racing. Did I do that?'

She had hold of my right wrist. As if she were a nurse, listening in on me.

'I been taking my medication, Doc.'

Which reminded me to find out about those prescriptions for Theresa Rojas.

'He's been bothering you, Jimmy. Don't lie to me.'

'Lie to you about what, Red?'

'Anglin. Everybody knows you've been a little tense over this guy.'

'Sure. It's nothing to worry about.'

'You better have a checkup. Your pulse is irregular. I was a nursing student for a year. Remember?'

'Really? It's off?'

'Not terrible. Just a little off. See the man, lover. Let go of this Anglin. Even if you don't catch him, someone else will. All else failing, Jimmy, God'll whack him Himself.'

'You really believe that?'

'Really believe what?'

'Do you really believe God deals with the perps who come floating his way?'

'Sure, Jimmy. We're Catholics. You recall all that parochial-school stuff?'

God would take care of Carl Anglin. I said it over and over in my head, but it didn't relieve the pressure. Now I could feel my heartbeat. Not a good sign. The blood-pressure medication must not have been working. Or it wasn't a sufficiently high dosage.

Anglin had a hold of me, inside and out. I could feel his grip on my temples, inside my chest. It was a crushing embrace he'd slapped on me. Like a bear hug.

'God will take care of Carl Anglin,' I said out loud.

'I'll get you a couple of Tylenol,' Natalie insisted as she crawled hurriedly out of bed.

Chapter Thirteen

[October 1968]

I feel them coming up behind me. I want to walk everywhere with my weapon drawn. The shrinks call it paranoia, but I think it's plain, healthy fear. They've defiled my house, whoever the hell-they-are. They broke in to kill me or to scare me and they sure as hell accomplished the latter.

I install new dead bolts on all the doors. I have new clasps put onto the windows to keep them locked. But anyone in the police knows that locks won't keep anybody out if they really want in. It's like with car boosters. You can put an air-raid horn under your hood and it won't keep them from stealing your automobile. It's just that spending some money and time on security gives you a feeling that at least you're trying.

Eddie hasn't had the pleasure of an intruder, but I've got him wary. He's sent his wife and kid to his mother's until things calm down or until we grab Anglin.

I still tail Carl. I let him see me once in a while. He smiles at me when he catches a glimpse, but I don't react with similar good humor. I just watch him to let him know we haven't let go of him. The strange thing is that we haven't heard from his lawyer about harassing him. He must still be amused by our stakeouts. He'll get bored with our presence soon.

Andrew Callan's death weighs heavily on me. I can't dismiss

him as a suicide, even if I were to set aside his sister's plea. I don't like his crime scene. It's too organized, too clean, too ready-made. Whoever prepared it was someone who understood Homicide investigative procedures. They laid everything out too neatly for us.

I go to our lab and ask them to reexamine the contents of Callan's stomach. I ask them to look at his blood again. Even though this is a slightly unusual request, Dr Brisco humors me and says he'll have a look, on his own time. I tell him not to mention the favor to anyone. Brisco eyes Eddie and me oddly, but he understands this is about the murder of someone from the Bureau, so he suppresses his curiosity.

'What could they do him with that wouldn't leave a trace?' Eddie asks as we drive toward Anglin's place to administer our daily dose of harassment.

'Digitalis,' I tell him.

Eddie nods. It's true, sometimes it doesn't leave much of a trace.

'Curare. That native stuff they put on the darts in the jungle. It paralyzes the victim. Cuts off their air,' I suggest.

'Spooks doing spooks?' Eddie asks.

'Callan wasn't a spook. He was just an FBI agent without any particular connections. He was disconnected on Anglin, that's for goddamn sure.'

We head toward the murderer of all those young girls. It's become something of a ritual for the two of us.

Dr Brisco makes a personal stop at my office on his way to lunch the next day. He motions for me to come walk with him. Eddie is reading *Sports Illustrated* in the shithouse in order to clear his mind for detective work.

We walk down toward the cafeteria. I stop at the soda machine and get us both Cokes. Brisco takes a sip, and then he indicates that we need to keep moving.

'You aren't wired, are you, Jake?' he asks, smiling.

'What'd you find?'

'Just the slightest of traces. But whoever did the original autopsy – and it wasn't me – missed it. Curare. That South

American stuff that the Jivaro Indians use. Modern medicine uses it now, but the Indians originally employed it to stun their prey, whatever they were hunting. But if you use too heavy a dose, it shuts down the victim's breathing so that you suffocate them. It leaves barely a trace of itself, Jake. The first M.E. might really have missed it legitimately. You have to be actively looking for it, it's so easy to miss . . . Whatever. It looks like your man Callan was stunned with this stuff before he was fed the pills that supposedly killed him. In order to get curare into him, someone might have given it to him in a drink. Or they could've just barely pierced his flesh with a fine-point needle. I don't know. We should probably exhume the remains.'

'They cremated him three days ago.'

'Then it's lucky they held onto his blood, his serum work-ups.'

'They seem to be very confident people, Doctor. They broke into a Homicide lieutenant's house. They murdered an FBI agent. That's just some of the small stuff they've probably done.'

'Well, Jake, I don't know what else to tell you, now that the body's gone. We've got the blood, true, but we would've needed some more of Agent Callan to bring anything into a court of law. I'm sorry.'

Brisco takes another sip of his soda and walks away from me.

I tell Eddie about the doctor's findings. He already knows about the cremation, so we're left with our peckers hanging out in the wind. Which is becoming a familiar routine in this case.

'Maybe God don't want us to solve this one, Jake,' Eddie laments.

I too am beginning to think cracking this case ain't in the cards for either of us.

Jimmy's letters talk mostly happy talk. He's seen Bob Hope and some other USO shows, last Christmas, and he's looking forward to Hope coming back again. He hates the guy's jokes, but his show reminds Jimmy of home. The broads that tour with the comedian are a little cheesy and they're aging poorly, he writes, but it reminds of him of being a kid and watching Sunday-night television with Eleanor, and with me whenever I was home on that evening.

He's definitely signing up for the second tour because the money will free him from college loans. I wrote him and told him I'd give him the cash – no repayment required – but he refused, saying he appreciated my gesture but he wanted to come out free and clear on his own. The second combat tour will pay his way.

This country is hanging out in the breeze, like my pecker on the Anglin case. It's anyone's guess which way we'll blow. That'll depend on the breeze. We've got hippies and yippies and dippies and shitbirds of every stripe, of every attitude and sentiment. We've got politicals and apoliticals and outright skullfucks who just want to get high and get laid. I can't keep them all separate in my head. I can't figure out who's for real and who's a lying sack of middle-class white kid with too much free time on his or her hands. I've given up trying to make the distinction. In my business everyone's really equal. They look much the same when I arrive on scene. That gray pallor. That waxlike look. The smell comes on a little later, like rigor, but human rot is the most unique stink on earth. When we dig up some corpse or open a door behind which lies a victim, the reek immediately hits your nostrils. It's at that point that you deny we are God's finest creation. We sure are his smelliest.

Maybe all this signals the end of the world. Or perhaps it's just my end, the end of my era. Frankly I'm tired, and like Scarlett's boyfriend, I don't much give a damn anymore. Except for the safety of my son, Jimmy. I want him to come home. I want his war to be over, and I don't give a shit who wins the conflict. Maybe it's time the country came down from the high we got from my war. Then we felt we could whip anyone – even after Korea. If Truman had let MacArthur drop those bombs across that Yalu River . . .

I'm just weary. My tiredness makes me depressed. And so does the booze. I may be an alcoholic, but I'm aware that the hooch is a depressant. I spend my off hours in a South Side saloon with a noble descendant of Plato and Aristotle. My wife does not share my bed any longer. My son who is biologically my nephew is in mortal danger in southeast Asia, fighting in a war I cannot comprehend, and my own life centers on catching a killer. A killer no one seems to want me to snag.

I drink, I sleep, I work. And in my nostrils I know it can't go on like this very much longer.

I take my suspicions about Agent Callan's demise to the head of the Chicago branch of the FBI, Dennis Murtaugh. He receives my information with a look of genuine shock on his face.

Murtaugh has a reputation for being straight, but I don't know him personally. I'm wondering how all this crap and corruption could be going on around him without him being aware of it. But I understand how it's possible.

'Curare?' he asks.

Eddie makes the leather of the chair next to me squeak. I'm a bit uncomfortable too, but I didn't know where else to turn. I know my own brother coppers too well. I know about the power a dollar sign wields.

'I know how it sounds, but there it is,' I tell Murtaugh.

'We'll have to look into it,' he says.

I sense I'm being dismissed.

'This is an outrage. I want to thank you for coming forward, and I hope I can depend on your cooperation in the coming days, Lieutenant Parisi.'

He stands up to shake hands. We're out of his office in another ten seconds.

'He either thinks we're nuts, or he's part of the whole deal,' Eddie concludes.

'I vote for we're nuts.'

'Jake, what'd you expect? This is all after the fact. The

official Medical Exam said he died of an overdose of those goodies in his apartment. Now, in some clandestine meeting, another physician lays this curare on you. What'd you think Murtaugh was going to do?'

'Slap my hand like my favorite uncle and tell me to have a nice day.'

I pull the unmarked squad car out into the city streets.

I can't sleep at night because I hear noises in the house. So I buy us a dog. One of those border collies that are trained to herd critters on farms. They're supposed to be extremely intelligent, as far as canines go, and they're supposed to make excellent watchdogs.

So I buy a year-old pup that I name Sonny. He simply looks like a Sonny.

He's extremely affectionate. Wants to nuzzle and kiss me all the time. Even Eleanor falls in love with this pooch. And he falls for my wife as well. Sonny is very territorial. He has pissed on every tree and bush around our bungalow, and he lets us know when anyone's about. He's better than any dead bolt, and he's much better company. The only thing he can't do is draw me an Old Style and a shot of Jim Beam.

So I've fallen in love with a dog. He gives me something to look forward to when I get home. Eleanor takes him everywhere with her, everywhere they'll allow an animal, at least. And she's written Jimmy about Sonny, too. Jimmy never had a dog when he was a child. When I write my son, I tell him I'll get Sonny mated with some excellent bitch and he can have a pup of his own.

Sonny keeps watch for me now. He's a very light sleeper. When I get up in the night, I never catch him zeeing out. He's always alert when my eyes are open. Sonny's a comfort. I'm becoming attached to him like he's the son I never had.

I'm at the hospital ten minutes after I get the call. Anglin's had a stroke, and no one knows how bad he is.

He's at Christ Mercy. We were on the streets when we received the radio message.

'Maybe the fucker'll die,' Eddie says, and smiles.

'Without admitting what he did?'

'There you have me,' my partner concedes.

When we arrive at Emergency, the doctor wants to know why we're there.

'We're friends of the family,' I say, smiling ingratiatingly.

The doctor is not convinced.

'You can't see him.'

So I show him my badge, and so does Eddie.

'You still can't see him,' the physician tells us.

'I really don't want to hold his hand. But if it looks fatal in there, I'd appreciate a moment with him before it's too late.'

'You want a confession from a dying man?' the ER doctor demands.

'Yeah. He's killed seven young women. If he's going to go, I want to put a period to his case.'

The physician stares at me and shakes his head.

'I thought he was cleared of the charges.'

'He was. I don't care. He killed them.'

Suddenly the ER resident looks at me and sees something in my eyes. What I see in *his* eyes is a fear that somehow I'll take out my obsession on him, instead of on Anglin.

'All right. If he goes bad, I'll let you see him before he checks out. I really shouldn't . . . But all right.'

'Thank you, Doctor,' I tell him, holding out my hand. He shakes it very tentatively, and then he withdraws back into the room where Anglin lies.

Two hours later, the doctor, Dr Arnold, reappears and tells us it was all a false alarm.

'Food poisoning. No stroke. He ate some bad mayonnaise at a restaurant. He seized up from the pain, but it wasn't a stroke . . . We'll clean his insides out, and he'll be fine.'

'Can I see him after they purge him?' I ask.

'I guess so. All right.'

We wait another three hours and finally Anglin's back in the land of the living, having had his stomach pumped.

'Hello, Carl,' I say.

He looks up blearily.

'Jesus Christ. Get out of here, will you? I'm in no condition to—'

Eddie's outside the door. Standing guard.

'You could relapse, Carl. Do you know how easily that could happen?'

Carl Anglin is a strong, lanky, athletic man, but he is very weak from the purge. He understands my threat, and he tries to sit up.

'Lie back, Carl. You got nothing to worry about . . . Unless one of your playmates decides to intrude onto my private property again.'

'I don't know what—'

'You might not, Carl, but I'm holding you responsible anyway. You come into my house, you or anyone you know, and I'll kill you. One of your old Navy buddies invades my space just once more, I'll find you and I'll kill you. And I know how to get away with it. Yeah, I could be as good at it as you are, if I felt the need. And to protect my wife and family, I wouldn't have any difficulty putting a hole behind your ear. I know where to find throwaway pieces, just like any other cop . . . Don't fuck with me again, Anglin, or I'll kill you myself . . . Now you take care, Carl. I'll be around.'

Anglin rests his head back on his pillow and closes his eyes as I leave the private hospital room.

Chapter Fourteen

[April 1999]

Mason of the FBI wanted to know why we were looking at Theresa Rojas after all these years. He came stomping into my office with his long-legged assistant, the choice morsel over whom Doc salivated, and he demanded to know what the story was. Why were we harassing an ex-witness to a dead case?

'Dead case?' I asked.

'You know what I mean, Lieutenant.'

The pretty assistant sat across from me. Doc was still in the head, relieving himself. With his prostate, it took a while.

'Why do you care if I take a look at Ms Rojas? If the case is dead—'

'We're watching her. If you hang around her, you might keep some interesting people away from her. You might inadvertently make her seem hot . . . Do you follow, Lieutenant?'

'Why don't you explain it to me?' I asked, smiling disingenuously.

Doc walked in with his *Poetry* magazine tucked under his right arm.

'The crapper and the muse,' he cracked. 'One cannot exist without the other. The duality of things. The beautiful and the obscene.'

My partner was eyeballing Mason's Number Two as he said it.

'I'm telling you, Jimmy. Leave her alone. You'll be messing with an ongoing—'

'And what the hell do you suppose my deal with Anglin is? That's been ongoing for thirty-one years!'

'Look. Just stay clear. It's a federal investigation.'

He stood. The beauty accompanying the beast rose. Doc murmured something lascivious, just out of anyone's earshot.

'What was that all about?' Doc asked me after Mason and his assistant had left my office.

We could hear the clicking of the assistant's high heels all the way down the hall.

'We're being told that Theresa Rojas is out of bounds to us.'

'By those federal pukes?'

I nodded.

'Hey . . . Have you got anything back about that woman's medication?'

'No. Not yet.'

'Let me show that list you made to Mari. I'm taking her out for lunch . . . Want to join us?'

When Doc assured me he was not taking his pediatrician wife to Garvin's saloon, I assented.

Mari, Doc's spouse, was very dark. A Hindu. The mother of an adopted young black child. A child my partner adored more than he did his own continued respiration.

We took Mari to an overpriced diner in Niles. It wasn't far from her office. She was very short on time because she had an overstocked list of patients.

I showed her what I had written down at Theresa Rojas's room at the hospital in Elgin.

'I'm not familiar with these three . . . But these two are very heavy sedatives. Why are you asking?' She looked over at me.

I took a sip from my Diet Coke. Then I looked back at her. She was so dark, her skin was almost a blue-black. She was also one of the most truly beautiful women I had ever personally met.

'I think someone has been keeping her in that hospital room for over thirty years. I don't know if it's sedation or some kind of psychosis-inducing stuff they're feeding her, but I think they're holding her prisoner with a hypodermic.'

'My God,' Mari gasped. 'How terrible . . . Can you prove any of this?'

'No.'

'The drugs on that list you showed me would not cause anyone to remain cut off from reality, I have to tell you that. Still they could be injecting her with any number of things that could recreate in her mind that episode of the murders thirty years ago . . . But you'd have to catch them at it – unless you can have her examined by a team of doctors and psychiatrists different from her current physicians.'

The overpriced lunch arrived. Doc attacked his food, but Mari was clearly upset.

'How could anyone . . .' Her voice trailed off. Then she peered up at me with her beautiful, darker-than-night eyes. 'They have murdered her, too, then, Jimmy. It's the same thing. They have stolen her life, if what you think is true . . . My God.'

Our M.E., Dr Gray, told me to go for a blood sample. It was the only way toxicology could help us.

We went to the Mental Facility with a court order. Theresa's blonde-haired shrink got her nose all out of joint when I produced the order, but she herself took the sample for us in spite of the fact that we'd brought a tech along with us for that purpose. The fuzzy-haired psychiatrist gave us a murderous glare when we were leaving, but Theresa Rojas looked over at me just before I departed and gave me the slightest nod. As if she was saying that what we were doing had her approval. As if she understood, wherever her consciousness was buried, that we were shoveling our way toward her.

Dr Gray said there was a slight trace of something unusual, something suspicious in Theresa Rojas's blood sample. But it was as if her blood had its own cloaking device, he said, because of the other drugs they'd prescribed – the ones I'd written down.

'You take all these drugs at the same time, it's gonna be difficult to separate out anything extra that someone's injecting into her – if they actually are using a needle, that is. But there's some kind of substance . . . Hell, Jimmy, if I were guessing,' the sixty-five-year-old Examiner scratched his stubbly chin, 'I'd say this woman has been given some form of synthetic drug that resembles LSD. But, as I say, the traces are slight, and the other drugs seem to be covering over most of the synthetic – like a raincoat or a cloak covers the clothes underneath.'

'Could you bring this to a grand jury?' I asked.

'Hell, Jimmy, I can't even identify the exact type of that shit. I said it looks something like LSD, but it's not a drug I've ever come across before. We'll have to bring this to the attention of the government folks.'

'That's like asking a cat if he swallowed Tweety Pie,' Doc moaned.

'I don't know where else to take this, Detective Gibron,' Gray said. 'I'm just a poor Medical Examiner for Cook County.'

Gray walked away from us and headed back to his examining room. He had plenty of other cadavers to look at.

'We have to take this to the very people who're trying to run us off the crime scene,' Doc concluded.

'You trust the FBI?' I asked.

He laughed out loud.

'How about the Food and Drug Administration?' I asked.

It took a week of pestering before we got the FDA's results. They wanted to know, in D.C., why we couldn't pursue the testing of this specimen through the usual channels. We gave them a very artful runaround, and finally they took us on because some doctor there became intrigued at the type of drug our earlier results indicated. He wondered how such a chemical mixture could exist.

The doctor's name was Engstrom. When he saw our stuff, it confused him at first. Then I brought up that word: synthetic.

Engstrom took our file to an older FDA scientist. Someone in his mid-fifties, Engstrom informed us over the phone. This guy proved conclusively that the chemistry was indeed synthetic. The drug was something the Feds had tested in the 1960s. It had been used in brainwashing experiments, which became all the rage after the Korean War. The stuff was created to induce long periods of total withdrawal from reality, Engstrom claimed, during which the victim – or the patient – would be highly susceptible to suggestion.

'Could these "long periods" last as much as thirty years?' I asked Engstrom over my office telephone.

'Dr Graham, my associate, says the stuff could remain effective almost indefinitely, if it were introduced regularly into the subject.'

End of conversation. The Army called this chemical stew MRS127. It was indeed a derivative of the street drug LSD.

We finally got a court order to have Theresa Rojas released to us. We were going to have her sequestered in a private hospital, St. Marion's, in the northwest part of town. All at the expense of the CPD. She was our number one witness against Carl Anglin. She always had been. But it seemed the Fibbies were at work trying to stop her release to us. Unfortunately for them, Special Agent Mason and the leggy blonde didn't have any muscle with Judge Peter Ault, a crusty old Cook County jurist who had a rep for being a loner and for being on no one's fucking pad.

Theresa got settled into her new room. With very strict orders. We kept a twenty-four-hour watch over her. She had no visitors, not even family. Not until she came out of whatever state this synthetic poison had put her into.

After just two days, her new nurse said Theresa was having brief spells of agitation. Which might have been the result of withdrawal from all those tranquilizers. Dr Meredith Wells was her new shrink. She prescribed exercise, rest and good food for Theresa. It'd be a while before all those toxins would be out of her system.

'It could be weeks, maybe months before she's even partially lucid. And there's a chance that all these drugs have done permanent damage. We'll have to wait and see,' said Dr Wells.

I talked to Theresa when I saw her on my weekly visits. I came alone.

'You're looking very good, young lady,' I said as I handed her a long-stemmed yellow rose on one occasion. Yellow was for faithfulness, my wife had told me.

She took the flower into her hand, but a thorn pricked the flesh of her thumb.

I went to her bathroom and got some Kleenex. I took her thumb and pressed at the scarlet droplet until the beading ceased. I tried to smile at her.

'That's the price of beauty. You get pierced by it sometimes,' I said.

No moods crossed Theresa Rojas's fifty-year-old face. Her visage was bland. No smiles, but no frowns either. When Theresa was anxious, Dr Wells explained to me, she roamed around the room ceaselessly. She wandered from the bed to the bathroom to her door and all around that circuit again and again.

No emotion showed on her countenance, however.

'I bet you can hear me, Theresa. I bet you heard me the other time I talked to you, too . . . This is all about Carl Anglin.'

She became restless. She stood and began to walk all around her room. From the bed to the washroom door to the main door. Theresa seemed like a mouse weaving its way through a maze it couldn't fathom.

'Carl's not here, Theresa. Carl will never be here. We'll be with you. We won't let him come close. I promise you . . . And the way to get rid of Carl forever is to tell me what you saw and heard, thirty-one years ago . . . I know you won't want to talk about it now. I know Dr Wells wants us – you and me – to go slow, and that's okay with me . . . Did you like your rose, Theresa?'

It might have been a hallucination, but I thought I saw a slight nod. Just a quiver of movement in the chin area.

I remembered what Mari, Doc's wife, had said about Theresa. They had indeed stolen her life. Except that she'd been imprisoned by all of us who'd colluded in her institutionalized existence. She picked up the rose from her nightstand. Her lips suddenly puckered, but no sound emerged from them, and she lightly dropped the flower back where she'd found it.

'So the situation is still pretty much the same. We have a woman who's been kept in a zombie state since the time of the assassination of Bobby Kennedy, and we now have a drug, MRS127, which the government does not acknowledge – and neither will Food and Drug, the people you took it to in the first place.'

So spoke the prosecutor, Henry Fields.

'No one acknowledges MRS127,' he emphasized. 'The man you went to originally – Engstrom? – will not go on record concerning what he told you over the phone about the origin of this synthetic, and Theresa Rojas is currently still a turnip, albeit now a non-medicated one . . . Am I getting this all accurately?' Fields barked.

'There's a good chance now that Ms. Rojas will become a witness against Mr. Anglin,' I reminded the prosecutor.

'Yeah, Jimmy. But when? Which century? I know it's not your fault, but – '

'She's coming around, Henry. I've seen her, too,' Doc countered.

'And where'd you receive your M.D.?' Henry returned.

'She'll help us. It'll be sooner than—'

'What if Anglin disappears again?' the counselor continued. 'He's done it before.'

'He likes the spotlight,' Doc insisted. 'He won't go away.'

'What if he does his thing with Theresa?' Henry shot back. 'He seems to find out a whole lot of supposedly confidential information when it comes to his personal safety. The guy has a line to someone somewhere.'

'He doesn't know where she is and neither do his federal friends.'

'I think I would rather pursue those government folks if, as you say, they have been shielding Carl Anglin for three decades.'

'It would give me a real woody too, sir,' Doc smiled.

Henry Fields blushed. Darkly. He was a pale, bald man. Very trim, like a cross-country runner who'd stayed in shape.

'You guys deal with the conspiracies, if they exist. I never watch *The X-Files*.'

'We want Anglin. Then we'll go after any accomplices,' I explained.

'You are either a fool or a real brave copper, Jimmy. I vote for nuts, with you and your playmate here. I hope you don't live to regret any success you might have from here on in.'

For some reason it sounded as if there were a veiled threat in the prosecutor's words, but I let it go.

We walked out of the district attorney's office and headed to the elevators.

'You think he's scared of what we're getting into, Jimmy?'

'He'd be a damn fool if he weren't.'

Red made dinner for the two of us. My mother had the kids, all three of them, and was taking them for ice cream at one of those multi-flavored joints after they'd got pizza at the mall. Eleanor loved taking the baby through the mall in a stroller, and my grown-up boy and girl loved Eleanor to spend money on them.

Natalie and I ate our Italian beef sandwiches and our fries slowly, without much relish. We watched the evening news together. It was the first time we'd both been on days in a while.

Theresa Rojas was not the only one whose life had been stolen.

Chapter Fifteen

[November 1968]

Anglin recovers well. And quickly. It was too much to ask that a piece of bad food take him out of the picture. He'll live to be an old man. I'm hoping that somehow most of that natural life will be spent in a cage.

My life continues as it has for months now. I see fleeting and transient images of my wife. I await letters from my son in Vietnam, and I dread anyone who's dressed in Army green coming up to my front door. In my war they knocked on your front door and told you the bad news about your loved one. In this conflict, I assume the SOP is the same. I know Eleanor must live in terror of seeing someone from the military walk up the sidewalk to our house. She survived World War Two without losing her brother and her father, but she remembers what it was like for her mother and for herself, wondering every day if bad news was on the way.

Eddie votes we shoot Anglin. We use a throwaway piece and we pop him on the street, some dark night, and we dispose of the gun in the Lake, part by part. I laugh and tell him I'll think about it. The joke is that I have indeed brooded about doing the unthinkable. I killed men in the war with far less provocation. Anglin tests me to my limits. He has crawled beneath my skin. But without that Army uniform the word for offing him would be 'murder'. I know there are those who might ask how a uniform affects the concept of murder, but I suppose I'm too old-fashioned to set aside my stubborn notions about propriety.

We cannot get the government to come clean about Carl Anglin's dark career as a pro assassin during the years of the Korean War and afterwards because the information is classified due to 'National Security'. All the doors have been slammed in our faces. And that is why I've become hell-bent on bringing it all to a close.

Anglin did something big enough to get himself protected by the G. Something serious enough for the horror of seven rapes and murders to be ignored and set aside.

I'm dialing Marty Genco's number again. My cousin, the Outfit guy. Originally I swore I'd never deal with him even once, let alone go running back to him. But I've got no other alternatives.

We meet at Luigi's, his favorite North Side eatery.

'You gonna get me killed, cousin,' Marty says and smiles. But it looks more like a weary grimace.

'How'm I going to get you whacked?'

'People notice. They know I haven't seen you in years and now they see we're practically brother goombahs. Twice in six months. What the fuck, Jake, people ain't stupid. They know who you are and what you're looking for . . . I gave you everything I know about that fuck Anglin. What else can I tell you?'

'You can tell me who he did to rate him all this juice, all this protection.'

'I can't tell you because I don't know.'

'Then find out for me or watch your business get visited by Burglary/Auto Theft.'

'You wouldn't be such a prick, Jake.'

I watch his brown, stupid eyes.

'I can't fuckin' believe it . . . We're blood and you'd turn me just to catch this prick Anglin?'

I keep watching his eyes.

'Jake . . . How do I convince you that I ain't got enough clout to know names the way you want—'

'You know who to ask.'

Marty groans and looks down at the appetizing plate of lasagna the waiter's just set down before him.

'You ruin a good meal, Lieutenant.'

But he takes his fork and stabs at his dinner, and then he takes a swallow of the food.

'Best lasagna in the freakin' city and you have to ruin my appetite. If I find this name for you, all other bets are off. I owe you nothing and you don't pull this *familia* shit on me anymore. And you personally don't get involved in busting my balls over my business. Does that sound fair, Jake?'

Marty's call comes to me downtown three days later. I'm to meet him at the Loop Laundry at noon. Eddie and I are there waiting at 11.52.

The time passes as we wait for my cousin. First fifteen minutes. And then it's suddenly 1.00 p.m.

A patrolman walks into the Laundry place, here on Monroe Street.

'Lieutenant Parisi?'

'Yeah,' I tell the uniform.

'You have a call from downtown. They said they couldn't get you on your radio.'

We've left our radio in our unmarked car.

Eddie and I go out to the vehicle on Monroe Street.

I make the call. I get the address, and then Eddie and I are on our way.

There's nothing of Marty Genco really remaining. The roof of his car has been blown forty feet away from his Cadillac Seville. The doors have been hurled twenty feet to either side of the explosion, and the only thing recognizable as a piece of the body is on fire. My cousin has been reduced to a charred, overcooked beefsteak. There's not enough of him left to fill a coffin.

There are plenty of other coppers on hand. Their word is that it's a mob hit, pure and simple.

This kind of explosion looks to me more like something military. The level of overkill is what strikes me first. The Outfit kills efficiently. They're usually very careful about trying to avoid hurting innocent bystanders. But this blast has sent shards of the auto's glass into the scalps of some pedestrians who were at least a hundred feet away from the vehicle when the bomb went off.

'It looks like they were blowing-up a fucking half-track, Jake, instead of a fucking Cadillac,' Eddie says.

'That's the way it looks to me, too.'

'You don't think it was his own people?'

I look over at him. There are numerous FBI agents in the vicinity, so I don't say anything more. We're not involved in this investigation. Clarence Cahill is the Homicide cop on scene. Calling me was a courtesy because they know Genco and I are related. So Eddie and I bow out and leave.

I call Marty's wife, Maria.

'I don't want to speak to you, you son of a bitch,' she says over the phone. I'm calling her from my house in the northwest part of town.

'I know you think I'm involved in this, but I'm not . . . Don't hang up, Maria . . . I always liked Marty. You know I wouldn't hurt him intentionally.'

'So you did this unintentionally,' she accuses me.

'No. Somebody outside the cops and outside the Outfit did him. But I don't want to talk about it over the phone.'

Her interest is aroused. She allows me to come over to their apartment in Berwyn.

Maria has kept her good looks. I was at their wedding, about twenty years ago. She's in her prime, actually. Early forties.

And now she's a widow.

But I sense anger more than grief in her attitude.

I walk into their flat on the third floor.

'Who killed Marty, Jake?'

'It wasn't us and it wasn't his own.'

'Who's that leave?' she demands.

'Did Marty say anything to you about why him and me were supposed to meet yesterday?'

'He said you were squeezing his balls. That's my job, Jake.' She's not smiling. Still angry. 'I'm a widow, now . . . And I hear you might as well be a widower, the way it's going for you and Eleanor . . . I never liked her much.'

'What'd he tell you, Maria? It's important. Much more important than starting a vendetta against me . . . Sure, I put his nuts in the vice, but that's the way it goes when you're in Marty's trade . . . Come on, this is important.'

'When's the last time you had a woman?'

She's not teasing me; she's tormenting me.

'Come on, Maria—'

'It's about this Anglin guy, no?'

'Yes. It's about Anglin.'

'Marty told me in bed three nights ago that this guy killed a major player and that if Marty even whispered the guy's name we all might wind up like my husband just did.'

'He didn't even suggest who this victim was?'

'I gathered it wasn't anyone in the crew or in any of the crews in this city. No. It had to be a bigger name than anyone in the Outfit's got. It'd be someone in the big headlines. You know, the bold print . . . You never answered my question, Jake. How long's it been?'

I sit down on their love seat.

'A long time . . . That make you feel better?'

'Yeah. Because it's going to be a long time before I have Marty again. A real long time, Jake. Does that make us even? I don't think so.'

I stand and let myself out her door. Her stare follows me all the way out.

The explosion is definitely a military-type operation. Bombers usually leave their signatures on their blasts. We go into the files to see if anyone's been using the kind of explosive utilized in this instance, and the only similar cases do indeed involve military-trained bombers.

My cousin was done by the same guys who're shielding Carl Anglin. I'm convinced of it. I was about to get that very important name and someone caught wind of it on Marty's side. Anglin's people must have high-level contacts on both sides of the fence.

'If you hear a click or two when you turn on your car's engine, Jake, turn around in a hurry and kiss it goodbye,' Eddie cracks as we sit at the lunch table by the vending machines downstairs.

'Kill a homicide copper? Why do that, when you can have so much more fun messing with his brains over this thing?'

'I hope you're right, Lieutenant. Otherwise we both might get scattered all over the Gold Coast and Lakeshore Drive, some early morning.'

Who'd Anglin whack? They got the guy who did Jack Kennedy. What other big names have been done lately? Maybe it isn't even an American. Maybe I'm thinking too close to home. Carl Anglin was a world traveler, after all. Perhaps it was some African overlord. Maybe a Sicilian family member.

And maybe it was a member of the American Spook Family who doesn't get his name in the papers but is someone everyone in that small, clandestine world knows. Perhaps Carl's killed a made man whose identity would prove embarrassing if it were brought out into the open.

My cousin was my last chance, I'm thinking. Now the avenues are all closed for me. The Feds and the Bad Guys won't tell me anything. The Spooks don't talk to each other, let alone to a Homicide cop, and Carl Anglin still lurks in the alleys, free as the feral cat he's always been.

Jimmy gets hit again. This time it's in the other leg, in the thigh. Some guy detonates a mine, gets blown to pieces, and my son is standing close enough to him in a rice paddy to get clipped with some more hot shrapnel. The fragment barely misses the kid's femoral artery, so Jimmy's smiling all the way to the bank, he confesses. He's not supposed to scare Eleanor, he understands, but he had to let us know of his 'good fortune'.

My son goes back on line within five days of his injury. It's his second Purple Heart, he tells us. He can't wait for his two tours of duty to be finished, and now that he's re-upped, he's got a wallet-sized calendar and he's marking off the days.

Jimmy asks me about the Anglin case. When I write him back, I tell him everything. I'm hoping my frustration might dissuade him from becoming the next gendarme in the family, but I don't hear anything encouraging when he writes back each time with a continuing interest in my caseload.

The Greek is my confidant. He fills my glass and he refills it until I've arrived at our mutually agreed quota. He won't let me stagger out of his place, and I keep telling him all the updates on the big murder cases I'm involved in.

There is only one case, no matter how many names are written on my section of the chalkboard downtown. There is only one.

The Greek's only concern is that I give him first rights to all the gory details. I sit in his tavern in the late afternoons. The place is pretty empty at that hour. I tell him about my days, as if he were my wife. But he just smiles and sends me on my way each evening, which is why we get along so well.

I get into the car and I head home to Eleanor. But she's not there even if she is there.

I remember Maria asking when was the last time I was with a woman. I can't remember. But I remember my prostate acting up last year and the doctor telling me then to 'use it or lose it'. And I can't handle the self-abuse alternative.

This night I walk into Eleanor's bedroom, which used to be our bedroom, and I burst right in. She sits up, shocked awake.

I begin to take off my clothes.

'You're drunk.'

'Only a little.'

'This is new. Tired of consorting with—'

'I've never whored in my life, Eleanor. I've been with no one else. Ever . . . Christ, Eleanor . . . I'm alone. I'm sick and I'm tired and I'm alone. For Jesus' sake, have pity on me.'

She rises from the bed and comes over to where I'm standing.

'I'm sick and tired and alone, too, Jacob. Where have you been, all this time?'

Chapter Sixteen

[May 1999]

Special Agent Mason required information from us about the relocation of a material witness in an ongoing federal investigation. He was very unhappy with our insistence that we were ignorant about the matter. He thought we were full of shit. I'd like to have agreed with him, but I bit my lip.

He'd been nosing around Homicide for the last day or two. In and out of my office. Bugging the captain, who didn't take well to irritants on account of his background in the Army Rangers in Vietnam. Our captain was more used to shooting people who pissed him off. He'd had a great deal of trouble adjusting to the politics of the police, but he'd made the change.

'Is there something I can do you for?' I asked, with the most malicious grin I could muster.

'Don't fuck with us, Parisi,' Mason threatened. His leggy, gorgeous assistant special agent was standing beside him inside my doorway.

'I'm sorry,' he said and gestured to the young lady. She must have been fresh out of Quantico.

She smiled, but didn't blush. I could picture her pulling the trigger on any perpetrator. Tough young woman.

'You've got Theresa Rojas, and you're going to be facing federal charges once we find out where you've stashed her.'

'It's been amusing, Mason.'

He wasn't amused at all.

'You don't have any idea what you're screwing around with, do you?' he declared.

'I heard that same message from someone else.'

'Who was that?'

'Carl Anglin. Himself.'

'Look, Lieutenant. Anglin is old news. Beyond history.'

'Then why does his name keep coming up?'

Mason reddened. Doc walked past them, into my rectangle of an office. He stood with his back blocking the view of Lake Michigan.

'Hello, everyone. Especially hello to you, ma'am,' he said warmly.

She did not return Doc's amicable, toothy smile.

'Ohh, I see. We're fighting,' Doc observed, grinning.

'Lieutenant . . . I'm not going to give you another . . . notice. You'd better deliver Theresa Rojas in twenty-four. Last chance.'

He turned and waited for the great-looking special agent to head toward the elevators.

We'd been duly warned.

The Dr Engstrom business gnawed at me. The last time I'd called up the Food and Drug Administration, they'd told me that Engstrom was on extended vacation and that he couldn't be reached – by beeper, cellphone, anything. If we ever got through to Theresa, we wouldn't have his expert testimony on how someone'd kept a murder witness in hibernation for three decades. Doors kept slamming.

Carl Anglin kept a low profile. We kept an eye on him, but we couldn't justify round-the-clock surveillance on him because he was not officially under investigation. The murders were over thirty years old. But we tried to maintain a daily check on his whereabouts by agreement with brother Homicide cops who went out of their way on their own time just to make Anglin sightings.

Well, the target had gone under for the last five days. His apartment was empty, according to the owner of the building on the nearby North Side. But Carl Anglin hadn't broken his lease, the owner claimed. He was still paid up for six months in advance. It appeared the book deals and the movie deals and all the other spin-offs of his memoirs had kept our man's head above water financially. He wouldn't starve – and he wouldn't pretend to go away permanently. We'd lost sight of him for two or three days on previous occasions but this was longer than usual.

On the sixth day Jack Brennan, a Homicide cop, called me and told me Carl was back in his place. Jack had seen him emerge onto the street from the North Side apartment just a few hours ago.

I wondered whether to be angry or relieved. I knew Anglin wouldn't just disappear. He wouldn't go under permanently. He wouldn't be found in the Lake, face down or with a .22 slug in the back of his head, behind one of his ears. Anglin had the Feds by the very short hairs, and I figured that if he was as cute as I thought he was, he had another manuscript containing a lot of fascinating details locked up somewhere safe. And that prick literary agent of his was salivating to get it into print – but of course that would only happen if Carl Anglin fell victim to a terrible accident. Whatever trump card Anglin held was keeping the G at bay. Otherwise one small-caliber round would've dispatched our man long ago. You had to give Anglin credit for learning how to survive against bigger jungle animals.

I visited Theresa on Sunday nights. I had to be extraordinarily careful about seeing her. My wife Natalie dropped me off at Doc's apartment building. Then I went out the rear exit of Doc's complex, and I used his car to make my way to the small private hospital where we kept her. I knew they were following me, and I knew I wouldn't be able to lose them for much longer.

I had members of our own surveillance team at CPD check my car and my house for tailing devices. The Feds were big on electric toys. So far we hadn't found anything, but they had very sophisticated devices that they used out on the street.

They'd find Theresa, if they hadn't already. They had the men, money and time.

This Sunday night, I brought her her usual yellow rose. Her lips puckered a bit, and she damn near smiled. Or maybe it was just the angle I was watching her from.

I didn't say much to Theresa. I'd already told her everything she needed to know. So I watched some TV with her, even though Sunday nights were vast wastelands on the tube. We sat together quietly and watched some movie-of-the-week nonsense. Occasionally she got up from her bedside chair and walked to her window. She looked out into the darkness, and then she went back to her chair and watched the rest of the show. Sometimes I bought her a bag of buttered popcorn from the cafeteria. Theresa enjoyed this treat. She ate every last kernel. I'd sip a Diet Coke and watch her gobble down the popcorn.

We moved Theresa to another hospital. This one was in rural Indiana, near a town named Lebanon. It was really isolated. And it meant I could pay her very few visits because of the distance and the greater chance of one of us getting spotted.

She was not happy with the move. She liked the view of the city from her old room. Now she had only a view of several cornfields for amusement – that and the TV, of course. The Indiana location offered her greater security, but she was used to the noise of Chicago. Now the relative solitude might become unbearable for her.

I had to make elaborate plans just to see her. A faked fishing trip to nearby Quinn, Indiana was my ruse for being out of state. When it got dark, Doc and I decamped and headed home – with a side trip to the hospital. I was fairly certain we weren't tailed from Quinn, but there was no way of telling for sure. Our security people swept our vehicle before we left, and I didn't see any aerial surveillance on our asses.

You never did see them, however.

Theresa seemed angry with me, this time. She wouldn't even look at the yellow rose.

'I won't be coming to see you for a very long time,' I told her.

This news seemed to soften her sullen expression.

'It's too dangerous. Someone might be following me, and they're so good at it that I won't even know they're out there. So I won't be coming out anymore unless . . . unless you get better.'

She flinched slightly.

'Theresa . . . Do you really hear me?'

She looked out into the cornfield. Perhaps the field was the backdrop upon which Theresa Rojas replayed the horrors of 1968.

We walked into Susan Malkin's North Shore apartment. We were almost out of the city limits – that was how far north we were. The lights had all been unplugged or broken. The blood on the carpet looked black, like oil on a concrete floor, in the darkness.

Doc trained his flashlight toward the woman's bedroom. Susan Malkin had not been heard from in three days. Her mother had become alarmed, had reported her to Missing Persons, and then the owner of this very elegant apartment complex had reported a strange smell emanating from the flat. But the owner was too spooked to enter the place himself, so it became a suspected homicide scene and here we were.

'Police,' Doc said loudly. 'If anyone is in here, come on out slowly with your hands visible.'

No response. We didn't think there would be one. Susan Malkin was dead. She was back in that bedroom and, Jesus, we could smell her.

Doc flipped the overhead light on. The two uniforms following us stopped dead in their tracks when they saw it. Susan's head had been stuck atop one of the bedposts. The headless body lay at the center of the bare mattress, the legs forced wide apart. It was almost as if she had been split up the middle, like a wishbone. There was a lot of blood around the genital area. She'd been stabbed in the torso repeatedly, so there was not much skin that wasn't lathered in gore.

One of the uniforms was already making use of Susan's bathroom, next to where we were. The eerie thing about the head was that the eyes were wide open, as if she had been forced to watch it all happening to herself.

On the neck were two very precise razor strokes. Very clinical. As distinct from the rest of the savagery. Doc knew without being told. The razor cuts had killed the woman. The killer had done much of the damage while Susan was bleeding to death. The beheading had been for our benefit. He'd left a witness for us.

We were at Anglin's apartment at 3.12 a.m. He was not there. Doc and I sat in the dark of his living room on a very expensive couch. The backups were all out on the street. They had this place surrounded. If Carl came in, he wouldn't get away without company.

'He didn't leave anything for us, of course,' Doc said.

'Of course not. He's a pro,' I concurred.

'So we'll just be going through the motions with him again.'

'Yeah. He'll lawyer up, and we'll have to let him go. There'll be no hair, no prints, no witnesses. He's very good. You have to give him that.'

I took out my nine-millimeter gun.

'No, Jimmy. You can't.'

'Yes, I can.'

'No. You won't. You have a wife and three children, and I'm a married man with a daughter of my own.'

We sat in the dark for some minutes.

'He'll get away with this one, too,' I reminded Doc.

'Maybe not. All the reports aren't in. You know how much time it takes to—'

'Too much time. This makes ten that we know about. He

likes to pick out individuals in his old age. Carl likes to work on single subjects now. Takes his time.'

We were sitting in a darkened apartment waiting for a killer to come home so that we could arrest him and then let him go again. It was a sick game we played with Carl Anglin. We knew. He knew we knew. We knew that he knew we knew. And so on.

'Maybe we should shoot that FBI agent, Mason,' Doc suggested.

'And leave the blonde assistant a widow?'

'You think he might be boning her?' Doc laughed.

'Jesus, I hope so.'

'If I weren't married, I would've offered my services to her long ago.'

'You're old enough to be her daddy.'

'True enough, Jimmy, but so are you.'

'Thanks for the vote of confidence.'

'The truth is the truth. We're both too old for the luscious assistant special agent.'

I was thinking about what he'd said about shooting Mason. Not that I was going to pop Mason. It was just that I hadn't considered going after him as a suspect in a homicide investigation. But why should the Feds be exempt from our scrutiny?

I got a squawk from my handheld radio. I told them I copied, and then I turned the radio off and Doc turned his off as well.

Someone was on the way up. So Doc and I positioned ourselves on either side of the doorway.

The key turned in the lock, and a dark, tall form entered.

When Anglin heard the click of Doc's .38, he froze.

'Stand still,' I told him.

I shoved him into the room, and then I flipped the overhead lights on.

'Oh – oh. I must've killed somebody,' he said, a grin on his face.

His green eyes seemed to pop out at you at first glance.

'Where you been, Carl?' Doc asked.

'More appropriately, how the hell did you two get into my—'

Doc showed him the search warrant.

'You found a conservative judge,' Anglin said and smiled bleakly.

'He's one of your fans,' I told him.

'Where you been, Carl?' Doc asked again.

'You still driving that Ford?' Anglin said.

'Yes,' I answered.

'Get it warmed up. Let's go downtown so I can call my lawyer and get this whole lame process over with.'

'What makes you so sure we haven't got something that ties you to the scene?' I queried.

'Shall we just get on with this?'

'All it takes is a thread, a fiber . . . Maybe you whacked off in the living room and just one small remnant of your DNA is swimming on her carpet,' Doc said.

'You both know better. Please. Can't we just go?'

Anglin's lawyer was downtown fifteen minutes after his call. Ten minutes after the lawyer's arrival, we were forced to let Carl Anglin go since he was not an official suspect in a crime where there was no workable evidence on the table. We would be offered no help by Henry Fields, the prosecutor. We had nothing and Anglin and his high-priced attorney were aware of our unsustainable suspicions. Out the door he walked, just the way he'd said he would.

We would now await the official word from the evidence specialists that we didn't have a goddamn thing on him, and then he would be out of the woods once more.

'The key is Mason,' I told my partner during our lunch break in Garvin's slovenly tavern. 'He's the guy. He knows why Carl Anglin wears this invincible ghost shirt. We have to proceed against him secretly, of course, but he's our guy. Our indirect route to Carl.'

'We investigate the G? Jimmy . . . I could retire any time. Why do I need my swan song to be a beef against the Feds?

Don't make our lives even more miserable. Why don't we just try to hit some Iranian or Libyan terrorist? It'd be a lot easier and a lot more fun.'

I watched his eyes, and then my partner surrendered.

'J. Edgar Hoover. Now I could've gone for a shot at him . . . Mason. Jesus, Jimmy. Special Agent Wyatt Earp Mason. Jesus.'

He put his hands flat on the table, and I began to tell him all about it.

Chapter Seventeen

[December 1968]

Marty gets blown to bits. Jimmy takes a tap in Southeast Asia. Carl Anglin is a free man. I'm looking for something that is right in the world, something that is just. I constantly encounter the word 'justice' in my business, but I have seen very little of it during this year and even during this decade. It seems like things had design, back in the 1940s. Then there was a world at war against evil, and evil was eventually rooted out. Hitler, Mussolini in Italy and Tojo in the Land of the Rising Sun all got theirs, finally.

Now, though, kids believe in pharmaceuticals. They believe they expand their horizons with drugs – the way some people used to embrace religion. I'm no great Catholic, but I still respect the Pope and his brother priests.

The world's flipped ass over teakettle or whatever, and I have no control over anything anymore. Justice isn't the only thing that's gone south lately. Cops used to be respected. Now we're called 'pigs'. The Yippies and Hippies really mean it when they call us that. They don't respect what we do.

Personally, I speak for the dead. I always thought there was dignity in my work despite the bloody nature of the scenes I have to witness.

I was never a complainer, but I find myself bitching more and more about the job. I don't know why any of us walk into those dark places anymore. They sure as hell don't pay us enough to do what we do. But here I am, whining again.

Maybe it's because of the recent false start with Eleanor. We were sleeping together, *living* together again for the first time in almost two years. Then the coldness crept back in when we got the news of Jimmy's second wound. Eleanor started to backpedal on me, and I was not exactly understanding about her anxiety.

Then it became the blood thing again. Jimmy is really hers. He belongs to her body, not mine. It came up in an argument, like it always does, and I'm back in the guest room once more.

The comfort she gave me for those few days of reconciliation was better than any I've had for longer than I can remember. She is a beautiful woman. She has aged well. A little more wrinkled than she was in her early twenties, but a beauty nonetheless. I never stopped loving my wife. We just couldn't cohabit very well. The usual reasons. But the usual reasons can't change the natural passion I have for her. The usual reasons will never diminish the craziness, the madness I feel when I know I can't have her or touch her or kiss her or embrace her . . .

It makes me physically ill to go over it all, again and again.

I have failed at the only relationship in my life that matters. I have failed to produce my own child with Eleanor's help. Carl Anglin walks free because I can find no trace, no footprint, that would link him with seven brutal rapes and murders. And now I get one of my own kin blown to hell by someone who knows what it was that Anglin did to help preserve his obscene existence.

All these failures lead me to think about swallowing a blue barrel and ending the fury in my head. But I am, as I say, a Catholic. I believe, fool that I am, in Heaven and in Hell. I think Jesus Christ died for my sins, and I don't want to anger God any more than he is already apparently angered at me. He'll let me off the hook when He's ready, not before.

I cannot shame my family by killing myself. The least I can do is take the pain. It was part of my Ranger training in

World War Two. I was at Normandy. I saw unholy hell on the beaches, there. All the carnage that the history books describe can never equal the true terror of actually being there on that sixth day of June in 1944. Then all the days after the landings. For almost a year we fought our way across a devastated Europe. I looked men in the eyes before I shot them. I cut German throats. I booby-trapped people I never saw get killed. Those images return to me from time to time. I never watch war movies. I have my own that I run in my head occasionally.

No, I was taught to survive, not to give in. The thought of surrendering to Hitler's forces was unthinkable. In my outfit we'd rather have died.

The war ended. Times changed. The world raced by me, and I began to feel like a mastodon. A furry old prehistoric elephant with a long memory.

Maybe it's just that I don't belong in this time, in this place. I should be moved back two decades to a time I could understand. This world belongs to Jimmy, not to me. Maybe Fate fucked up. Perhaps I should have been left lying face down in the sand at Normandy where a lot of my brothers in arms fell, the impact of the bullets that killed them the last sensations they were conscious of.

Morbidity comes with my job. I deal with the dead. I try to speak for them and take the place of the living tongues they've forfeited.

I've done a lousy job for seven young women who were learning to help people. Nursing. Now there's a job with integrity.

Killers survive in the jungle. They flourish all over the world. The meanest of us were the most likely to live through the nightmare of June 6, 1944, I believe. There must be a final cruelty somewhere in my makeup. It shows in the subtle rejection of me by my wife and son. It doesn't matter that he's not mine by blood. He's always looked to me as his father, and that should've been good enough for me. He was there for me to love, and I never loved him enough. Now I can't tell him those things in the few letters I mail him. I wind up talking about my caseload instead. I write to him about unfinished business like Carl Anglin. I tell Jimmy that when he gets on the force there will be someone like Anglin to haunt him too, if he ever makes it to Homicide. Don't be a cop, Jimmy, I tell him. Be a schoolteacher or a doctor or a lawyer – anything but a 'pig'.

He remains resolute. He tells me in his own letters that he wishes he could help me nail my one outstanding case. He'd like to be my partner on the day I slam the door of the cell that holds Anglin. Jimmy insists I'll get my man, just like the Mounties. My son wants to be Stateside when I cuff the monster with the dangling locks and the jungle-green eyes.

'I'll call the cab,' the Greek insists.

'No. No . . . I'm fine. Really. It's all right,' I tell the barman.

I manage to rise from my bar stool and then I'm navigating toward the door. Out I go into the frigid December evening air.

I get the car rolling toward home. Driving at an abnormally slow speed, I am able to keep it steered accurately toward my residence. Like all drunks, I have the idiotic notion that I drive better when I'm stiff.

I'm lucky and I know it.

When I arrive at the house, I cut the left front tire over the curb, and then I pull back the other way and the auto comes to a clunking stop as the wheel hits back down on the street.

It's dark already. Eleanor and I went round and round last night. My drinking has become too much for her to bear. She despises me for turning my back on her just when it appeared we might be coming back together for the first time since we married.

I open the door. I turn on the hall light. Eleanor awaits me at the top of the twenty-six steps that lead to the upper level of the house.

'I can smell you. By God, I can,' she growls.

'Can you really, Eleanor? Can that lovely nose of yours tell you all about my day?'

I begin the ascent, but I stagger about five stairs up.

'You'll kill yourself.'

'Me? Never, darlin'. I love my life too much.'

I continue up. I look at my bride's beautiful face. It's the face of a twenty-year-old beauty who's consented to make me the happiest man in the world.

'Why don't you sleep there? Eat there? There's nothing for you in this house, nothing that you really want—'

'Shut up!' I bellow.

'It's my house too. I'm the one who lives here, Jake. You're just a boarder, here for a meal from time to time, but you're still just a boarder.'

'A short-timer.'

'Yes.'

I'm almost up the stairs. A vicious notion grabs me. I should take her by her long brown hair and drag her down this flight with me. We could tumble to our deaths together.

Suddenly, the hostile impulse flees. I want to touch her. I want to make love to her. I want her back. Close to me.

I do indeed reach out with my hands as I nearly make it to the top of the flight, but her right hand shoots out at me. I don't know if she's trying to take my hand or if she's trying to shove me backward, but I stumble on the penultimate step and I've lost my balance and I'm leaning dangerously backward and I can hear Eleanor cry out and now my heel is dislodged from the step and I'm tumbling backwards head over heels like in a comedy movie as if it's some kind of sight gag but I can't stop rolling over and over backwards and I can hear something snapping beneath the back of my skull and the last sound I hear is the clean soprano shriek of my beautiful wife Eleanor.

PART TWO

Chapter Eighteen

[May 1999]

Susan Malkin, Martha Eisner, and Renee Jackson. The list of murders beyond the original seven sat with Doc Gibron and me. We were all there was between Anglin and his complete freedom. No one else seemed inclined to go after the son of a bitch.

Until this twenty-eighth day of the month that celebrated the Virgin. We received a call from Anglin telling us that he'd been assaulted. Homicide didn't get the call originally, but we heard about it from Violent Crimes. Renee Jackson had a nineteen-year-old brother, Wayne. Wayne was a member of the Regals, a South Side street gang. He was near the top of his outfit and he didn't see justice being done by our letting Carl Anglin walk the streets of Chicago. Wayne Jackson had put out a contract with his own crew to get Carl Anglin.

So Carl came home with one of his many doper girlfriends who had an IQ of seven in the hole and the young lady got her face slashed. Anglin broke the cutter's neck with a move Carl had perfected in Asia while he was in the military.

We knew it was the Regals because the Violent Crimes investigator recognized the stiff. When the homey was ID'd at the hospital, and when he was pronounced dead, we received the call. It was in our hands now.

Carl looked shaken. We saw him at Presbyterian Hospital,

on the North Side. He was there for his lady, Dolores Claiment. Exotic dancer. Soft-porn star. Brain dead.

'She's gonna have to have extensive plastic surgery, man,' Anglin complained to us.

'Send the bill to the Regals,' Doc told him.

Anglin appeared to ignore my partner.

'They got a claim on me,' Carl said. 'Are you gonna do anything about it?' he demanded.

'We investigate all homicides. You killed a man named Arthur Wells . . . You broke his neck, like you were wringing a chicken's.'

'Military training comes in handy once in a while.'

'You must really be up on your old self-defense,' Doc said.

'I go to the gym five days a week.'

'Got to keep in shape for your next bestseller,' Doc added.

Anglin was unfazed. 'Are you going to do anything about these punks?'

'We'll look into it. Sure,' I told him.

'I don't like your low level of enthusiasm.'

'I don't either,' I told him. 'Maybe it's those ten kills you've got on your fuselage, Anglin. But I will look into it anyway . . . You might want to change your address and your habits. These kids are deadly. Just ask anyone from Tactical.'

'You ain't funny, Parisi.'

'I don't mean to be . . . You remember my father? His name was Jacob.'

Anglin's face lit up, a twisted grin appearing on his lined features.

'Whatever happened to your old man? I lost track.'

'He died. In an accident at the house. Fell down some stairs.'

'Oh yeah! I seem to remember reading about it. Sad, that.'

He never took his stare from my face.

'You ain't blaming me for the old man too, are you, Lieutenant?'

'It's comforting to know there are people out there who want to get close to you.'

Now Anglin's smirk began to fade.

'I heard there was something strange about the way your old man checked out. I heard—'

'It was an accident. It was over thirty years ago. Back when you were able to do more than one girl at a time. Back when you weren't a sad old bastard who had to screw female sewers like Dolores to make you think your little cheesedick still works.'

The grin was completely gone. He moved closer to me, and I stepped up to him. Doc edged his way between us.

'Gentlemen,' Doc murmured placatingly.

'Your old man laid hands on me once. He got away with it,' Anglin hissed.

'If I ever lay hands on you, I'll break you piece by piece.'

'You think you're badder than that homey I wasted?'

'Gentlemen,' Doc said again. He was still keeping us apart.

'You're real expert at killing hundred-pound females and one crack cocaine addict who should've stuck you and forgot about slashing the sewer . . . No. We'll handle this by the numbers, Anglin. You got me provoked, but this is as far as it goes. Next guy to talk to you will be the County Prosecutor.' I stepped back, but I didn't lose eye contact with him. This was one pissing contest I wouldn't back down from.

Finally Anglin turned his gaze toward my partner, the referee. 'My attorney is just slobbering over the chance to do you two.'

'Maybe you ought to hire a counsel with two legs instead of four,' Doc said, grinning.

'I assume you think you're quite the badass too,' Anglin told Doc.

'If I ever got really mad at you, Carl, I'd use a baseball bat. See, the guinea there believes in coming up on a guy from the front. Me, though, I don't have any problems busting animals like you from behind. I mean, why would I want to make a contest out of it? I'm too old and impatient. No, if I came for you, Carl, the first thing you'd know about it was when you were picking splinters out of the back of your skull. But now, with aluminum bats, you probably would never be conscious long enough to wonder what it was that laid you low in one swipe.'

We were through threatening Anglin. He was through baiting us. It had gone to the brink. Someone was about to get hurt. You could smell it in the atmosphere, there in the waiting room at the hospital where Anglin's paramour was getting stitched from cheek to chin.

'You have anything else you want to say?' He was looking at both of us. He had assumed the stance. He'd learned karate and judo during his hitch. Standard training.

'The Lieutenant's a black belt. Which degree was it, Jimmy?' asked Doc.

I didn't answer him. I was waiting for Anglin to move.

'Same training I had, I bet.'

'My father was a Ranger in 1944–45. I didn't want to disappoint him.'

I was waiting for the first kick, the first jab, but it never arrived.

Finally Anglin turned his back. I was relieved. I was fifty-two, Anglin was well into his sixties and Doc was only a bit younger than him. I could just see hospital security breaking up a bout between three geezers our age. It was an embarrassing image.

'We'll look into this Regals thing,' I said. 'But I think you'll have made them even more pissed off with you this time.'

We took a ride to the far southwest part of town. Regal Territory. Gangbanger Central. We found Wayne Jackson on the street with several of his bros. It was a bright, clean day, there on a playground in bangerland. The bros were engaged in a trash-talking marathon game of hoops, while Wayne, Renee Jackson's brother, watched at the sidelines.

'You the two Homicide Ds ain't caught shit with this Anglin motherfucker.'

The brother seemed bright, in spite of the homey dialogue.

'We're the two,' I responded. Doc watched the ongoing trash-a-thon. There was not much basketball going on, however.

'He kill ten fuckin' women and he been walkin' the streets for over thirty motherfuckin' years, and you here gon' tell me about somebody tried to nail that cocksucker.'

I nodded and he laughed.

'You think I'm the dude behind the hit?'

I nodded again.

'So you roustin' me or what?'

'I want you to let us take care of Carl Anglin. He already killed your sister.'

Doc turned toward our conversation now.

'You know my sister?' Wayne asked.

'I'm investigating her death. You know I never knew her.'

Wayne was a tall, very black African-American. Very good-looking, very athletic-looking. Which made me wonder why he wasn't out there on the court.

'We wasn't close. I mean I love her because she my sister, but she had her way and I got mine. She was a school girl. Always in her books. Momma love her, but she got no use for me, and hey, I unnerstan'. Momma believe in makin' your dream come true. Renee her dream. It was comin' true, too. Girl was gon' graduate, be a nurse, all that fly shit . . . Now she as dead as . . . We wadn't close, but we was blood. Renee never look away when I come around. She still care about what I do. Told me to go to school and shit like that, but she never could get it in her head that me and her . . . We was the same blood, but we was different.'

'Call it off, Wayne. He's not worth your death as well.'

The young black man looked at me oddly, like he couldn't follow my words.

'That motherfucker is dead.'

Now there was no trace of his homey accent. He'd simply made a straight-up statement.

'That motherfucker is dead,' he repeated.

'Then we'll put you in the hole and your sister's still gone,' Doc explained.

'You all come get me when you ready. You know where I lives.'

He turned away from us, and the conversation was over.

The apartment was in the federally subsidized complex, there in the far southwest part of town. It was 4.29 a.m. The sun wouldn't rise for an hour and a half. Doc and I had plenty to fear, being two white spots in an all-black hood. So we took four black patrolmen along with us. They were a little nervous, as well.

The call came through 911. Sounds of gunfire. Which wasn't unusual for this area. But a good citizen called it in and a patrolman found the body in the bedroom. The cop didn't see the other body in the bathroom until he went to squeak a leak in the toilet.

Wayne Jackson had a hole in the back of his head about the size of a baseball. He was lying on the mattress in the bedroom. There were fragments of skull and bits of gray matter sticking to his pillow and the wall behind the bed's headboard.

The female in the bathroom had been shot similarly. One hole, the size of a hardball, in the back of her noggin. The shooter had done Wayne and then caught the female taking a dump or a whiz in the head and dispatched her soul along with Wayne's.

'High-caliber. Big hole,' Dr Gray, the M.E., told us. He'd beaten us to the scene. I couldn't help wondering how come he'd got here so quickly. But he probably just wanted to get in and out before the sun rose and all those friendly neighborhood faces could welcome him.

It was a tense scene. No one felt comfortable there.

'Not a gangbanger job, do you think?' Doc asked.

'If it were, I'd expect some more violence to the bodies. Doesn't look like anger. Looks like a professional execution.'

Doc knew it was Anglin's associates. You had to hand it to them for balls, coming into a black enclave, here in the southwest part of town, and doing a tap on a honcho banger while he was balling his old lady. Real brass balls, it must have taken.

'We better get this show on the road before Wayne's troops and the media show up,' I told my partner.

It was a very quiet crime scene. No one was cracking wiseass jokes. No one was making snide remarks about the girl getting hers in the shithouse.

'They're out of control, Doc. Nothing stops them. These people are insane. They shield a murderer. They hit a gang leader in his own crib. This goes beyond nuts. These guys don't care who they have to kill.'

'You think they'd go this far to protect Anglin?'

'Look at their track record. He gets them to remove anybody who's a threat to him.'

'And what about us, then?'

'It has to have a side story. No, the papers can call this business with the Regals something internal. Inter-gang warfare. There's no conspiracy here. Nothing you can grab hold of, at least . . . And who knows? Maybe they're going to be right. Maybe I'm reading this all wrong, just like my old man did. We got this common obsession, and it's fried both our brains. Carl Anglin has become the fucking boogeyman. There's a monster in everybody's closet. Maybe I need to go back into therapy, Doc.'

'Then I'll be in the next chair, sitting right beside you.'

We got through with the on-scene investigation in another half-hour. The sun was just barely up in the east as we pulled away from the complex.

Wayne Jackson joined his sister on a list that Carl Anglin had been composing for the last three decades.

The key was Mason. I told Doc that more than once, and even though he was nervous about going after a federal agent, I couldn't see any other way to get to the roots of the Anglin problem. He was like a weed. You had to get him all the way out of his soil or he just kept popping back up.

We couldn't do this with the blessing of the Chicago Police Department. It was going to be Doc and me on our own against him. On our own time.

We watched Mason's house when we were off shift. We

did the surveillance in Doc's Chevy Celebrity. It was an old beater like that some teenager would use to drag his ass to college. Didn't look like a cop vehicle. The thing was painted mauve, for Jesus' sake. It stood out so badly that it didn't stand out, for our purposes.

Mason lived alone. We saw no trace of the lovely assistant.

'I'll bet she's gay,' Doc snickered.

'Then life as we know it would not be worth living,' I replied.

We were listening to Doc's all-night jazz station on a portable battery radio that my partner always dragged along on stakeout.

'You think anyone funny'll show up here?' Doc asked.

'That's why we're here,' I moaned. I hadn't had enough sleep lately. Natalie had been questioning me about all the 'overtime'.

'We need to tap his phone,' Doc concluded.

We got one of our own technicians to do the illicit deed for us. He owed Doc big time on a woman my partner had set the technician up with a few years ago. The blind date became his wife. His wife was a major babe, so Ralph Krenski could hardly refuse Doc's request.

'I'm tapping a freakin' Fed's residence?' Ralph gulped.

'They'll never get us to squeal on you,' Doc said to the tech.

'Jesus, we could all go away for a long freakin' time—'

'Think how lonely you were until I helped you out,' Doc reminded him.

'If you really don't want to, Ralph, I understand,' I told him.

'This is about Anglin, Doc tells me.'

I nodded.

'The varmint who killed all those nurses?'

'Yes.'

'My beeper goes off and I'm comin' out of there like the speed of bleedin' light.'

Doc got out of the Celebrity.

'Where'd you acquire this ride?' Ralph asked.

They walked toward the darkened house of the FBI agent. Mason was not due home for three hours. We'd made sure he was at his headquarters before we'd come to this northwestern suburb. We were not far from Arlington Race Track.

Doc had his magic bag with him, and in moments Ralph the Techie was inside.

Chapter Nineteen

[April 1978]

Erin clutched hold of me and kissed me. My young wife cried as we shared the award of my detective's shield. All the years prior to this moment had finally come to fruition. This was the moment for which I've been waiting all my professional life as a police officer. Detective James Parisi. And it didn't stop with my assignment at Burglary/Auto Theft. I was headed to Homicide. It was clear in my mind as my wife's lovely face was as she stood near enough to me to make me go cross-eyed.

I held her at arm's length to look at her properly. Erin Galagher, now Erin Parisi. Schoolteacher. Lover. Wife. The mother, someday, of my children.

I'd left her to go to Vietnam. I served two tours in spite of her begging me to come home after twelve months. Explaining how the second tour would pay our bills for my schooling didn't seem to stop her pleading. She wanted me out of Asia. Erin didn't care about our finances. But I knew that lack of money would become a factor adversely affecting our ability to get married as soon as I returned home, so she more or less gave up the battle over my second hitch in Vietnam.

The war was part of my preparation for my career. I looked at it that way so I could endure the heat, the mosquitoes, the lunatic lifers – all the horseshit attendant on the misery that ended a few years ago. When I returned Stateside in 1970, the war was already lost. The will to defeat the communists was long gone. The country wanted to shrink back inside its borders and refused to become the superpower watchdog of the so-called free world. It was a time, I suppose, much like the 1920s. It was a decade of reaction against sacrifice, brutality, and loss. I understood why people began to turn inward. They wanted this nation to reject the notion that we were conscience and copper to the world. Music, sex, drugs, booze, property. We became the nightmare antithesis of anti-materialism.

All these things that I heard about in college turned out to be pure politics. The world I came back to was interested primarily in the pleasures of the groin. Life was meant to become painless. The Big Aspirin was the cure-all of an ancient malady.

That was the big lie of the 1960s and 1970s. At least it was the bullshit that my nose got a whiff of when I came back, when I arrived home in 1970. The war didn't make a philosopher out of me. It made me more resolute. I was going to get the bad guys. It was as simple as the plot of a Hollywood western. Good prevails over the shitheels of the world. There is a God, He is just, and we are His instruments. Just like in Catholic grade school. Very simple and straightforward.

After the ceremony for the award of my detective's shield, I took Erin back to our ginchy apartment in the Old Town District, and we made love standing up in the middle of our living room floor. Then I took her out to dinner at a Czech joint about five blocks up the street from our residence. We walked together in the sweet air of spring, with a breath of Lake scent wafting toward us from the east. We were only a half-mile from Lake Michigan. Here I was, a young cop with a beautiful bride on my arm in a city I loved. My war was over. I had survived it. I had survived the last half-dozen years as a patrolman, doing duty on the West and South Sides, the real shit beats in the city, and I had attained the goal my life had been aimed at. Now there was only one more step upward. Homicide. Where the best of the best live. The pinnacle of copperdom. But I was definitely on my way.

My wife was an exceptional educator. She was a natural with children. They love her. I've talked to some of her co-workers, and I kept hearing it over and over. Erin was a natural.

Eleanor, my mother, was at the ceremony where I received my shield. My father, Jacob, has been gone all these years, and I regret his absence. I miss him.

He didn't survive my second tour. The accident happened just as I was leaving a hospital in Japan. I'd been there for the third whack I took. Shrapnel in the lower back. Got it while we were deep in the bush. After that hit, I was re-assigned as a Rear-Echelon Motherfucker, an REMF. I had fulfilled my combat obligations, the Army informed me, so I spent the rest of my tour in country lecturing to newcomers to the war about how to survive the first two weeks. Everyone believed that if you made it past the first fortnight, your odds of making it home alive had somehow increased dramatically. That was the legend, anyway.

I had to make myself cold and remote to look into their innocent eyes and tell them that this was no joke, this war business. I could see death prefigured in some of those fresh faces, but I hoped I was wrong in my forecasts. I figured some of the wisdom I handed down to them might come in handy in their next twelve months.

I came home, I got married, I became a cop, and now, a half-dozen and more years later, I had the gold badge I had been aiming at for a lifetime. Aiming at to show Jake Parisi my worth. And then he goes and trips and falls down twenty-six steps at our home, and when I get back for the funeral, via a special dispensation from our Uncle Sam, I find out there is a mystery about his demise.

Did my mother shove the old man down those stairs? Was it, as it was finally decided, an accident?

My mother answered no questions. I went into therapy, at the Department's expense, to come up with answers of my own.

Detectives solve mysteries, as everyone knows. That is what they do. They look into the heart of matters and discover the truth or what passes for the truth and they bring matters to closure. Closure. That dramatically necessary word and concept.

My father left Carl Anglin hanging in Jacob Parisi's conscience. My dad could very well haunt our family home, there in the northwest part of town. He left matters unresolved. It's like an ended love affair in which things are left unsaid, incomplete.

My job right then did not entail Carl Anglin and his seven murders. I had a caseload that revolved around stolen vehicles. I dealt with boosters. But if I could distinguish myself quickly, I might be able to reach the top level, Homicide. The cream of the coppers.

I listened to the Homicide cops talk about Anglin. For some of them, that decade-old case was not history, it was not closed. My father's partner Eddie still worked in Homicide. He talked to me quite often and told me all the old details about the nurses' murders. Eddie knew where I wanted to be someday. I asked him all the routine specifics about what Homicide cops did do during each shift. Eddie Lezniak told me I'd be moving up soon. The word was already out that I was a comer, a surefire big-league player. I hoped he wasn't saying nice things just because I was his erstwhile partner's son.

Anglin was out of the news. He wrote a book ten years ago, the last I heard, and tried to peddle his story to the movies. But he'd disappeared from the daily media. He didn't show up on the evening news denying everything as he always used to. There were no magazine interviews with this creature who fascinated the public— How could anyone human do what the murderer of those seven women did? It was like watching a hooded cobra do its thing. There was something magnetic about someone that evil.

Some said he'd disappeared and gone out West. New hunting grounds. Chicago had focused too intensely on

Anglin. Wherever he went, coppers recognized him. He was no longer just the drifter, the ex-Navy killer, that no one had known before 1968.

My father never found out why Anglin was under the wing of someone extraordinarily powerful in the government, or the 'G' as it was referred to by the police. Jake's cousin Marty was blown up in a car, and that branch of the family never forgave my old man for involving one of its crew in the Anglin mess.

I have cousins in the Outfit. I wasn't proud of those familial ties, but there was nothing you could do about blood. It came with your equipment.

In fact I talked to Marty's nephew, Petey Mancari, after I arrived Stateside. Petey was still pissed, seven years later, about his uncle's death too. I talked to Petey about a month ago, right before the beginning of spring when there was still snow on the ground.

We met at Presto's Pizza in the far southwest part of town. Presto's has the best thin-crust in the city. It's like eating pastry, the crust is.

'You catchin' all them boosters with the fine rides?' Petey smiled.

Petey had movie-star looks, even though he was a small-time member of the outfit who collected bets. He was a bagman, I mean.

'From time to time,' I told him.

'I hear you're really hot shit, Jimmy. The terror of northwest Chicago.'

He wanted me to get on with it. He knew this was business, that I didn't have anything personal to do with his side of the clan.

'Don't your people wonder about why Marty was blown to hell?'

I put it as straight up as I could. Petey was no genius.

'Yeah. There are some hard feelings. Some of which were aimed at your dad for involvin' my uncle with that rapist – whatsisname.'

'Carl Anglin.'

'Yeah, yeah – I know his name . . . There was talk about reciprocatin' the blast, but it died down after about a year or two. You was still out of the country. Hittin' someone over Marty didn't make good business sense, Jimmy. That's all.'

We took a few bites out of our pizzas and a few tugs at our beers. Presto's Pizza had the green and blue Christmas lights still strung up all over the restaurant and bar areas.

'You tryin' to get me zapped, cousin?' Petey asked. He was dead serious about the question.

'No. I don't want you hurting yourself . . . But I got unfinished business with Carl Anglin.'

Petey took another sip of his draft. He was a killer with females. His looks more than offset his natural stupidity. But he was clever enough to survive within his crew. He had smart instincts, at least.

'It's bad business, like I said, Jimmy. You're a car-thief cop. Stick with it. You can grow old and get a decent pension and not face jail or pissed-off Outfit guys, like some of my associates.'

Maybe he wasn't as dumb as he looked.

'He killed your uncle, indirectly, Petey. He made my father . . . he hurt my old man the worst way you can. With his pride. The son of a bitch is trash and we allow him to walk the streets like any other man. I don't give a shit what you do for a living, Petey. That's not my job. But you can do something right if you can aim me at who's helping Anglin piss on our feet.'

'You're takin' all this far too personal, Jimmy . . . All I know, all I *heard*, is that this guy is connected to the government. He did them a favor. He did a job for them, and then he was smart enough to hand over the story to somebody who can hurt the Feds if Anglin takes the heat for the girls' murders. You've heard this story before.'

I nodded. I'd made him edgy. He started tapping the table with his forefinger.

'I need a name, Petey. Somewhere to start.'

'It ain't your fuckin' business, Jimmy! I told you. You can

get people hurt. Includin' yourself. I can't help you. Not with this. It's over my head and out of my league.'

I'd come to the end of the line with him. The avenue to the illicit side of the *familia* was closed. If they wanted vengeance, I was out of the loop.

But I knew they hadn't forgotten Marty Genco. They didn't allow hits on made men unless there was absolute justification for the whack. Somebody's personal safety or fortune must have been on the line.

I did some homework on my own. I hit the libraries and the archives in my spare time. Finding traces of Anglin after his military duty became very difficult. But there was the Freedom of Information thing that opened one tiny door.

Anglin had been officially demobilized in 1960. Then he disappeared into the miasma of the Far East. But IRS records showed that Anglin was in the States from 1962 to 1965, at least. He worked as a fisherman in Key West during those years. At least, that was what his income tax returns said.

The suspicion was that he was CIA or CIA-affiliated during all of those post-Korean War years. The CIA denied any connection to Carl Anglin. It was old news. If he'd worked for someone in Washington or Quantico or Arlington, they'd have had no official name for themselves.

I tried to find out if Anglin had any politics. I found that he was a registered Democrat but had not voted in more than two elections since his return from Asia. He had not shown allegiance to anyone, particularly. He'd been a member of the National Rifle Association, but he'd stopped paying dues in 1964.

On my own time I contacted the police in Key West and asked for information about Anglin during his residence there. Some deputy sheriff let me know that Anglin had been arrested three times on suspicion of armed violence, but that each beef had ended in a dismissal of charges. A lawyer waltzed him right out of the shithouse on all three occasions.

Then he gave me the name of the lawyer – Preston Ramsey. I knew I'd heard the name, but I couldn't place him.

I asked for more information about Ramsey from the deputy in Key West, and he filled in the missing piece. Ramsey had been involved in the investigation of the John Kennedy assassination. He'd been in the middle of all the accusations when the conspiracy theories abounded in the early 1960s. But Preston Ramsey came away free and pristine, and his name faded away, just like that Congressional report about the President's demise.

They got the guy who did Kennedy. And then someone got Oswald's killer. Old news. Case closed. Books and movies tried to resurrect the mystery of the killing of JFK, but Oswald remained the lone gunman. The FBI supposedly proved that no single man could have shot as quickly as Lee Harvey Oswald was supposed to have shot. No one could've hit the target with such deadly accuracy, either.

I felt a great chill come over me. I had a notion I could not share with anyone. Not even with my wife. Nearly fifteen years had passed since this country had mourned the loss of its leader. Wounds were supposed to have healed, time was supposed to have distanced us from the trauma of what had happened. Theories about FBI or CIA involvement . . . Ideas about the Mafia carrying out a whack on the President . . . nothing ever came of any of it. There was just one strange ex-Marine who pulled off some of the fanciest marksmanship in history. Grassy knolls.

Jesus. A chill hit me again when I remembered the Zapruder film. The top of Kennedy's scalp being blasted off by the bullet.

Picture Anglin as another of the shooters. Envision this pride of the Navy, now gone bad, taking big money to hit any target. As long as the price was right . . . Carl Anglin. One-time war hero. Now a mercenary. He was the sniper out in the weeds. He was the man with the real ability to pull off a kill like that. He wasn't some lame loser who'd almost defected to the Soviets. He could actually have pulled it off. He'd got the skills.

Again, the cold crept up my back. *Leave it alone,* I told myself. *It's silly and scary. Kennedy's dead.* The burden of proof selected Lee Harvey Oswald, and there were no more boogeymen to pursue. Let the damned dogs stay lying and sleeping.

It grasped me and wouldn't let go. But I could never speak of it to anyone else. It would be like spotting a UFO and reporting it. You'd have to be crazy. No one'd think of you as a serious human being ever again.

And how would I make the last move upward in the CPD if people heard my theory about the murder of a US President? I'd be back on the street in uniform, watching out for parking offenders.

I had to bury the idea so deep inside myself that I couldn't even come back to it in dreams. If Anglin really had been in Dallas that fall, I didn't want to know about it. This city was a big enough territory. I was a local copper trying to keep tabs on my own turf. Dallas, Texas was too big, too distant. I'd begun my career and I'd got a new wife and we were about to create a family of our own.

I left the archives and I promised myself I'd stick to car thieves. Boosters. I could deal with them.

I could deal with them. I couldn't deal with ghosts and grassy knolls and snipers who couldn't hit a cow in the ass if that sniper were standing right next to that goddamned bovine beast. It was only a fantasy, a set of coincidences, I told myself.

I'm a lowly car-thief copper, I told myself. *I'll stick to the job they gave me. And I'll think about Carl Anglin no more.*

Chapter Twenty

[May 1999]

The surviving Regals, lords of 111th Street in the southeast part of town, right over by the Lake, were angry. And there were plenty of them still around. The word from Tactical and Gangs was that there was going to be payback. They were not frightened that one of their higher-ups had got waxed with his girlfriend on their own turf. Like most gangs, they were brain dead and didn't learn easily. Striking out at an opponent was SOP. Trouble was that they hadn't isolated their target. They knew Anglin had something to do with the shooting, but they knew also that it was likely more than one shooter had done Wayne Jackson and his significant other . . . Who to pop? That was the question.

Anglin had changed his residence. He was living somewhere in the New Town District. It was where the wannabe yuppies lived before they got married and headed off to the burbs with their brats in tow.

We knew where he was, and if we did, the Regals had their intelligence too. I wasn't worried about Anglin's safety, but I wanted him to go down by the numbers. I didn't want any outside influence affecting him. Not the Feds or the Regals or that mysterious outfit hiding somewhere behind the Spooks of D.C.

I had shared my suspicion about Anglin's target, my JFK theory, only with Doc. I had not talked about it with anyone else, not even with either of my two wives. It was too crazy to share any more widely. Anyone except Doc would think that this investigator had become overly obsessed with catching this particular killer, and that with the JFK idea I was making him some kind of super-villain—

Wasn't he already that, with seven victims, perhaps ten? Was the explosive secret of Kennedy's assassination worth more than the sum of all their lives?

I had to back away from the notion. It scared me, as I said. I had to concentrate on Anglin as a murderous psycho in his own right.

Carl had plenty of problems besides me. There was a large group of African-American male gangbangers who would dearly love to use his entrails as lawn cover. So Anglin had better watch his back. Whoever was shepherding him had better keep a close watch on their boy.

And finding out about that guardian angel of Anglin's still depended on Special Agent Mason. The tap had been on his phone for two weeks, but we'd come up with nothing to stir our interest. Like most agents, he understood how easily he himself could become a target for surveillance. Paranoia was the Bureau's watchword. It was a legacy from J. Edgar Crossdresser.

But one night Mason might become overly confident that no one was listening out there. Someone might call him on what he – and the caller – thought was an ordinary unsecured home phone. We had to hope he thought we thought he was beyond reach.

That lucky call happened on a Thursday evening. Ralph the Techie was on hand. He was sitting in a station wagon with his tape running, just 100 yards from Mason's residence.

Early on Friday morning, Doc and Ralph and I were listening to the recording at my office in Homicide.

'Yes?' Mason's voice.

'I have the document.' Female voice.

'This is an unsecured line.'

'I understand.'

Pause.

'What the hell,' Mason went on. 'What have you got for me?'

'Are you sure?' the female voice asked.

'I don't feel like going all the way downtown to my office to find an encrypted—'

'Okay, then . . . The Major says that group with the royal name is planning to take our boy into a downward spiral this very weekend. You had better provide security. You know how our man is about his personal safety—'

'You'd better stop right there and tell me the rest over a secured line. And don't call me at home again.'

'This is considered a One Priority. Time is a factor, Mason.'

Female voice hung up, and so did Mason.

'Major?' Doc asked.

'Major Motherfucker,' Ralph quipped.

No one smiled back at him.

'Ralphie, do you realize the deep shit you've just waded into with the two of us?'

Ralph the Techie looked over to Doc.

'What? I just record messages. That's all I . . . What deep shit?'

'You're listening to an FBI guy who has another master, other than Louis Freeh. You follow me, dummy?' Doc told him, glaring at him in a deadly serious manner.

'You mean Special Agent Mason is—'

'Yeah. If you want to bail, now's the time to grab a bucket,' I warned him.

'Oh man. I didn't know we were digging into dirt that's not for human consumption. I mean I thought this was just routine police . . . I can get myself killed here?'

We both looked right at him.

'Oh man, oh man. I got a family, Doc.'

'So do we, Ralph,' Doc returned.

'How shitty is this shit?'

'The shittiest you can imagine,' I replied, grinning harshly.

'Oh man, oh man . . . Who're we going after?'

'Anglin. It's always been him. But we have to get past his friends too.'

'And they are well-placed individuals within the framework of our government?'

'Yes, Ralphie. But no one elected *these* sons of bitches. They were spawned by some lazy bastards who like to hire out to have their garbage removed.'

'Doc, this is crazy. You're scaring me. We were just after a murderer—'

'The safest way for us to go is to get them, expose them. We don't have to arrest them. The daylight kills them on contact, Ralph. Like in the vampire movies. You remember what happens to the Count when the sun's rays hit him?'

Ralph watched Doc's eyes. 'What've you two got me into?'

'I'm sorry, Ralph, it was my fault,' I told him. 'And you can still walk out now. We're never going to speak your name. You can trust us. No one else knows about this recording.'

He looked down at his shoes.

'Christ, I gotta think Doc's right. I won't feel safe unless you can root these mothers out. I don't want to be watching over my shoulder for— Christ, I have my family to protect, too.'

'So do you think the three of us could invade Special Agent Mason's office?' I asked.

Ralph sat up with a start. 'You want me to trap his freaking office? His *federal* office?'

We watched him again.

'Oh man, oh man. I could've gone into insurance, accounting . . . A Fed's home field.'

'We'd do it, actually. You'd look a little strange, walking in there with us. We have legit business with Mason. One of us could distract him while the other planted the bug . . . You got something simple enough for us to put into operation?' I asked.

'I suppose I could show you how to . . . Yeah . . . Has he got a big desk, like this one here, Lieutenant?'

'I think it's similar.'

'Look, tapping a G's office telephone is way too risky. But we could get a bug in the room so you could hear what he's saying, at least.'

'Sounds like a plan,' Doc confirmed.

Ralphie the Techie started to give us our first lecture on audio surveillance.

Doc diverted Mason into the hallway while I asked to use the Fibbie's telephone for what I explained was a private call. I dug into my pocket for the tiny transmitter. I took the ball of adhesive goo that Ralph had supplied me, stuck the goo on the underside of the wooden desktop and then pushed the transmitter into the goo. All we had to do now, Ralphie suggested, was hope that the Feds didn't sweep their own offices for bugs for the next few days.

When Mason and Doc walked back in, I was just hanging up from my call to the National Weather Service. Sunny and warm, the man had said.

The attack on Anglin was coming this Saturday night, we found out. We didn't hear who Mason was talking to, but we got the idea from his responses to a call on Saturday morning. Our luck had held up. The Feds hadn't found the crude transmitter we'd planted. They had no reason to believe that anyone would dare invade their space, so I guessed we were banking on their arrogance. Something that was indeed usually a bankable notion.

We had to involve SWAT in this business. Homicide took care of bodies after the fact. Special Weapons and Tactics, of course, was something of a preventative measure, when they were not actually eliminating targets. Since we had notified the SWAT people, though, Doc and I were allowed to accompany our friends in the anti-terrorist garb to the scene of what we hoped would not become a reenactment of the serious disagreement between the Clantons and the Earps in Tombstone at that famous corral.

The first precaution was to get Anglin's neighbors out of their apartments. The operation was due to take place there in the new neighborhood that Carl Anglin had invaded. Three-flat apartment buildings made up most of the blocks there on the near by North Side. We cleared out the occupants for a half-block on either side of Anglin's abode.

Carl Anglin was the only tenant home tonight. As soon as the sun went down, the evacuation went ahead. You had to admire the SWAT guys. They could've cleared out Wrigley Field and the ballplayers would never have noticed. It was done that quietly and quickly.

The hit itself was scheduled for 2.00 a.m. Sunday morning, officially. So we had about six hours to prepare for the Regals.

Doc and I sat in our Taurus, about two hundred yards from Anglin's place. Doc had brought along the usual gear for a stakeout. His portable radio, a bucket of Brown's chicken – which he finished solo – and a flashlight and a paperback of poetry by a guy named Pinsky. He left not a second to chance or to boredom.

I tried to sleep when I could while on a stakeout. At least, I did once I was sure that Doc was awake with his jazz station and his poetry and his 'six clucks for a buck' or whatever the cooked poultry cost him.

I couldn't zee that night. I was waiting for the Regals' arrival long before they were scheduled. What mystified me was how Mason's friends had infiltrated them. They were a gang upon whom Tactical had made no dent for the last ten years. They were an extraordinarily hostile clan. None of our black undercovers had been able to get inside to date. The Regals were very clever and very paranoid. If you wanted to be one of them they had to know you since you were in grade school. They were extremely selective about new recruits.

It was the witching hour. Only two more to go. The neighborhood was too quiet. God knew where Tactical had taken the residents. They'd herded them off somewhere, far away from this site. Maybe the quiet would tip off the Regals, and perhaps they'd abort.

Our man was nestled quietly in his apartment with yet another young devotee who wanted to be near this dangerous suspected killer of ten girls. Anglin must have seemed exciting to whoever was up there in bed with him. I didn't know how some women reasoned – especially those who fell in love with cons on Death Row.

I settled back and tried to listen to Ahmad Jamal on Doc's all-night jazz station. The man could play the piano. Very smooth. Doc had extraordinary taste, it seemed to me. But I was not an aficionado of jazz.

1:30 a.m. rolled around, and the people in black out there had been fully deployed. If the Regals tried to enter Anglin's apartment building, they were in for a shock.

Doc turned off the radio. It was now ten minutes before the hour. And the Regals were early. We saw the two vehicles cruising down the street toward the three-flat in question. They were four-door cars, the kind of vehicle that drive-by shooters tended to use.

But the Pontiac and Buick late models passed by Anglin's location.

'They see something?'

'No,' I answered. 'They're just being cautious.'

I was vindicated when we saw them coming back down the street after having made their first pass. Now they slowed before they got to the address. The Pontiac pulled over first, and then the Buick followed behind it to stop at the curb outside the building where Carl Anglin rested with – or on top of – his company for tonight.

There were seven of them. Four from the first car and three from the second. They were carrying some kind of sawed-off weapons, something compact.

Doc pulled out his Nine and I gripped my own weapon. We were letting the SWAT team handle the takedown, but we were taking no chances about getting caught in some cross fire if things went south.

The seven Regals glided toward the entry. Three of them split off from the main party and circled around toward the rear exit.

As soon as the first banger touched the handle of the door, ten SWAT guys were on top of them. Gun barrels were immediately jammed behind the four bangers' ears, and we could hear the clunk of their weapons as they hit the sidewalk.

Doc and I got out of our vehicle. We heard one gunshot, and then there was another burst of gunfire from behind the apartment building. But the firefight there was over in seconds. We rushed up to the scene. The four men who had been going in via the front were on the ground and were already cuffed. Doc and I circled to the rear and found the SWAT standing over three dead Regals.

'They tried to act,' a hooded figure informed me.

The bangers' heads looked like exploded melons. All that damage had been done with one deadly burst of automatic fire.

Mason wanted to know how we'd known about the attack on Anglin. I smiled and said we had some intelligence on these mean streets too, but the special agent was not happy with my response.

We'd got there before his own folks had arrived – that was what really stuck in his throat. We'd had the area cleared and secured before his Spook friends could set up and deploy. And if they'd got there before us, I'm certain there would have been seven corpses at County instead of the three that our SWAT fellows had had to neutralize.

Mason wanted information from me, but I was not forthcoming. He'd find the transmitter within twenty-four hours. He'd figure it out. He'd find the tap on his home phone within thirty-six hours as well. He was, when it came down to it, no fool. And then he'd know who his opposition really was. It wasn't the Regals. It was me. And Doc. Then we'd have a war of our own.

I was not convinced this raid would put the street gang off the vendetta trail. They wouldn't forget. But maybe it'd give Doc and me time to focus on Mason and this 'major' who supplied Mason with intelligence about our subject of mutual interest, Carl Anglin.

For the first time since the newest rash of rapes and murders, I felt like some kind of door was opening. But I didn't know if the opening was something any of us wanted to look through.

Chapter Twenty-One

[May 1986]

The bulbs popped and the ceremony was over. I had my new shield and I'd become an official member of the elite: Homicide. All those years of preparation were ended and I was where I belonged.

Jake had been gone all those years, as well. Nick, my uncle (or father, biologically), Erin, my wife, and Eleanor, my mother, were all there with me.

The labor had ended fruitfully. I'd scoured the streets for the common variety of auto booster, and now it was time to play in the big leagues. It was where I was born to be.

My first partner was John Matuzak. A veteran of ten years in Homicide. He was a natural teacher, showed me all the moves. Orthodox and not-so-kosher moves. In other words he taught me to expedite, to get the job done. But John instructed me too about not losing sight of the smallest details. He showed me how to defend myself in a courtroom against a greaseball shyster who was paid for an acquittal. I never realized the survival moves you had to employ as a homicide investigator. It was absolutely adversarial in a court of law, and you couldn't let your ass hang out naked in the breeze.

Then Johnny M. had a heart attack two years after we become partners, and he spent six months recovering in a hospital, and then he took his retirement because he'd put his thirty annums in. We had a big party for him in Cicero, and Johnny retired in Williams Bay, Wisconsin, where he fished and hung at the beach by the shores of Lake Geneva.

He survived the heart thing and Homicide.

My next partner was a guy named Harold Gibron. They called him Doc because he was going after his Master's in English or European Literature – I couldn't remember which. So I was thinking they'd stuck me with some wiseass academic who'd correct my grammar.

But Doc was just another street guy with a shield who happened to enjoy fine literature but who didn't foist blue-blood fine arts onto his ignorant guinea younger partner.

We got along from the beginning. He told me everything. About his divorce, about his living alone, about his dream of copping that PhD and teaching compliant coeds. Harold was, of course, a bullshit artist, but he never lied to me. He saved the lies for his troop of lady friends – none of whom fell into the 'serious' category. It seemed that the divorce had turned him away from thoughts of settling down and having children.

When he met Erin, they became fast buddies. Doc told her dirty jokes that made her laugh and made me a little embarrassed, but when I saw the fun she was having listening to this old Korea hand, I couldn't get angry with him.

We had an impressive turnover rate for our caseload. We worked well together, and we put together a string of solved murders. I was a sergeant, as was Doc, but I was going to take the exam for lieutenant in the fall. It meant more money, and Erin and I were starting a family. We already had a little girl and we wanted a boy next.

Doc and I started off making a few waves with the arrest of a TV anchor who'd been wasting young women on the North Side. We got our names in the paper, and then the media knew me. They'd already become acquainted with the good doctor.

Our next big headline case was the murder of several teenaged girls – done by an ex-nun. This deal also made the media. The lieutenant thing looked closer to reality now. All I had to do was pass the written test.

Lurking behind everything I accomplished, everything we got closed, was Carl Anglin. I had spent six months in therapy, courtesy of the Department, talking to a shrink about what I thought had happened with my father the night he'd rolled down those stairs at the family house. Had the old lady shoved him? If so, had she done it deliberately? The verdict had been accidental death. There hadn't been much argument about the cause of death from the detectives who'd been called to the Parisi house that night. They had been able to smell the booze on my father's clothes, on his body. It had been an accident. He'd simply slipped and tumbled down all those twenty-six steps, and he'd broken his neck on the way down.

Case closed.

But not Carl Anglin's. Every so often I got the urge to look into the old man's files. I tried to get a fix on Anglin's whereabouts. Which was difficult because he moved about quite often. He stayed in no place for very long, and it would have taken full-time surveillance to keep good tabs on him. He was in and out. But there were no more slayings that carried his signature. We saw plenty of savagery, but nothing that resembled that crime in 1968.

Almost twenty years had passed. The unnamed witness to the killings was still hidden away at Elgin Mental Hospital. According to the doctors I'd talked to there, Theresa Rojas was still cut adrift from our world, and so there was no new development in the case. The only other witness was dead, and we hadn't been able to crack the military or the Feds for any new information about Carl Anglin's wartime exploits. It was still just a theory that he'd been shielded from prosecution because of something he'd done after the infamous Bay of Pigs fiasco, and we couldn't break their silence.

So we went about our work as if Anglin had departed the world along with Theresa Rojas – who might as well have been dead for all the use she was to any investigation – and the other seven nurses. Doc told me obsession was unhealthy, and I confirmed his notion. But that didn't stop me from looking over the old files from 1968, from time to time.

And yet the pieces meshed. It explained why Carl had heavy-duty help in avoiding the murder rap for the nurses. He must have had his story on tape somewhere. He must have had it written down and arranged for its exposure to the world's media. Something was preventing this 'Tactical Five' from calling on Carl Anglin with 'extreme prejudice'. They couldn't hit him because he'd insured himself. With whom?

He could have given a tape or a transcript to a lawyer. Or the material could have been stuck in a Swiss account box. It would have been impossible to pinpoint the hiding place of Carl's blackmail data among the complexities of the history of the United States during the last quarter-century.

Carl Anglin had blown the top of JFK's head off. Oswald had been the schmuck. He couldn't have nailed a moving target three times in six seconds, or whatever it was. But Anglin and an accomplice could have done. It was their job. They were skilled assassins, not disgruntled fanatics like Oswald. Then Oswald got wasted with cops all around him and we were supposed to buy into that kind of copper incompetence. The man who was supposed to have shot Kennedy was allowed out in the open and Jack Ruby just happened to be there.

I understood closure. I understood how important it was to let old wounds heal. But a lie of this size would never close. The wound would stay open. There was no possibility that it would heal. Shakespeare had once said something about murder crying out for resolution, but I couldn't remember which play that was in.

Approaching Doc about the matter was something I hadn't so far been able to do. But on our dinner break at the

White Castle at 3.16 a.m. on a Wednesday morning, the words just seemed to rush out of my mouth.

There was no one at the counter with us, no one in earshot. The employees of the White Castle were either very busy or half asleep. The dawn was still hours away.

I turned to Doc as he bit into a cheese slider.

'I think Carl Anglin shot John Kennedy in the head. I think he's got something on tape or in writing that he's hidden with a lawyer or somebody, and I think he's hanging it over the heads of the FBI. I think that's why they had to help him with the nurses.'

Doc swallowed the remainder of his cheese slider. He took a sip from his black coffee.

'I've been thinking the same goddamned thing for about six years.'

'Why the hell didn't you tell me, then?'

'Because I thought you'd think I was a lunatic, of course. Why else do you suppose?'

'*Are* we lunatics?'

'I guess. We're the craziest dicks on the block,' Doc said, smiling ruefully.

'What the hell can we do about it?'

'We can shut up and forget it forever.'

'How, Doc? How the hell can we—'

'My cousin saw a UFO when he was in the Army in 1956. He saw it out in the woods where they were involved in war games or something. He and his buddy got chased through the woods by some kind of miniature flying craft, like a little saucer. Do you think those two reported anything to their superiors? Fuck no, they didn't. They would've been accused of being smashed on duty. They would've been tossed in the brig until they rotted. You don't come down the road with news like that. Elvis is dead. UFOs are explainable phenomena. JFK caught it from a lone shooter. It's going on a quarter-century, Jimmy. Nobody wants to revisit that horror in Dallas.'

'I'm not crazy. You're not nuts. And Anglin was there, in Dallas. He did the President, probably with another shooter.

It was what he was trained to do. He had the motive, he had the ability. He had the lack of conscience, for Jesus Christ's sake! He pulled the trigger and killed Kennedy, goddammit!'

The guy flattening the tiny burgers turned and looked at the two of us.

Doc smiled at him.

'Can you get us a waitress to refill our coffees?' Doc asked the grill man.

'Sure,' the cook replied, smiling. He walked off toward the back.

'Keep it down, Jimmy. It's goofy enough without yelling it aloud.'

'We can't prove it. I understand that. Unless . . . '

'Unless what?'

'Unless we can pressure the Feds by telling them that we know where Anglin's hiding his blackmail material.'

'I'm sure Carl's got all the angles covered. He knows the kind of people he's working for.'

'Yeah. Pricks who allow the murder of seven women to go unsolved and unpunished. That's the kind of people we're talking about, so I'm not worried about ruffling their feathers.'

'Think about it, Jimmy. You've got a daughter. You've got a wife. You want more children. Who's going to keep the boogeyman out of your house? You can count on me, but I'm just one guy in your little army.'

'That's how all these assholes operate. Keep everyone scared shitless. It's like *omerta* with the guineas. Talk and you float with your nose in the sewer water.'

'Facts is facts, Jimmy. What can I tell you? And this isn't the first conspiracy theory about the Golden Boy from Hyannis Port. Why should our notion be smarter than all those others?'

I couldn't come up with an answer for him. And now I was thinking about the harm that could come to my wife and my daughter. It was a real threat. Not something you could shrug off, like a warning from some city thug. These guys played for keeps. They played in the biggest ballpark.

'So we swallow our paranoia,' I suggested.

'You got another way to go with all this?'

'You're saying we never speak of this again. We keep it quiet because these animals have all the cards.'

'We're just no-name Homicide cops from the city. We keep our own yard clean. We try to do something that's out of our league . . . hey, it's a good recipe for getting it up the ass without a condom in play. You follow?'

I felt sick. Helpless. Doc was right, and there was nowhere to turn for help.

Anglin got away with it the way he did almost twenty years ago. Some little faction of nutcases was getting away with another big-time evil and our hands were still tied. Carl had himself protected. I wondered if we could get ourselves the same kind of lifetime warranty. What if Doc and I went to the papers?

They'd want documentation. They'd want witnesses. We weren't talking about going to the trash tabloids because the *Star* and the *Enquirer* publish outright bullshit all the time. To get the legitimate press on our side we'd have to have something besides the unsubstantiated theories of two Homicide investigators. We'd need a witness. Someone who'd worked with Anglin in the field.

But there was no list of co-workers. The government had shredded any evidence of the exploits of Tactical Five. They were just fantasy, anyway. That's what any prosecutor in the country would say if we brought all this up in public.

Our theory was just another Halloween scare, like the Orson Welles hoax about the Martian invasion.

'Let it lie, Jimmy. It can't go anywhere. They've covered their tracks with a mountain of sand. Anglin disappeared into it when he pulled the trigger. He's a survivor. He understands what it takes to keep breathing in a river full of snakes.'

'What if he goes back to our streets and starts it up again with some new young girls?'

'We'll have to deal with him if he does. Right now he's gone beneath the surface. Maybe he'll leave Chicago alone.

Maybe he'll go after a colony of prairie dogs in Nebraska. Maybe the fucker'll slip and fall in the shower and he'll break his sly little neck.'

The waitress finally emerged from her hiding place. She filled our cups and then she retreated to wherever it was she'd been hiding, waiting for the sun to come up and end her shift of slinging cheese sliders and pouring coffee.

'You never thought you'd be involved in the murder of a President of the United States, did you, Jimmy?'

'No. You're right. We're wading into deep water. It's time to move on back where we can operate.'

'That's my boy. Don't take it personal. Everybody's gotta learn their limitations. It's painful to reach that point of awareness, but there it is. We don't get to hunt down Judas Iscariot, nor do we get to cuff Hitler or Mussolini. We miss out on a lot of justice. You just have to put things in perspective, James.'

We had to keep the evil genie confined inside the jar. We could never unscrew the lid and let him loose. Our caseload did not include the assassination of John Fitzgerald Kennedy.

And Carl Anglin's name had apparently been deleted, too.

Chapter Twenty-Two

[June 1999]

The gang had been put on hold as far as Anglin was concerned. We had Tactical on round-the-clock watch over the Regals. The bangers had been told by our people to lay off. If they didn't cool down, Tactical had promised them a roust like they'd never seen before. Our people let them know that all their business in the hood would be effectively shut down for as long as it took. The pressure seemed to work, since money was more important to them than one gang member's sister. The urge to vengeance went only so far, then it was back to business as usual.

My mind wandered back to the conversation that Doc and I had had late at night a number of years ago. We'd been talking about Anglin's big hit. The one that got him all this federal aid. I'd blurted out that I thought Carl Anglin had fired the head shot that had killed Kennedy. To my amazement my partner had agreed. We'd sat in some White Castle at near-dawn, having a few burgers and some coffee, and I remembered the chill that had hit my spine when Doc went along with my spoken-out-loud nightmare. Anglin had assassinated JFK, not Lee Harvey Oswald. And Anglin had had help.

Renny Charles was the help I'd had in mind when that horrible theory came into my head. Renny Charles, who'd taken a header out of his front-room window when Doc and I had first made contact with him.

I was going back to Charles. He might have been the key to finding out what had happened back in the 1960s. I was hoping that I was wrong. I truly was. I wanted Oswald to be the shooter. I wanted this whole matter to boil down to the murders of ten young women and nothing more. I didn't need the complications. But the idea of a lone assassin still stuck in my throat like a dry hunk of Thanksgiving turkey.

I was not involving my partner in this one. He'd been right the first time we discussed this insanity. We should have got on with our caseload and kept our noses out of shit we couldn't shovel.

I made my way back to Renny Charles's North Side apartment in my family Chevy. This was off the clock.

When I approached his apartment building, it was 9.46 p.m. I checked my watch with the help of the nearby streetlamp. It was a moonless night. Hot, humid, the usual June Chicago evening just before the real summer hit the streets.

I didn't have Doc's little burglary kit, so I had to enter in the normal fashion, via a ring of the doorbell. I buzzed Charles's apartment. No answer. I rang again. Same silence. So I buzzed his neighbors on the other two floors, and fortunately one of them responded. When I arrived at Renny Charles's door, I knocked four times.

I could hear the guy who'd buzzed me in cursing when he realized no one was there for him.

I knocked four more times. Then I simply reached for the knob, and found that the door was unlocked.

I took the Bulldog .38 from my ankle holster, and then I walked inside.

Darkness. I reached for a switch. I clicked it up, but no light-bulb came on. The drapes were closed, so no illumination streamed in from the sidewalk outside. Light from the streetlamps was shut out.

I took two more steps – and a blow to my head sent me plunging down into Renny Charles's carpet.

When I came round, I found I was sitting in a chair in the apartment. I thought I was still in the living room, but I couldn't be sure.

'Good evening, Lieutenant.'

I couldn't see the source of the voice, but whoever it was was apparently seated directly in front of me. I decided to stand up. Then I remembered I'd dropped the .38. The Nine too was missing from my shoulder holster. The guy in front of me was holding all the cards. So I stayed seated.

'Who are you?' I asked.

'I'm the Major.'

It hit me with a shock of revelation. He was the man in Tactical Five. The vague name we'd got for Anglin's splinter group of spooks.

'Why'd you sap me?' I demanded.

'Because it'd be a bit inconvenient for you to see me. Don't you agree?'

'All right.'

'You were looking for Renny Charles?'

'That must appear obvious . . . Major.'

'I really am a major, you know.'

'I'm sure you are.'

'Lieutenant . . . I'm here because I want to try to help you.'

'So you crack my noggin as a way to get acquainted.'

'We could not meet in any usual way, but I'm sorry for the pain nonetheless.'

'Where's Charles?'

'He's deeply hidden, Lieutenant.'

'Does that mean dead?'

'No. You see, he comes under the umbrella that Mr Anglin has opened. We have an understanding with Carl. I'm sure you've guessed as much by now.'

'Yeah. I figured he had your nuts in a vise over something pretty valuable to himself.'

'Indeed. He has the greatest life insurance policy ever written. The big companies would be envious of Mr Anglin's coverage.'

'You didn't kill me.'

'No. I'm hoping I won't have to.'

'Why would you have to?'

'Please, Lieutenant Parisi. Please. You know what this involves. You know that Anglin worked for us and that he was clever enough to insure his survival by leaving documents in the hands of people who could do this country very great harm. You're a policeman, and that's why I'm giving you this courtesy. But if you continue to look into Anglin as a suspect for the murders of—'

'He killed all ten of them, you son of a bitch!'

I was standing by then. But I remembered he had the weapons, and it was a useless gesture. I sat back down.

'Yes, he did. He killed them all.'

'And you want me to allow him to go on doing—'

'We are negotiating a solution for Mr Anglin. We are attempting to locate the owner or owners of the documents that serve as his protection from us – and from you, as well. Let us find the documents at their source, Lieutenant, and justice will be served. But if you insist on bulling your way into matters that don't concern you . . . Well, that would be unfortunate for both of us. Let us negotiate a settlement with Mr Anglin—'

'You haven't been able to for thirty years. Why now?'

'Remember there are things we are only just now discovering about World War Two. It takes decades, sometimes, to unearth evidence, facts . . . You have a family to consider, Lieutenant. Your wife is a police officer, too. You have three lovely children—'

'You threaten my family – you come near my house, you or any of—'

'None of that will be necessary if you just leave him to us. Think, Jimmy. Think.'

I wanted to grab one of my missing weapons and light up this room with gunfire.

The Major went on: 'I have no desire to harm you or your family. You must provide them with protection. You must ask yourself if an animal like Carl Anglin is worth the risk . . . Is he?'

'It's my job. It's what I do.'

'Your job does not entail digging up the agony that this country endured over thirty-five years ago. This nation survived the pain. We put matters to rest. It serves no purpose of justice to dredge it all back up. And those girls will have their justice if you will only allow us to pursue Mr Anglin in our own way. Doesn't that satisfy your personal and professional needs?'

'Why should I trust you? You've let him slide, and because you did, he's murdered three more young women.'

'Carl Anglin was one of the best field operatives I have ever trained. His hard heart made him the perfect assassin. It didn't matter who his target was. It was simply a task to be performed. He was also one of the best shots I have ever seen. Anglin could do head shots at more than 200 meters. The best pair of eyes I've ever encountered. Then he came home and did jobs in South America and Central America. And finally he was on the beach at the Bay of Pigs. Anglin was taken prisoner. He was raped and mutilated in prison. They cut off one of his testicles in that jail. But he escaped with some Cuban nationals and made it back to Key West. The jail thing turned him into something worse than an assassin. He'd always had a problem with women . . . You see, it was a female at the prison who cut off one of his balls.'

'And I'm supposed to feel sorry for the puke.'

'No. I just thought you might be interested in Anglin's history . . . Let me take care of him, Jimmy. We're almost home. Can you trust me for, say, one more month?'

'He and Charles did John Kennedy, didn't they?'

'Ridiculous.'

'Lee Oswald couldn't hit a barn with a bowling ball.'

'Absurd. No one would believe such a lunatic story.'

'But it's true anyway, isn't it, Major?'

'This is my last offer. Let him go. Things will become very unpleasant for you if I ever have to talk to you again.'

Then it was silent in the apartment.

'Major?'

No response. I waited a full two minutes before I got to

my feet. Then I stumbled toward where the voice had come from. I found the chair, its seat still warm from the Major's body. And I found my .38 and my Nine lying on top of the seat. There was a lamp next to the chair. I switched it on, and the dull glow from the low-wattage bulb barely illuminated the living room. He must have run out the back, through the kitchen. I switched lights on as I proceeded to the back.

There was no trace, though, of the Major.

He'd slid out of the place as noiselessly as he'd arrived. I felt the welt his sap had made on the back of my head. Then I remembered my most dangerous blunder: Telling him about Anglin and the Presidential whack. My idea was so humiliatingly idiotic when spoken aloud that the Major knew no one would believe me if I repeated it. So many conspiracy nuts had claimed to know the identity of the 'real' slayer of JFK that even to speak about the subject had become a joke. Like Elvis sightings and UFO abductions. I wouldn't be able to get a soul to believe my theory about the true history of Carl Anglin, so the Major didn't really feel threatened by me.

But he wanted me to back off from Carl because he thought he could free the G from the threat of Anglin's blackmail document. That document had to be a hell of a lot more convincing than a lone Chicago Homicide cop with a squirrelly notion of who'd killed a famous American President.

The Major must have come across new information about where Carl had stashed the goodies that kept the Spooks from his door.

Anglin had no such deal with me or the Chicago Police Department. He was just another piece of shit to us – and especially to me.

No, the Major wouldn't come after me unless I put Anglin in a position to tell all to the media. He wanted a month. He'd already had three decades.

He couldn't stop going after this butcher. And neither could I.

I told Doc about my evening at Renny Charles's place and my partner went into a rage.

'Let's go have a talk with Mason.'

'Wouldn't do any good. I don't think Mason knows the Major. This guy is Superspook. I never heard him before he conked me, and I never heard him get out the room, either.'

'He's flesh and blood, Jimmy. Screw him. Let's go find him.'

'No. He made his threat. He wants us to lay off Carl for a while because he thinks he can take off his other nut. He thinks he can defuse him. They must have located Anglin's "representative".'

'When they do, they'll kill Carl.'

'Like swatting a fly hovering over shit.'

'And we're supposed to sit back and let them do our business?'

'I was hoping you'd see it that way.'

'Shit, you scared me.'

'Anglin put his piss-scent on our territory. He doesn't get any free rides . . . Tell your wife to keep her eyes open, anyhow.'

The first look of personal concern crossed Doc's face. He was a husband and a father, just like me.

I tried to reassure him: 'I don't think this spook wants to put the hurt to any of ours – or to us, either. I think he just wants us to know he could, if he felt like it. Power ball, with the big dogs playing.'

'I taught Mari how to shoot. She carries a legal weapon in her purse. I'll tell her to stay heads-up.'

Doc had set me thinking about Natalie and my three kids. Natalie could take care of herself. But my three children were innocents, of course.

'He doesn't want a shit storm with the CPD,' I said.

'No. Hell no, he doesn't.'

We were whistling in the dark, past the graveyard.

So I had our evidence people dust Renny Charles's apartment for prints.

One day later we got some positive news. There was a clear thumbprint on the back doorknob. The print was scanned by the FBI's lab, and we had a name.

Frederick K. Martinson.

Frederick K. Martinson had been killed in Desert Storm. A major in the Army's Ranger Unit.

The other prints in the flat came from Renny Charles and a few other sources that had no copy in the FBI files. Which meant they were neither criminals nor military.

The Major really was a ghost. He had the hands of a man who'd been dead for eight years.

I put Natalie on high alert. I explained to my two older children that they were to be very wary of any adult they didn't know who tried to get them to go off somewhere by telling them that Natalie or I had been injured and was in a hospital. I told them to be aware of the bullshit spiels that'd trick them into getting into someone's vehicle. My boy and girl were pretty street-smart, so I was confident they wouldn't fall for some line.

I'd warned my mother to be wary of anyone coming to our door with a story that would require her to take off, with the baby in tow, toward a hospital.

I'd asked too for a squad car to keep a very high profile in our neighborhood. Especially at night when I was at work. The desk sergeant had been very cooperative. He knew I was working on Anglin.

If the Major didn't take Anglin out of play in a month, I'd be waiting. But I was not going to sleep much during the next four weeks. I was still after him. Full-time. Just as it was before.

Because Carl Anglin was not finished. He'd never have enough. Losing half of his manhood might have been the spark for all this carnage, but there'd been plenty of hate and viciousness in that scrawny-assed body even before that female Cuban cop had started to cut at him.

Anglin was my business. He was in my district, my parish. The Major wouldn't beat me to him. My father had started this long chase, and I was going to be there, waiting for Carl Anglin, at the end of the line.

PART THREE

Chapter Twenty-Three

[July 1999]

After two years in Burglary/Auto Theft, my wife Natalie joined the crew. She became a Homicide cop. A member of the fraternity. Doc and I and Eleanor and Mari, Doc's wife, and my three children were at the ceremony where she got her promotion.

'Detective,' I said to her.

'Lieutenant,' she responded. And then she began to cry. And Eleanor and my eldest daughter Kelly begin to sob along with her. Soon Mari had to join in. Doc and I and my son and the baby, Mary, had the only dry eyes in the vicinity. Natalie's side of the family had moved to Pennsylvania and couldn't make the trip because they were coming to see us over Christmas. It was crowded enough around my wife. I couldn't remember the last time I felt as up as I did then.

There hadn't been much to feel elated about recently. The welt on my head had finally started to go down, though. The Major apparently knew how to use a sap. It told me he might once have been an M.P. in the military. At least he was no pencil pusher. He'd showed up in person to contact me, and that also told me something about him. He didn't always pass the dirty work to underlings. He had the sack to do it himself when necessary.

We took the newest member of Homicide to a fancy place in Oak Park – The Elms. It served over-priced food, but it was good, and my wife deserved the swank of it. For too long I hadn't seen her as much as I'd have liked because of the Anglin case, and she'd been busy moving upward in her career too. I told myself that we were going to take our vacation days together, and later, at The Elms, I confirmed that with Natalie. We were taking five days in southern Wisconsin. We were going to lie on the beach during the daylight hours and we were going to become reacquainted in the bedroom in the evenings.

By the third day on the beach in Delavan, Wisconsin, Natalie was literally grinding her chompers to get back to work. She'd waded through three paperback thrillers and one romance. She said she preferred the detective books because they made her laugh out loud.

We were sitting on this same beach on the fourth day – it was the week after the Fourth of July – and she laid the news on me.

'We're not going to be able to have another baby for a few years.'

I looked over at her with the appropriate surprise on my face.

'What brought that announcement on?' I asked.

'I have to get settled into the new job. I can't be taking maternity leave as soon as I arrive at Homicide.'

'No one expected you to.'

'You mean you understand?'

'Of course I understand. And maybe we ought to be happy we've had the one little girl together. Do we need a flock?'

'Not necessarily. I thought you might've—'

'We have our baby. If you want more, that'll be up to you. I'm happy with the three live ones we've got . . . The big ones belong to you too, you know. They're kind of attached to you by now. You don't need to produce your own train of offspring if you're happy with where we're at.'

She leaned over to me from her lawn chair. We'd been watching the sailboats and the water-skiers. When the heat became uncomfortable, we walked into the lake and doused ourselves. It was pleasant and uneventful. My kind of vacation. She gave me a kiss on the lips.

'I want to help you with Anglin, but they won't let us work together.'

'That's SOP. It makes life a little simpler. If we hadn't already been married, you might've had a harder time getting into Homicide. They like to discourage the fraternization stuff.'

'Is that what you've been doing to me the last four nights? Fraternizing me?'

'Yeah. Extreme fraternizing.'

A look clouded Natalie's bright, freckled face. Her auburn hair seemed redder in the sunlight.

'Is Anglin a dead case, Jimmy? Are you just going through the motions?'

'No. It's active.'

'You never talk about it much . . . And you never explained the bump on the back of your head, either.'

I reached up and touched the small pill-sized lump that was my souvenir from the Major.

'The less you know, the better I feel about it.'

'It has to do with the G.'

'Yeah. You're talking like an old vet already.'

'What're they doing with Anglin?'

'If I tell you, Natalie, you're involved.'

'I *am* involved – with you. Till death do us part is the way I remember it.'

'It's dangerous.'

I was telling this to a woman who had faced down a sociopath in our own home. Faced him down and calmly blasted him into our furniture.

'You're right . . . Okay.'

I told her all there was to know about Anglin. I included the Major. I explained my idea about Anglin shooting the President of the United States, and then she sat up, alert and straight-backed in the chair.

'So now you think I'm an idiot.'

'Jimmy.'

'I know. I'm nuts. I'll be speaking in tongues next.'

'The President? Kennedy?'

I told her about Anglin and Renny Charles and their erstwhile membership of the assassin community.

'It's . . . It's a little hard to digest.'

'Yeah. It's the weight I've been carrying for about fourteen years. The only other person I've told it to is Doc. Who recommended I shut the hell up and never utter a word about it again. He's probably right. And I hope you don't pass it on to anyone.'

'Of course I won't . . . My God. John Kennedy . . . '

'I'm probably wrong. It's just a hunch, you know, a theory?'

She looked over to me and her stare was severe.

'What if you're right?'

'I don't see justice being done any time soon, if that's what you mean.'

'Jimmy . . . How can you sleep at night?'

'Sometimes I don't.'

She took hold of my hand. Then she narrowed her gaze as she looked out across the placid water of Lake Geneva. Only an occasional sailboat broke the line of the horizon out on the blue water. And the touring paddleboat that came by with the sightseers every hour on the hour.

I squeezed my wife's hand and I shut my eyes.

Mason the Fibbie stood as I entered his office. His assistant was sitting in a chair across from Mason's seat.

'I still haven't heard your name,' I told her.

Doc was standing next to me, waiting to hear her lovely voice, but she didn't speak.

'And you're here to tell me what?' Mason asked coldly.

I tore my gaze away from the blonde. I left the scrutiny of her to my partner.

'I got a nice bump on my noggin from your Major.'

That got Mason's attention. He stopped dicking around with the papers on his tabletop.

'Major who?'

'You know. Tactical Five. Those spooks who float around the D.C. area with a clandestine title. You know. The CIA with different initials.'

'I don't know what you're talking—'

'Ah, c'mon, Mason, please. He's as real as the lump on my head. I'd say he was an M.P. at one point. Christ, he knocked me down and out with one swipe. Very professional . . . He tried to swing a deal with me.'

'A deal?'

'Yeah. He wants me to lay off Anglin for about a month because he says he's got a line on his blackmail data. You know, the material that's incriminating enough to get you and the Major to obstruct a homicide investigation that's been going on for thirty-one years?'

'And you think I know this Major guy and that I'm somehow involved in his plans to eliminate Anglin from your playing field. Is that right?'

'That is first-rate stuff, Special Agent Mason. You take acting lessons at the college?'

'Look, I don't know any Major—'

'You're a liar. But I'll tell you what I'm going to do. I'm going to tell you so you can tell the Major. I've got my own little document about the Anglin case and about the interference you and your boss have thrown my way since we began looking into the more recent murders. I've got that paper with both major newspapers in Chicago, and I'm working on a third publisher in New York. They're very interested in printing the piece. But there's a stipulation.'

'What stipulation?'

'They can run the story only if I or one of my family or Doc here, or any of *his* family, meet with an untimely death. I've given them enough tasty morsels as appetizers for them to be willing to wait and see if any of us have bad luck. So if I break my neck falling in the shower, you are all going to become the recipients of a great deal of unwelcome publicity.'

'You can't back up anything you're saying. It's all bluff. It's all bullshit.'

'Try me, Mason. I know how to please a pack of journalists. I've had lots of experience with them.'

'You're lying.'

I was looking right into his eyes.

'Tell the Major to back off. He's got his fingers in my sandwich and they're about to get bitten off. I don't care who he's connected to. I'll put all that dirty laundry in my basket and I'll hang it up in every federal office in this county. You wanna play chicken?'

Mason's brown face darkened to midnight blue. 'You bastard – you wouldn't . . . ' he spluttered, enraged.

'Try me, Mason. Try me.'

Doc looked at me in the elevator and he began to giggle.

'What a performance. You talk about what an actor Mason is—'

'Mine was no act. I've contacted the papers. The *Tribune* and the *Times* are slobbering at the chance to get an exposé piece from a Chicago Homicide cop.'

'You didn't say anything about the Kennedy business.'

'No. Hell no . . . But I whet their appetite when I told them it had to do with putting a monkey wrench in the Anglin affair. I didn't get specific. I just told them I had something extraordinarily juicy for them if they'd agree to publish only—'

'Only if something bad happens to any of us,' Doc finished my sentence for me.

'They don't have anything except my word that I could have something very special for them. They don't have a story now, but they're willing to keep an open mind for a future possibility.'

'You think you can threaten this Major guy?'

'No. I want him to know we're still players, though. I don't think he wants the mess of popping Chicago policemen. He knows how the Department is about losing any of its own. I just want him to give us the room to go after Carl Anglin ourselves. Because the Major's going to make him disappear, if he has his way. That'd be too easy for the son of a bitch.

I want him in the lockup with no way out, this time. I want him staring at life in the shitter or lethal injection. I don't care. I want Carl Anglin to be frightened, the way his young women all were. I want him to face the terror they did, knowing they were going to die.'

'And how are we going to get Anglin where we want him?' Doc asked.

'We've got a month, it sounds like.'

I got the call from the psychiatrist on a Saturday morning. So I got Natalie up – it was 6.35 a.m. – and we dressed as though we were going to the beach at Lake Michigan. When we arrived at the Oak Street Beach, I left Natalie at the parking lot with our Cavalier, and I jumped into the waiting car that Doc Gibron drove. We tried to make sure that we weren't being followed, and it seemed we were clear.

We headed out to the Outer Drive and went south toward Indiana. The drive took an hour and forty-five minutes in light Sunday-morning traffic.

The psychiatrist left us alone with Theresa Rojas.

'Hello, Theresa,' I said, smiling gently.

Doc greeted her with a familiar yellow rose.

'Hello,' she said. It was more like a whisper.

'Theresa?' I asked.

'Yes,' she answered.

'You're back?' I asked her.

She smiled. 'I was never anywhere else.'

'Can you talk to us? I mean, can you tell us about what happened all those years ago?'

'You mean what he did to my friends.'

'Yes.'

Doc was mute. All he could do was stare.

'Who knows you're able to speak, Theresa?' I asked.

She looked at the yellow rose and smiled. 'You gave me flowers.'

'I gave you yellow roses. They're supposed to stand for loyalty.'

'You were loyal to me . . . You look like him. Like your father.'

I was not going to educate her on my genetic background. I was too excited to see her lucid, alive, clear-headed.

'They drugged me, Lieutenant Parisi.'

'My name is Jimmy. This is Doc Gibron.'

She smiled over at Doc.

'They gave me something and then those other doctors all talked to me – like in hypnosis. I was studying to be a nurse. I know what they did to me.'

'It was called MRS127. It's a synthetic drug, like LSD. It kept you tied up, in your head.'

'I still have flashbacks. The doctor says I probably will continue to have them.'

'But you're back, and you're here to stay, this time,' I insisted.

'Am I? Am I really, Jimmy?'

Her eyes were brimming with tears.

I took hold of Theresa and hugged her tightly.

'Who did this to me? *Why* would they do this to me, Jimmy?'

I had a lot of explaining to do to her. And her talk about 'flashbacks' had me wondering if she was indeed all the way home, in her head.

'You remember the night Carl Anglin killed all your friends?'

Theresa looked down for a moment. Then she looked back up at me before glancing over at Doc.

'I remember every second of every minute. I saw him. I saw him kill two of the girls. I was under the bed, but he never saw me. I saw him. Yes. I remember everything.'

Chapter Twenty-Four

[July 1999]

Mason didn't find the crude transmitter that I'd slapped under his desk, so we still had an ear in his office. When he got another call from the Major, we picked up something interesting. A meeting place for Special Agent Mason and this enforcer from Tactical Five.

Grant Park. Eight p.m. on the button. I myself heard Mason repeating the Major's instructions.

'I can't believe they haven't located the bug,' Ralphie told Doc and me after he removed his earphones. 'Or maybe they're playing it cute.'

'You think they know we're listening and this meeting is to set us up?' Doc asked. My partner looked over at me. 'The Major's no dummy. I can't believe he's taking risks,' he explained.

'But the bug is crude. They're used to playing high-tech and maybe they reckon everyone thinks the way they do,' I told them.

'Are we going after the Major?' Doc wanted to know.

When he looked at me again, he had his answer.

Ralphie uttered his usual groan.

We were at Grant Park at 7.30. Just the two of us, Doc and I. Ralphie was excused. He was done with this project. It'd been dangerous enough, so we cut him loose.

It was a hot, early summer's night. Truly breathless. High humidity and just a hint of a breeze coming off the Lake in the east. We were sitting on a park bench near the softball diamond where Mason was supposed to meet the Major. It was Diamond Number 13. We'd heard Mason repeat the number, so we should have been near where they'd be – if they weren't setting us up, as Ralphie the Tech suggested.

We were armed as always, but the weaponry didn't make me feel any more confident.

Fifteen minutes went by, along with a few pairs of neckers. Two couples were heterosexual and one twosome was humming Bette Midler tunes in low, masculine voices.

Doc giggled. 'Hey.' He gestured to me when I looked over to him.

It was now five minutes to the hour. And we spotted Mason's blonde assistant. But no Mason. We were far enough away – perhaps the length of a football field – from the baseball diamond for her not to notice us. Doc had a set of opera glasses.

'It's the girl. Mason's girl,' he confirmed. 'She's standing right behind the screen, right behind home plate. I don't see anyone coming up on her . . . Wait a minute.'

The light was going. Dusk was on us, and I had to rely on Doc and his opera glasses to keep me informed. I could just barely make out the figure of the girl. And now I saw a male approaching her. He was tall, wearing a black cloth jacket on this hot-as-hell evening. When he reached her, he directed the blonde toward the nearest park bench.

'He's very unhappy with her. They're arguing,' Doc said. 'He's got his hands in his jacket pockets, so it doesn't look like he's going to get physical . . . Shit, Jimmy, it's getting dim out here. I can barely make them out anymore. Maybe we ought to approach—'

'He'll bolt. He's got those kind of reflexes. You can bet on it.'

The male in the dark jacket rose. Both of us could see at least that much. The traffic in the park was very light this evening. Most people were probably down by the Lake to get the cooler breezes from the water.

'He's taking off, Jimmy. We're going to lose him . . . '

We were both off the bench and half-trotting toward the assistant. We closed the 300 feet in seconds. We were moving at a fast clip.

We stopped about twenty feet in front of the blonde woman on the bench. She was sitting, oddly still.

Doc walked up to her.

'I don't recall your name, but . . . '

Then he reached down to touch her, and she slumped over onto the bench.

I walked over to the two of them.

It was then that we both spied the red splotch on her white-bloused chest. The tall guy had pumped a slug through her. He must have had a silenced gun in his jacket pocket.

'Stay with her and call an ambulance,' I told my partner.

I took off to the west, the direction the tall man in the black jacket had gone.

It would soon be full dark and then I wouldn't have a prayer of spotting him. He'd been moving off at a near gallop when we'd started to approach the dead FBI woman.

But I saw him jogging up to the stop sign at the boulevard. He stopped, looked around, and snapped back into motion when he saw me a hundred yards behind him. He bolted across the busy intersection – and I was after him. He was trying to head toward the Loop, toward some crowded streets where he could vanish.

Soon I was running out of steam. My breath was growing ragged from the running, from trying to close the gap between us. But I had shortened the tall man's lead. We were out of the park and were heading toward the downtown district. I had my handheld radio and I told Doc where I was headed. He responded and said he'd send some help my way if I gave him the general location.

My quarry was headed toward State Street. By now I was really almost out of gas, but the memory of that lump on my head and his threats to me and my family spurred me on. Anger overcame fatigue and I somehow got my second wind.

Now he was on State, nearing Lake. The streets were still crowded from the tourists visiting the downtown shopping locations, and I was afraid that he'd vanish into the pedestrian traffic. But I found that I was still gaining on him.

He had the piece in the right pocket of his jacket. I was picturing it even though I hadn't actually seen it.

I stopped briefly and removed the Nine from my shoulder holster. I was wearing the weapon under a very light nylon jacket. Light as it was it was still too warm, so I was sweating heavily in this steamy air. I palmed the gun in my right hand and held it against my right thigh. It was dark enough that no one on the street saw the pistol. They were too busy scoping out the tourist traps.

I was within a half-block of the Major – I assumed it was him. I was still edging closer to him. He had slowed down noticeably. He was approaching a crowd of people who were waiting outside a movie theater. They were standing in line for some film – I couldn't see what was on the billboard outside the place.

He turned back toward me. He waited for me, his hands inside his jacket.

I kept on coming until only 100 feet separated us. The Major placed himself directly in front of a crowd of two hundred movie patrons. He had them as a shield, except that his cover was behind instead of in front of him. It was effective, nonetheless.

At fifty feet, I halted. Stalemate. He knew I wasn't going to cut loose with all those civilians standing behind him.

Under the glare of the bright theatrical lights of the marquee, I could see his face. He was blond, like his FBI victim. He had what was called an aquiline nose – like an eagle's beak. But it wasn't overly large. There was a distinct dimple in his chin. He looked like a Hollywood leading man. A handsome specimen. Tall, athletic, rugged. Like the advertisement for the Marlboro Man. A man's man.

He was smiling at me. Perfectly white teeth, naturally. I might have been shooting at Gregory Peck when he was younger, the thought occurred to me.

Then I remembered his threats to my family. I watched him smile. The line outside the theater refused to move. The movie might not have been scheduled for another half-hour. I had no way of knowing.

He was still showing me those teeth. And my backups were either lost or late.

His grin vanished when I raised the nine-millimeter pistol. Deliberately, I fired three rounds into the air.

The sound of the shots brought screams from the people in line, and then the crowd scattered and headed for any sort of shelter they could find. The throng in front of the show disappeared in less than five seconds. It was like a magic trick.

And just as the last of the bystanders got out of our way, I saw the Major pull the gun with its silencer attached out of his right jacket pocket. I watched him raise the weapon in my direction, and then I pulled the Nine's trigger. My first round spun him around and knocked him to the ground. I rushed toward him, and as I closed in he tried to raise his gun again. My second bullet hit him in the belly and doubled him over, but he still tried to stand up and get off a shot at me. My third and final round found his throat, and the shock of this impact knocked him flat on his back.

I stood over his supine body. Blood was jetting from his neck wound, but the other hits showed simply as black holes in his clothing.

I removed the handgun and silencer from his grasp. His grip had very little strength left in it, so there was no struggle. There were new shrieks coming from the sidewalk behind me. Female onlookers who'd just realized they'd witnessed a killing.

Except that the Major, if this was really the boss of Tactical Five, was not quite history yet.

I tried to press my fingers over the little gouts of blood coming out of the wound in his throat, but I couldn't get them properly plugged in. If the paramedics didn't arrive soon, he'd bleed to death. I tried my handheld radio, but the spurts of blood frightened me into reapplying the pressure on his throat.

Finally a patrol car arrived. I told the uniforms who I was and ordered them to call for the paramedics. There was a first aid kit in their car, so I was able to get a bandage over the Major's neck wound.

But he'd lost too much blood already. I'd blown an artery in half with the Nine, I thought.

I bent down close to his face.

'Tell me. Tell me before you die. Tell me how to get to Anglin. How to get his juice turned off at the roots.'

The handsome spook tried to smile, but his own juice had nearly run out.

He tried to mouth some words, but his wound stopped him speaking.

I got close to his face, close enough so no one else could hear, what with all the street noise around us.

'Anglin killed the President, didn't he? Tell me . . . just tell me.'

But all the Major could do was blink his eyes once. And then his stare became focused far, far beyond me – and beyond all of us.

'Why the hell did he shoot the girl?' Doc lamented.

'Maybe he thought she was with us. Maybe he scoped us out and thought she was the Judas goat. I don't imagine the Major handled betrayal very well.'

'Why'd Mason send her?'

'Fear. The Major was a scary guy, Doc. I don't know. Maybe Mason had no clue the spook would take out that pretty little woman just because the Major sniffed something in the air. The Major isn't talking anymore, and Mason'll find a little hole to hide in as soon as possible. Bet on it.'

'Now there's no way to link Anglin with the President.'

Doc peered out into the darkness from my office's window. He looked off into the east, where the Lake lay.

'I can't think of anybody who's likely to come forward on the matter. No. It seems our conspiracy theory has sunk with the fortunes of the leader of Tactical Five. I'm sure all his partners will slide into their drains when the papers find out this guy was attached to the secret G.'

'But they won't go any further than the Feds will allow.'

'Of course not.'

He turned and sat down in the leather chair opposite my desk.

'We have only one card left to play.'

'Theresa. Yes,' I agreed.

'We need to take extraordinary steps to keep her in the pink.'

'Yes. We do.'

'There can be no press. No media. Until we're headed to court.'

'Our friend Henry Field will not prosecute until he's sure, damn dead sure, that we have a real live witness in her, Doc. If Theresa regresses, if she goes south on us again, we lose Anglin forever. His deal with the Feds is still active, now that the Major's croaked. He has his armor in good repair now that his boss isn't around to remove his insurance policy. We don't get him with Theresa Rojas, he doesn't get got.'

'She has to remain in our world.'

'There it is. There it truly is.'

Theresa made great strides, the Indiana shrinks told us. She had become very vocal, very articulate. Her solitary confinement in the prison of her mind was over and she talked all the time. She was lucid and clear, and there was very little to remind her doctors and therapists of the mental recluse that Theresa Rojas had been.

Doc and I had to take very careful precautions about visiting her and communicating with her over the phone. I didn't know if the FBI was worried about finding the witness we'd hidden from them, now that they had the Major's death – and life – to cover up. Except that they knew Anglin would spill everything once we took him in. He'd want all the rats to drown with him. He was that kind of rodent. It'd make great press, and he enjoyed the spotlight.

The thing that disturbed me then was that Anglin would hear about Theresa's recovery. It would be in the interest of the members of Tactical Five, if any remained, to let Anglin know about her. Then his self-defense mechanism would pop into place, and that clique of spooks would get Theresa done for free.

We had to keep Carl under full-time surveillance until we were sure about Theresa's recovery. Once we'd cuffed him, I'd feel better. I'd have liked to be able to cuff the Major's surviving 'relatives', too, but I didn't know their names. But I could locate Anglin, at least. He was her most direct threat.

The Chicago Police Department was not exactly an example of optimum security. We couldn't trust anyone with information about Ms. Rojas. Not the captain. No one. We were going to make a lot of enemies once people around here found out we'd been sitting on a witness like our girl. There would be men who would want to take credit for nailing Anglin, but I didn't give a shit about ruffling those assholes' feathers.

I was going to keep Theresa alive. I was going to be sitting there when she placed the noose over his head. I was going to watch something like justice happen in a Chicago court of law. All these miracles would come to pass if I could keep Theresa in one piece for the next few weeks while her doctors finished her therapy.

Theresa was coming out into the open. Back into the world. She smiled and talked to people. She'd finally been able to free herself, and she'd crawled out from underneath that bloody, thirty-one-year-old dormitory mattress.

Chapter Twenty-Five

[July 1999]

The Major's fingerprints belonged to a man who'd died years ago. We went to the Federal Bureau of Investigation for an explanation. We received nothing for a response. They simply didn't know. It was a mystery.

And Special Agent Mason was nowhere to be found. He had been reassigned – and his new whereabouts were classified, John Rush, the FBI guy who talked to us, explained. Rush was an old-timer. He had no use for clandestine splinter groups and spooks, he said, and I believed him. There was disgust on his middle-aged face as he had to deliver this perfunctory rap. He was just doing his job, he apologized.

We told him this was a murder investigation. He replied that killing the Major – whoever he was – had been simple self-defense on my part. No murder there, he stated. I explained that the Major was linked to Anglin and that it was Anglin who was the murder case. Special Agent Rush shrugged his shoulders. He had nothing else to give us. The Major was gone. I imagined the Feds had secured the remains, and his carcass would now belong to the apparatus of 'National Security'. The mills of government were already grinding up his bones. The story of the gunfight in the street was relegated to a few sentences in both of the major Chicago newspapers. Just another shooting in a big city, according to the media. And their source of information was not the Chicago Police Department. The government itself had given them the story on this incident.

So, as quickly as he'd popped up in front of me, the Major had disappeared on the night he'd blown a hole in Doc's Fibbie girlfriend. I thought my partner was still in mourning over her loss.

'The world has too few truly beautiful women, Jimmy. I know what we think of her profession, but that's no reason to be prejudiced toward such a miracle of genetics,' Doc lamented after the ambulance had taken Joyce Carlson's dead body away. We'd finally found out who she was after the Major had slotted her.

There would be no more talk of conspiracies, of Presidential assassinations. Doc and I had come to the end of the line. Everywhere there was an opening, there was a dead end to match it. No wonder the Warren Commission people came up with a report as quickly as they did.

No one wanted to know who did it. I was convinced that we were through with what had happened almost forty years ago in Dallas. A few movies and books, a few half-cracked theorists on the talk shows. We just wanted it to be finished.

As far as Doc and I were concerned, it was done. We were focusing on Anglin. If he wanted to share something with the world after we locked his ass up for no less than ten murders, that was his business.

Carl Anglin might have wanted to let his pent-up dogs of vengeance loose when he went down, but that was not going to stop his prosecution this time. The race was on to get him to trial before the remnants of Tactical Five, if there were any, got to him to shut him up.

We had surveillance people on the ex-Navy killer round the clock. Our captain was very interested to know why we had the heat on high, but we kept him at arm's length about where we were. It was between Doc and me. That was the only way to keep Theresa Rojas's status secret.

She was getting stronger all the time. All we told our superior was that Anglin's arrest was imminent. He was the only law enforcement person we shared that information with, but we needed to move quickly before other people became involved, as inevitably they would.

We were about to take Theresa's deposition. On the next Tuesday. This was Friday. We were waiting to see if she had any 'episodes'. To this point she hadn't had the flashbacks that might have occurred, her therapist warned us. That was the LSD factor in MRS127. But the doctor in Indiana had never dealt with a victim of this synthetic, so everything was new to him too.

Renny Charles was another person we'd have liked to bring in as a witness against Anglin. Not that Charles could put Anglin on scene, whether back in 1968 or in the other three cases. But he could help a jury understand what kind of creature it was who was on trial.

I tried to put the Kennedy killing out of my mind – and off my conscience. I was too young to have voted for the man. I didn't much like any of his relatives or their offspring, and I was never much taken with his aristocratic wife. His sex life didn't concern me, although I couldn't fully respect a man who couldn't keep his word or his vows. But that was his private life.

It was like being privy to a secret. The more you had to keep it to yourself, the more you wanted to shout it to the crowd. Human nature at its worst, I supposed.

With the death of the Marlboro Man, alias the Major, we'd have to leave the conspiracy behind John Fitzgerald Kennedy's demise to other people. We had a job to do. We had to bring the murderer of ten young women to justice. It was about time, for them and for their families.

We had a stenographer and we would be running a tape. Theresa was a natural beauty. The passing years hadn't stripped her of what God had originally endowed her with. There was a natural grace, a femininity about her. When she stood, you wanted to touch her shoulders. They were fragile and elegant. She stood straight, no stoop in her posture. There was no sense that nature was aging her. She looked almost like the file photographs that showed her as a nursing student at the end of the 1960s.

'Theresa, we'd like to begin. If you're all set,' Doc told her.

I sat next to her. I reached out and touched the back of her hand. She looked over at me and smiled gently. She resembled the Madonna, I thought. At least, all the pictures and other renderings I'd seen of the Virgin Mary. Her smile made the room warmer, more comfortable. It was almost scary, supernatural. She was the other side of the Anglin coin.

'Go ahead and tell us what happened on that night in 1968,' Doc prompted.

'It was a Saturday night.'

Theresa took hold of my hand and held on firmly.

'I didn't know what was happening to the other girls. I only found out what he did to the last two, because they were in the same room as I was . . . I was in the bathroom when he came into our suite. The door was shut. I heard them struggling with him, and then he must have tied the two of them up because I didn't hear any more struggling. I was going to try and hide in the bathroom, but I thought he'd surely check there when he came back. I came out of the toilet and I was going to try and look for a knife or a scissors or something to cut them loose. Then I heard him turning the handle of the door, and I fell to the floor and I crawled under the bed.

'He had his back to me at first. But when he turned I saw his face. My head was at the edge of the box spring, and I could see him as he watched my two roommates. One of them was on the bed I was underneath, and one was on the bottom bunk of the bunk beds across the room. After I got a good look at him, I inched my way further beneath the bed.'

'Why did you chance it by taking a look at him, Theresa?' I asked.

She gripped my hand even tighter.

'Because I knew he was going to kill them. I knew he would kill me too if he found me. I had to see him . . . Maybe he wouldn't find me, I thought, and then he wouldn't get away with what I knew he was going to do.'

'What kind of weapon did he use?' Doc asked.

'I saw a straight razor in his hand. I don't know what else he used . . . He went to the bunk bed and hit her. She was tied up like a pig. She couldn't move. I saw him beating her when I crawled back to the edge of the box spring. I wanted to scream, I wanted to cry out. But I knew he would do the same things to me if I made a sound.

'He beat her and beat her . . . and then he raped her. Twice, I think. Once when she was lying on her back and the other time . . . '

She squeezed my hand again.

'He sodomized her. Her name was Carolina. He attacked her as if she were not even human. It was like watching an animal in the barnyard . . . Then he turned her back over and cut her throat with the straight razor. Carolina couldn't make a sound because of the gag he used on both of them. She bled badly. Spurts of blood. I almost got sick, and I inched my way back under the center of the bed.

'I didn't see him kill Marita. She was on top of the mattress above me. I saw the bedding come down at me as his weight went on top of her. He must have raped her twice or three times. I can't be sure. But I heard her groan when he killed her. I knew he had killed because the blood ran down the wall next to me and began to pool beside me. Then there was less weight on the bed. I saw him walk across the room. I moved myself closer to the edge where I could see.

'He took the razor and cut Carolina from her breasts to her privates. He opened her up like a cow. I could see her insides . . . '

Theresa halted. I asked her if she needed a break or if she wanted some water.

'No. Let me finish this . . . He slaughtered her like a steer or a pig, and then he came back to the other bed and cut

Marita. Again I knew what he did because more blood came dripping down the wall next to me, and the smell was . . . was unbelievable.'

She stopped there.

'What did he do then?' Doc asked.

'He left. He wiped his straight razor on Carolina's sheets, and he left.'

'And what did you do then?' I asked her.

'I waited. I waited for hours. I wet my own nightgown because I was afraid to get up . . . But I did get out from under the bed, and when I saw what that man had done . . . I blacked out, I think, because the next thing I knew I was at Elgin.'

'How do you know Carl Anglin was the man you saw in that dormitory room?' Doc asked.

'From the pictures of him that you showed me.'

'You are positive the man who murdered Carolina and Marita was Carl Anglin?' Doc asked again.

'It was Carl Anglin. I'm sure.'

'With all the drugs that have been put into your body, you're certain the killer was—'

'What I saw was the truth. Nothing I saw that night was a hallucination. My hallucinations came *after* the murders. Someone drugged me for thirty years, Detective Gibron. Someone stole my life, or at least thirty years of it, with a drug, but that night he killed all those girls . . . There was no drug in my body that night. I did not hallucinate what he did. Carl Anglin killed Marita and Carolina and I know he killed the others as well.'

We stopped the tape.

'Have you had any visions? You know, flashbacks?' Doc asked.

'No. Not yet, anyway.'

'We need the jury to know you're lucid, Theresa. They mustn't be distracted by thinking you're having visions or episodes,' I explained.

'I understand . . . No. My head is free of that drug now. I know it. I know what I remember. I saw Carl Anglin butcher my two friends. No one should have witnessed what I saw, but it is God's truth, what I'm telling you.'

I held her hand firmly. Then I released her.

'Do you need any more?' she asked.

I wanted to embrace her. To hug those frail shoulders. But I couldn't.

'You'll have to tell the prosecutor – he's called Mr Field – the same story, Theresa. Then you'll have to say it again to a jury. And to a defense attorney who'll most likely want people to believe you've had a bad acid trip,' Doc warned her.

'I know what I've told you is the truth.'

'I believe you. We both do,' I said. 'But we've got to make sure that the jury buys your version. Anglin's attorney will do anything and everything to make you look like a lunatic. I want you to know what you're going up against,' I told her.

'I don't care what they think. I have to say what I know.'

I nodded and took her hand again.

'Take it easy. We're both on your side, here.'

We had the shrink's word Theresa could be ready to leave Indiana in two weeks. Then, he said, they'd be sure that she was free of the threat of any possible 'episodes'.

Our first stop was with Henry Field, the prosecutor.

His jaw almost literally dropped when he heard about the return of Theresa Rojas to the real world.

'Christ! How long have you two been sitting on her?'

'About a month,' I admitted.

'And you didn't see fit to—'

'Would you have liked to have a semi-comatose star witness?' Doc said. 'We had to be certain she was back. And she *is* back.'

'I ought to be very pissed off . . . Did you take a deposition?'

I nodded.

'Did she ID Anglin?'

'Yes,' Doc told him.

'How?' Field wanted to know.

'From the photos . . . She saw him do one of the roommates from her position under the bed. But she actually witnessed a killing with her own eyes.'

'They'll try to make it look like she's tripping her way through the past. They'll make her look like a drugged-out—'

'When you hear her, you'll believe her,' I interrupted. 'So will the jury. Henry, it's like listening to Mother Teresa. Our Theresa, like her namesake, has a very high believability rating, I'd say.'

'She'd better have. She's all we've got.'

'She's all we need, Henry,' Doc said firmly. 'She'll help those twelve honest souls on the jury to shove that lethal-injection syringe all the way up Anglin's skinny ass.'

'Here are the tapes,' I said, passing them over to Field. 'You listen to them and decide.'

In a half-hour we were back in his office.

'I'll have a warrant for Anglin's arrest in about twenty minutes. Make sure he doesn't flee the county,' Henry Field warned us.

There would be a small army present at the cuffing of Carl Anglin. A dozen squads. A backup SWAT team, just in case Carl got testy.

Anglin had relocated to the far northwest part of town. Our street people had pinpointed his new digs just two days ago, Tactical informed us. There would be no stakeout. It was the middle of a hot July afternoon, and we were going straight in. We weren't sure he was in there, but we were about to find out.

The block was swarming with police vehicles. We had got the street cordoned off at either end as well as the two streets east and west that ran parallel to Dempsy Street, where Anglin now lived.

Doc and I led the way up to the second-floor apartment. There were no federal people accompanying us on this raid.

The entry at the ground level had no lock, so Doc could put his burglary tools back in his pocket. He and I and four uniforms made our way up to the second flight.

'Anglin! Police! Open the door!' Doc yelled.

We waited five beats, and then the uniforms rammed the door with their metal apparatus that splintered the entryway open after three hits.

We went into the flat with our guns aimed waist high. There was no one in the living room. Nor in the dining room or kitchenette. All that remained was the bedroom.

I was at point. We opened the bedroom door.

On the mattress sprawled that gorgeous brunette from Anglin's other apartment who'd greeted us in the buff a few months prior.

She was naked except for her thong panties again, but this time her face was a mess, a collection of bruises and lacerations.

I propped her head up on the bloody pillow.

'Can you talk?' I asked.

She tried to blink her eyes, but one of them was swollen shut, thanks to Anglin's fists.

'Please. Where is he? Can you talk at all?' I repeated.

She managed only a whisper.

'Carl . . . He said he was on his way . . . '

'Where?' I urged her.

'He said he was on his way . . . Unfinished business. He said he was on his way to . . . Indiana.'

Chapter Twenty-Six

[July 1999]

This was my first helicopter ride since my second tour in Vietnam. The chopper took off from the top of our downtown headquarters. It had taken us a half-hour of speeding through city traffic to get from Anglin's apartment to HQ, but Doc had the siren and the lights going, and we made it quickly through the snarl-ups. I hated high-speed pursuits. Doc understood my fear, but he had no choice. We barely missed a few other cars and several pedestrians. But we made it.

I also had no love of heights. I made my nervousness clear to our chopper pilot, who laughed and lifted off from the multiple-storeyed headquarters building. The pilot, Jack McDade, had also been a helicopter pilot in the Vietnam War. The pilots were, as I recall, the goofiest bastards in country.

'We'll get you there in minutes,' Jack grinned.

Doc's face was already green. This was his first ride in one of these rickety-ass miracles of aviation.

'We may not have minutes,' I reminded the pilot.

'I hear you,' Jack told me. This time he was all business.

We headed east-southeast, toward Indiana and Theresa Rojas.

'The Major told him. The Major got it from the Fibbies who got it by surveillance that we weren't aware of, someone at the hospital who shot their mouth off—'

'What difference does it make now, Doc?' I asked.

He nodded resignedly. Who knew what kind of a lead Anglin had on us? Maybe the helicopter would even the odds. Maybe he wouldn't be able to penetrate the hospital's security . . . which I knew wouldn't stop him. When he got there, he'd get in. That was his kind of thing. After all those years of experience, it'd be like walking through the front doors of a church on Sunday.

The Indiana State Police had been notified. They were on their way. But the hospital was in a remote area, and it'd take some time for them to arrive. Also, the choppers in Indiana were all engaged at the moment. It'd be an hour before any of them came free, so the cops had to go by automobile. There was no place near the hospital for an ordinary airplane to land.

So we were it. We were the closest available helping hand.

I'd already contacted the hospital by phone. They were on high alert – whatever that meant. Doc and I and Jack were likely to be the only cops on scene in about fifteen minutes.

The crosswinds began to pick up, so Jack's job was made more difficult.

'No problem. We'll get there. But we're going to have to go in lower than I'd like to. Let's all of us keep our eyes open for power lines.'

'Shit,' Doc declared.

'Indeed. Shit,' Jack repeated and smiled.

We swooped down to about a hundred feet from ground level and the pilot changed course slightly to fly directly above Indiana Highway 96. Jack claimed it would be the quickest way to the mental facility.

It began to rain, complete with lightning and thunder.

'Isn't this stuff supposed to ground us?' Doc asked.

'Yeah. Usually,' Jack snorted.

But he pressed on above the light traffic below us. We were moving faster than the cars, but I couldn't figure out the speed. I was too terrified. I clutched the arm of my seat like it was a buoy in a shark-infested ocean.

In another ten minutes we saw the building where Theresa Rojas lived. There was a small park just a few blocks from the actual site, so Jack wanted to put us down there.

The sky was nearly as green as Doc's face. I could imagine tornado sirens going off in the distance. But just then the wind died down to nothing. We landed with rain streaming down the bubble canopy of the chopper. When we got out of the helicopter, lightning daggered down out of the east, and suddenly we couldn't see the hospital's lights.

'Jesus. The power's out . . . Jack, you can stay here if you—'

'Bullshit,' he laughed. 'I'm going in with the troops. That creep could be out here somewhere. I like your company a whole lot, Jimmy.'

'All right. Are you packing?' I asked the pilot.

He patted his shoulder holster.

'Always,' he said softly, and grinned.

The rain began to come down as we tried to make sure we had all our weapons in tact. I checked the ankle holster, and I drew out the Bulldog .38. It was my gun of choice in close encounters. It'd halt Anglin – a whole platoon of Anglins – with its stopping power.

We moved out quickly toward the hospital. By now the rain was coming down furiously, making it almost impossible to stay on a straight line to the facility, but we pressed on in spite of the deluge. I was first; Doc and Jack followed with their weapons in their hands.

The front gate, one of those black wrought-iron deals, was wide open. I looked at Doc. I could barely see his face until another streak of lightning lit up the sky. There was more than concern in his expression as we approached and passed the opened gate.

We ran up to the entrance. We could see nothing through the glass door because there was no light on inside. I would've thought they'd have used candles or a backup generator, but there was no illumination inside that I could see.

'He'd take care of the generator even without the storm, Jimmy. He knows how to create a friendly atmosphere for his business.'

We walked into the darkened building. Doc's railroad flashlight gave us some help in finding our way. Outside the rain swirled everything into an opaque green soup. Inside we had a slightly better chance of seeing what was in front of us.

We reached the admissions desk. No one there.

Until Doc aimed the flashlight's beam behind the desk and found the unconscious body of the receptionist. My partner reached down and found that she still had a pulse.

'He hasn't had time to have fun with the staff,' I told Doc and Jack. 'He's gone directly to the target.'

We left the still-breathing receptionist where she lay, and we moved on down the hall toward Theresa's room, number 226. There was a knocked-flat orderly about twenty feet down the hallway. He was still alive as well, Doc discovered.

When we arrived at Theresa's room, we found the door had been opened. Jagged streaks of lightning outside illuminated the inside of her cubicle just for a second. Anglin was holding her from behind. He was sitting on the bed. Doc leveled the flashlight at the two of them. Anglin had his forearm underneath Theresa's chin, and we could see that he was squeezing hard. The beam of the flashlight showed us the razor that he was gripping tightly in his right hand while he methodically, expertly choked the life out of our only witness with that forearm.

I could hear Theresa gurgling. Anglin was looking at the three of us pointing our pistols at his forehead.

'Turn that fuckin' thing off or I'll cut her right now.'

Doc extinguished the flashlight.

'This is pointless, Carl,' I reminded him. 'You aren't leaving here and you know—'

'She's the last one. The one I missed, back when your daddy couldn't cuff me . . . You know how many staff members they got here? Eight. That's how many.

I chloroformed five of them and had to club the rest. Picked them off one by one. Mother Nature made it too easy . . . And then you three had to show up. The cavalry, right?'

'You should've whacked that big-titted brunette. She pointed us at you,' Doc told him.

'That's what you get when you leave your enemies alive. Can't hurt you if they ain't breathing.'

'You hurt her and you won't get your day in court,' I reminded him.

'She ain't going to testify against me . . . Are you, girl? See, we've been sitting here for the past few minutes, just before you so rudely interrupted us, and we've been discussing the past. You know. The history that we shared all those years ago. Theresa was jabbering when we first began, but I think she's done had a relapse . . . And you've already noticed that all those lovely folks here at the home are still breathing. They're just taking a nap. Now, you all might get me for assault and breaking and entering and whatever else you want to cook up, but you ain't getting me for the nurses because you just lost your best witness again . . . She was a talkative little thing when I first got in here. Even a bit feisty . . . Bit me on the forearm. See?'

He pulled up a sleeve and showed Doc the marks of her teeth. The flashlight beam revealed little droplets of blood.

Lightning shocked the green sky outside alive, and the blooming pressure of a thunderclap burst Theresa's window open. All of us jerked in shock. But Anglin never let go of her, and he was still clutching the razor tightly.

'Yeah. I'm going to skip out on all those charges you're getting ready, Lieutenant. My friends will make sure that I don't pay for too long because of what you might throw at me on account of tonight's little get-together. You aren't wired, are you, Parisi? No. You were in too big a hurry to haul ass down here and save your favorite witness . . . Her roommates were good, Lieutenant. They fought a little, and I always liked fight in a woman . . . You ever choked a bitch almost to the point of killing her when you were both about to come? No? Too bad. You could see the come in their eyes when I squeezed them almost to the point of dyin'. It sure is some kind of rush . . . '

'What were their names?'

Anglin loosened his grip on her neck.

The voice belonged to Theresa Rojas.

Lightning spiked the green sky with yellow pitchforks. The thunder hit just seconds later.

Doc pointed the flashlight beam at Anglin's face. We could see the green of his cat's eyes raging back at us.

'I'm walking this little lady right out the front door, Lieutenant. You and your boyfriends there blink, and I cut her throat. And there goes your sole witness.'

'And you die the second she bleeds,' I told him.

'I ain't afraid to die, Parisi. Anyway, I wouldn't want to go into a cage over the likes of this cunt. I'm hoping you really would pull the trigger. You'd be doing me a favor. But she'd still be dead and you don't want that to happen, now do you?'

Anglin began to back out of the room with Theresa in tow. He held the razor precariously close to her jugular vein. He would cut her just the way he'd cut the other nurses, and he knew that we knew it.

The lights were still out in the hospital. Only the flashes from the electrical storm outside illuminated our way toward the hospital's entrance. All I could see of Anglin's face were his eyes as the lightning flashed outside. The razor never moved from its place against Theresa's exposed throat. We had our guns pointed at Anglin's head, but I never felt so powerless as I did then as we followed him and Theresa toward the entry.

A lightning flash lit up the reception area. Anglin pulled open the glass door, and then he snatched Theresa violently backward through it.

We followed them along the concrete driveway. Anglin was headed toward an old Jeep that sat in the circular drive in front of the hospital entrance. He was reaching into his pocket for the key, I supposed, as another booming jolt of lightning struck not far from where we stood.

'I won't let you leave here,' I shouted through the rolling thunder of the storm that was pelting us with a mixture of heavy rain and pea-sized hailstones. The hail felt like little stabbings on our faces and heads. Doc and Jack and myself were drenched by the downpour, but we managed to keep our weapons pointed at the man struggling to get Theresa Rojas into that Jeep.

Another boom shook the five of us standing on that drive. Yet another concussion followed. Then the sky lit up in a ghastly flickering yellow and green flash as pitchforks of lightning pocked the sky.

Just for a moment Anglin let his attention wander from the razor that nestled against Theresa's vulnerable throat, and he dropped the hand that held the blade as he peered skyward.

I cocked my piece, but before I could put a round through one of his green eyes, another batch of lightning pitchforks flared as the thunder reached a crescendo. A bolt of pure white electrical energy hurled itself toward the power lines that stood at the edge of the drive, and we all jumped at the resulting explosion. We saw the power line snap away from its couplings, and down it came, writhing and twisting like a furious snake about to strike whatever stood before it.

Theresa dove away from Anglin once she realized he'd released his hold on her neck, and she scrambled away from him with feral speed. Anglin tried to duck the thrashing power line, but he moved too slowly this time and the wild black snake sprang at his throat as if it were a real serpent. The force of the blow whipped Anglin down onto his back, and it was then that he screamed, just as blue arcs of high-voltage sparks came crackling out of his mouth and ears and eyes.

Anglin's scream didn't last long, but the stink of scorched flesh started to come at us almost immediately. Black smoke rose from his fried corpse as the rain continued to drench us and as arcs of lethal blue force continued to burst out of every orifice in his dead body.

I rushed over to Theresa, who lay in a sobbing heap about ten yards from the electrified remains of Anglin. I picked her up and hustled her back inside the hospital. I yelled for Doc and Jack to get out of the fury of the storm, but they stood there mesmerized, watching Anglin burn up in a coruscating blue blaze. Their guns were still pointed at him as if he might still escape from the cable that had wrapped itself around his throat.

'Doc! Jack! For God's sake!' I yelled at the two of them.

But they just stayed there, watching.

I held Theresa tightly as the ferocious noise outside began to subside just slightly.

After a few more minutes the lightning had ceased altogether. Doc and Jack finally walked back inside the hospital.

I looked into their eyes as I continued to hold Theresa. They didn't say anything, so we all simply stood there as I held our surviving witness with all the strength I had left in me.

The phones were still working, Doc found out. He dialed 911 and asked for several squads of paramedics to be sent out to this remote location. As he put the receiver down, we heard the approach of the Indiana state troopers.

I walked Theresa out to the lobby. All the lights were back on and the receptionist at the door had come round on her own. She was sitting behind her desk, looking distinctly groggy. When she saw Theresa and me, she screamed.

I showed her my badge, and then she began to sob.

'We've got help coming. You just sit down and take it easy. We're all safe now. Don't worry.'

The receptionist leaned forward, lowered her head and sobbed into her folded arms.

I sat Theresa on a couch in the lobby next to admissions.

I hugged her tightly. She was the sibling I'd never had, I was thinking. She was the sister I might have had if the old man hadn't been sterile. I felt like her big brother, although we were actually very close in age. Theresa had a family of her own, I understood, but it had just grown by one member. Emotionally, I'd adopted her as my sister. Hell, she wasn't even Italian, but Mexican was close enough. We both spoke those Romance languages, I'd heard, so it was close enough.

'I wish my father could see you tonight. He wrote about you in his files. He wrote about you so much, I felt like I already knew you the way he seemed to.'

'Where will I go from here, Jimmy?'

'I don't know. Where do you want to go?'

'I wanted to be a nurse. I wanted to make people feel better.'

'Why not go back to school and finish what you started? You're not too old. You'll never be too old. Hell, you're younger than I am, and we just had a new baby.'

'I'll never have a baby of my own.'

'Doc's wife is fifty-something, just like you. She just adopted a little girl . . . Anything's possible these days. Almost anything.'

She kissed my cheek.

The Indiana cops were all over the building then. The paramedics were rushing through the corridors, trying to revive all the hospital staff whom Anglin had decked one by one.

Doc came back to us with the good news that there were no fatalities in the place – other than Anglin.

Theresa was squeezing me so hard I was afraid she'd shut off my air. Then she relaxed her grip and let go.

'How would you like to spend the night at my house?' I asked her.

I wouldn't let her argue.

I called Natalie from the front desk and told her we were having a visitor to stay with us until we could arrange things with Theresa's family. Natalie said she was happy to help her out, especially after she heard about Anglin's demise.

Jack came up to the three of us.

He smiled and walked off toward his copter. Doc told him we'd get a ride back in a vehicle borrowed from the Indiana state troopers. Jack waved farewell to the three of us.

I had to go to the shift supervisor, who was halfway

coherent and conscious, and explain that I was taking their patient out of the hospital on my authority. The supervisor was dazed enough to go along with me.

We arranged with the state troopers to use one of their squad cars to transport Doc, Theresa and me back to the city. When we'd given our statements to the local coppers about Anglin's death, we walked out to the car, the three of us, and headed home.

Epilogue

[August 1999]

I watched them cremate Carl Anglin's meager remains. His mother was the only witness from his family. I and a few other coppers were present too. Cremation was the best way to finish things, as far as I was concerned. I knew that Catholics generally preferred burial, but me, I wanted to go out clean. Anglin got the consuming, cleansing fire that stopped his body rotting in the ground.

His mother said not a word to anyone present, and she scurried off somewhere as soon as it was over.

Renny Charles did not show up. I hadn't reckoned he would. He'd either disappeared or he was deep under. Perhaps he was like the seven-year locust that emerged periodically to make everyone's life just that bit more miserable. Wherever he was, I'd have liked to nab him on general principles.

He and Anglin had killed the President of the United States. I'd carry that powerful suspicion to my own cremation. I couldn't prove it and I couldn't even talk about it. So they were ghosts. All of them. JFK, Anglin, the Major, Special Agent Mason, his leggy blonde assistant. Seven nurses in 1968. Three more this year. History, all of them.

Doc didn't want to rehash the past, and I couldn't blame him. He was too busy trying to keep up with his daughter and Mari.

And I had my own crosses to bear. Maybe they were more like responsibilities than crosses. Three children at various stages of maturity, from infant to young adult. I had a young wife who could run me ragged because she was over twenty years younger than I was.

Nick, my biological father, came around sometimes. He said he didn't want to intrude on us, but I knew he wanted to see me and find out what was going on. It was the pull of our shared DNA. I didn't deny him. In fact, I tried to get him to come around more often. He was my children's true grandfather. The two older kids had been told the truth about my roots. The baby would find out when she was old enough to understand.

It was a matter of coming to terms. With the private matters of my own past, with the public events of years gone by. I had to deal with evil. Less often with outright goodness. It was a matter of how much I could endure. Why Carl Anglin had to plague my father's already painful life, I didn't know anymore than I understood why Anglin was still hanging around when I took my tour of duty with the Chicago Homicide team. But there he'd been. Carl Anglin and all the other creatures like him were facts of existence. Another one just like him was waiting out in the weeds. I could count on it; I wouldn't be surprised when the new guy emerged.

After all, he and all the others like him kept me in business. I found them. Someone else judged them and tried to figure out 'why'.

Doc kept talking about retiring and getting familiar with the coeds at some college. And I reminded him he didn't have the balls to cheat on Mari. He nodded at me, grinning ruefully. I had him pegged.

Theresa Rojas told me she was going back to school to finish her nursing degree.

I visited Jake Parisi's grave from time to time. He was interred in the far southwest part of town, not too far from his favorite after-work tavern. The place was now owned by Jimmy Karras's son, Jimmy Junior.

The afternoon after Anglin's valedictory barbecue, I drove down to visit my father. I placed a yellow rose, one like those I'd kept giving Theresa Rojas, on his grave. I didn't spend much time at his final resting-place. But I uttered a few Hail Marys and then I walked back to the car.

I headed over to Karras's saloon where I ordered two beers. I drank mine slowly, but I left the other one untouched. When I got up to leave, Karras Junior wanted to know why I'd left the extra draft.

'He'll be along in a while. He comes in after every shift,' I told him.

I gave the Greek a grin. Then I walked out his door into the heat of the late afternoon.